EMPTY FOOTSTEPS

by the same author

novels
(From the Chronicles of Invernevis)
Cruel in the Shadow
The Blind Bend

biography
Sir David Russell

Empty Footsteps

From the Chronicles of Invernevis

Lorn Macintyre

BLACK ACE BOOKS

First published in 1996 by Black Ace Books
Ellemford, Duns, TD11 3SG, Scotland

© Lorn Macintyre 1996

Typeset by Black Ace Editorial
Ellemford, Duns, TD11 3SG, Scotland

Printed in England by Antony Rowe Ltd
Bumper's Farm, Chippenham, SN14 6QA

A CIP catalogue record for this book
is available from the British Library

ISBN   1–872988–76–8

The publishers gratefully acknowledge
subsidy from the Scottish Arts Council
towards the production of this first edition

ACKNOWLEDGEMENTS

Grateful thanks to Hunter Steele
for all his help and patience.
Also to Chris Dillon,
for the translation of Father Allan's poem,
and for editorial advice and assistance.

Thanks to the School of Scottish Studies,
University of Edinburgh, for permission to quote
from the following items from *Tocher* magazine:

'Rann ri Ghabhail a dh'Aon Anail'
(A Rhyme to be said in One Breath),
recorded from Donald Allan McQueen, South Uist,
by Donald Archie MacDonald.

'Fhuaras Naidheachd an De'
(News Came Yesterday),
recorded from William Matheson
by James Ross.

BHA CEOTHRAGACH MIN AM MUIGH

Bha ceothragach mìn am muigh,
   'S cha chluinnteadh osna na gaoithe,
Bha solus an latha mùchte,
   'S cha mhuthaichinn guth nan daoine;
Thàinig cianalas air m'anam,
   Thog mi mo cheann bhar na cluasaig;
Cha do shiubhail an anail ach ainneamh,
   'S bu làidir mo chridhe a' bualadh;
Tha fuaim 'nam chluais 's nam cheann
   A tha fàgail geilt air mo chridhe,
Mar cheum nam mìltean ag imeachd 'san ùr-shneachd
   Dol gu gleac as nach till iad.

A FINE DAMP SEA-MIST

The day was dark outside because of the fine, damp sea-mist
and I could not hear the slightest sigh of the wind;
Daylight itself was subdued and I could not distinguish
the voices of the people speaking;
My soul filled with anxiety and pain,
I raised my head from the pillow;
I could not breathe properly and my
heart began to pound and palpitate;
There's a noise now in my ear
going through my head
which leaves a tense fear in my heart;
like the empty footsteps of thousands trudging
through the fresh new snow
setting off for a fray from which they will never return.

Father Allan MacDonald foresees the First World War.

1

There was a plague of wasps that summer, and several of the women had veils hanging from their straw hats. They were the guests of the officers at the sports at the annual camp of the 8th Territorial Battalion of the Argyll & Sutherland Highlanders. Behind the party, in the pegged-back coolness of the marquee, orderlies in white jackets were waiting to serve the strawberries and champagne.

Major Niall Macdonald of Invernevis had decided that Alanna Richardson sitting across from him in the crescent of chairs was the most beautiful woman he had ever seen. Alanna, who was wearing cream, with lace at her cuffs, was in animated conversation with Ian Malcolm of Poltalloch, whose party had come in two motors from their mock Jacobean palace at Calltuinn Mor, the place of the great hazel trees. Poltalloch, younger, had been Salisbury's Assistant Private Secretary, and he and Alanna were discussing the suffragettes.

'It's not votes I would give them,' Poltalloch, younger, said.

'I agree with them,' Alanna announced.

Heads turned to her. Her husband the Brigadier was signalling, but she wasn't going to be put off. This was her cause too.

'But surely you don't condone arson,' Campbell of Jura, the Adjutant, said.

'I didn't say that I condoned arson. I said I agreed with their cause. Women are equal to men.' She was looking around for support, but the other women seemed to be occupied with their gloves or hats. Lady Campbell-Walton, in black tulle on such a day, was glaring at her as if she should be done away with.

'But they're superior,' Campbell of Kilberry said, trying to ease the situation.

'Equality will do, thank you,' Alanna told them.

'But we're all equal here,' Jura said.

'Only in numbers,' she replied.

Invernevis was watching her. He was fascinated by the way

the veil moved when she spoke, and waited for the next outburst to blow it aside.

Poltalloch, younger, turned to confront her. 'And what would you do if you got back to London to find that your house had been burnt to the ground by a pack of harpies?'

'It wouldn't happen,' she said haughtily.

'Because you are a friend of the Pankhurst woman?'

'I have met Mrs Pankhurst.'

'And you admire her?'

'I do admire her, she's very brave.' The veil was lifted back in her spread fingers, like a knight opening his visor in challenge. 'And what would *you* do, if they tried to force-feed you, sticking a tube down your throat?'

'These women deserve it,' he said vehemently. 'They destroy property.'

'So they've to be treated as men please. This is the example King Edward set.'

In the silence Invernevis searched his pockets for his cigarette case. Poltalloch younger's wife was sitting beside him. Her mother, the Jersey Lily, had been Edward's mistress.

'Carson knows how to deal with them,' Poltalloch, younger, told the company. 'One of them chained herself to the railings outside his house in Eaton Place. He sent his butler out with a jug of water.'

'To cool her down,' Lady Campbell-Walton said appreciatively. 'Women never behaved like that in my younger days.'

'Not to cool her down,' Poltalloch, younger, continued. 'He poured the water in a thin stream from the woman to the gutter. A crowd collected and began to laugh at her, so she unlocked herself and made off pretty quick.'

Some of the women joined in the male laughter.

But Alanna had more to say. 'The suffragettes got their own back on you clever politicians last week. They carried Sylvia Pankhurst from her sick-bed and laid her on the steps at the entrance to the Strangers' Entrance at the House of Commons. Asquith had to agree to see her. Not only that – he has received a deputation of six working women.'

'You're remarkably well informed,' Poltalloch, younger, said suspiciously.

'You need to be well informed when you're dealing with men. One of the women took along a brush head. She explained to the Prime Minister that she only got a few pence for putting the hundreds of bristles in all the holes. I understand that he's seen the light at last about how women are exploited. The Liberals are courting us, and so is Labour, so you Conservatives have no choice if you're to get back to power.'

'So you would let Ramsay MacDonald and his rabble in, just for the sake of securing a vote?' he challenged her. 'Wouldn't that be betrayal?'

'Betrayal of what?'

'Your own class.'

'My class is being a woman. What is this, Ian Malcolm, am I on trial?'

The great doors of Calltuinn Mor had just slammed shut on her for good, but she didn't care. These Malcolms were so damned pompous, with their money made from the sweat of black backs on sugar-cane plantations. Mrs Pankhurst had as much right to be in society as the Jersey Lily.

'What do you think about the suffragette cause, Niall?' she asked sweetly, turning to Invernevis.

It was wickedly done, to put him on the spot.

'I don't keep up with such things at Invernevis,' was all he could think of saying.

'But your servants aren't slaves, are they?'

The Duke of Argyll, the honorary Colonel, had fallen asleep in the sun. He was wearing a black armband for the ninth Duke, who had been carried to the mausoleum at Kilmun in the spring, with half a ton of flowers and eight thousand of his tenants in attendance. The new Duke was boyish-looking, with fair hair, and had inherited much intellect as well as much land. His sister, Lady Elspeth, was with him, looking bored. She and her brother would rather sit on stools in a smoke-filled black house in Glen Aray, listening to an old woman singing a Gaelic lament, than be in a flower-filled box at Covent Garden as Caruso sang

Leoncavallo. Each night exquisite small dishes of bread and milk were set out for the fairies in the policies of Inverary Castle. When they retired for the night, preceded by the old butler with the lamp, His Grace and his sister said, '*Oidhche mhath,*' to the dead they passed on the stairs.

The Duke jerked awake as a motor car roared up behind the marquee.

'Who is that?' Lady Elspeth asked indignantly.

'Young Lauder,' Campbell of Kilberry explained.

'Who is he?'

'Harry Lauder's son.'

'And what is Harry Lauder's son doing here?'

'He's joined the battalion, Elspeth.'

A young man in rimless spectacles came in with a young woman and stood awkwardly while an orderly fetched chairs.

'How do you do?' Alanna gave her hand.

'This is Miss Thomson,' he said.

'I adore your father's songs,' Alanna told him.

'We'd better get on with the sports,' Kilberry advised the Adjutant.

An officer's revolver started the first race, a dozen men in shorts down to their knees, numbers pinned to their vests, their elbows going as they approached the tape where another officer was kneeling to pick out the first three prize-winners.

'They're fitter than you give them credit for!' Kilberry called across to Jura.

'That's only a hundred yards,' the Adjutant answered. 'Try them on a ten-mile march with a pack on their back.'

'At least they're having a good time,' Kilberry said.

Invernevis was watching Alanna Richardson again. The veil was up on the brim of her hat, her long neck with its loops of pearls rippling as she laughed at the antics of grown men running with eggs wobbling on spoons. How was it that this woman could give as good as she got from any man, yet, so soon afterwards, look the society beauty again? He wanted to move his chair beside hers for the infectiousness of her personality, as if he could carry some of it back to his lonely existence.

The men loved the sports, pulling on a rope in teams in the tug-o'-war, then wrestling together. An interval was called and bottles of beer were distributed while the strawberries and cream and champagne were served in the officers' tent.

'Aren't they all so – wonderful?' Alanna called to the company around her.

'Wonderful men,' Kilberry agreed with paternalistic pride. 'You'd better make the announcement before they empty their bottles,' he advised Jura.

The Adjutant used a megaphone to tell them that Princess Louise had done them the honour of becoming their Colonel-in-Chief. They stood cheering, raising their dark bottles of ale while Invernevis's glass chimed against Alanna's.

It took three men to carry the caber on to the field. Several competitors tried to lift it, but went away again. It was Dochie MacDougall's turn. He swivelled his sporran onto his hip, then spat on his palms. The great tree stripped of its bark was now balanced against his shoulder, his hands locked under its end. Alanna Richardson had taken mother-of-pearl glasses from her bag, as if she was watching an opera. MacDougall took a tottering step. The crowd went silent as the tree swayed, as if it wanted to slip back to the earth and take root again, but he steadied it in time. Now he was running with it towards the officers' tent, trying to keep the caber in line with the lady in the cream dress who was sitting beside the laird, her hat with the veil now to one side, now to the other. When it was obscured he heaved. The pole swayed as it stood on its end, then went over with a bump, making the turf reverberate.

Alanna Richardson was on her feet, clapping.

'Well done!'

'That's the strongest man in the battalion,' Kilberry told her. 'He's one of yours, isn't he, Niall?'

'Yes he is,' Invernevis said proudly.

The heavy hammer competition was called. As MacDougall spun round and round his kilt began to ride up till it was level

11

with his waist, as if he was going to take off. But he let go and the hammer soared into the sky, scattering some of the spectators before it thudded into the turf well beyond the other marks.

Lauder was hurrying across the park.

'You're not throwing again till you're properly dressed,' he told the big man.

'What's wrong with my dress?' MacDougall asked truculently.

'You've got nothing on under your kilt. There are ladies present.'

Other competitors were gathering to hear the confrontation.

'I haven't got anything they won't have seen before,' MacDougall said, turning away.

'I'm ordering you, go and get properly dressed or you're not competing.'

MacDougall said something in Gaelic, and the men laughed.

'What did you say?' Lauder demanded.

'I said, maybe I could borrow your pants, sir, but they'll be too fine for me I expect.'

'You were quite right to tell him to be more careful with his next throw,' Jura said when the Lieutenant arrived back at the enclosure. 'He could hit somebody.'

'A man like that doesn't know his own strength,' Kilberry said with admiration.

The first piping competition was under way, and whisky was now being served by an orderly. Invernevis sat back with his glass, most contented. The sun caught the silver filigree on the drones as the player paced the platform. Kilberry had his fingers clasped over his chest, apparently nodding to sleep, but he was listening to every note, and winced at the slippage of a finger as if a wasp had stung him.

It was the perfect afternoon, Invernevis was thinking as he lit a cigarette. There hadn't been a better camp. It wasn't only the weather; it was the men lying on their sides on the grass, listening to the pipes, something that never changed. Maybe Alanna would have her vote by next year's camp, but what difference would that make? Now his personal piper, Hector

Macdonald, was on the platform, and from the expression on Kilberry's face it was a good performance.

Macdonald was announced as the winner of the march, and strathspey and reel. Alanna had been asked to present the prizes. As she handed over the medals for the heavy events it looked as if she was going to give MacDougall a kiss.

'*Bheir mi siùcar thugad an ath thuras,*' ('I'll bring you sugar the next time,') Maggie promised the carthorse walking her home on the other side of the drystone dyke.

There was a painting like this in the big white house across the river, brought back by an early nineteenth-century traveller to Barbizon, a pistol in the coach with him. In the golden glow of day's end the peasant woman's arm circles the basin, her fingers gripping the green rim. But the details were different. She was a small woman of perfect complexion, her black hair pinned up, and her overall seemed to get whiter in the deepening dusk as she walked along the road with the basin of seaweed she had gathered on the loch shore to make the delicate pudding *carraigein*. She would have a bowl made by the time the Master came back from the camp because it was so good for the stomach and he would need it, after all the drink the others would make him take.

She felt the basin beginning to vibrate against her hipbone as the late train from Glasgow emerged from the mountain pass, clattering across the iron bridge over the river, then swinging across the moor for the village, beyond the three darkening standing stones on the hill.

Her laceless canvas shoes moved through the dust, horse-drawn wheels still the mode here. There were rare wild flowers in the ditch, pale yellow petals like a little shrine among the brambles.

The road went on, but she turned left, over the quaint hump-backed bridge. The evening sky was like a burst yolk as she turned between the crumbling stone pillars. She heard the owl's wavering vowel amplified in the leafy tunnel of the avenue. She began to sing to herself in Gaelic, the basin swaying against her hip. But her voice failed her as she reached the blind bend. She should have crossed the river at the stepping stones, terrified as she was to go past this place where the gig had overturned, leaving her to look after a widower.

Then she heard the clip-clop at her back. One of her mother's stories had been about a road where a coach could be heard but never seen, the invisible horses whinnying to warn of an accident that had already happened. If you stood in its way you would be swept into the other world, so she stumbled down among the trees, the water from the basin slopping over her shoes.

'Maggie!'

Roddy the coachman was a dark hump sitting up among the branches.

'What the hell are you playing at, woman? There's a fellow here for you.'

She stepped behind a tree, trying to tidy her hair with one hand before she went up.

'I was collecting a parcel off the train and he was on it,' the bad-tempered coachman explained. 'This is the new groom – at last. I was beginning to think I was going to die in this seat.'

In the dusk boots gleamed level with her flustered face.

'The Master didn't tell me that anyone was coming. He's not at home,' she added, as if that proved it was a mistake.

'Show her,' Roddy said, elbowing his passenger. 'That one's worse than a policeman.'

He fumbled in his waistcoat pocket and smoothed out a paper on his knee before he passed it to her. Then a match spurted, a cupped hand carrying its steady glow to her face. It was Invernevis House notepaper – the Master's blue scrawl, all right.

'Sam Raeburn,' the man said.

She gave him back the letter, but his hand was out again, for hers.

'Pleased to meet you.' It was a considerate grip.

'I'm Maggie Macdonald.'

'He knows that already,' the coachman fretted. 'I've been

telling him to keep in with you. Put that damn thing on the back so I can get home.'

'I'll manage.'

'Suit yourself – you always do,' the coachman said, casting the whip. 'This fellow will need feeding!' he shouted over his shoulder.

The house was in sight, its whitewash dulling by the second, its windows deepening pools. She took the moss-covered path for the back door. She felt excited about having someone new about the place as she put the basin on the big table, then clashed the poker between the bars of the stove. As she lifted the globe from the lamp and lit the wick, her brother Hector's postcard from Dunoon gleamed where it was propped on the dresser. She went outside, putting her head into the cool of the slatted larder, carrying the ham shank on the ashet in to the table.

She should really send this stranger through to set his own place in the servants' hall, but it would be lonely there. She took out her own cutlery from the table drawer and made a square of it at the end, a thing she'd never done before, not even for her own brother.

'Could I have some butter, please?'

She watched the yellowness melting into the steaming clefts of the new potatoes. When she realized she was staring at him she turned away, finding that she was holding his cap to her breasts, its maker's name faded by his sweat. She put it on the rack above the stove, then attended to the complaining kettle.

'This is very tasty.'

'I wish there was a glass of beer to go with it,' she said earnestly.

'I don't drink, but I wouldn't say no to a glass of milk.'

She was even more pleased as she poured the frothing whiteness into the glass, setting it down by his hand. He would be the only man in the house who didn't indulge.

He had a nice fresh open face, neat fair hair above biggish ears. He didn't eat like the rest, all jaws, but more like the Master. The hands working the cutlery were big but gentle-looking.

He must be about the same age as her brother Hector, and he was ten years younger than her. That made a difference.

'That was worth waiting for,' he said, his knife and fork crossed on a cleaned plate.

He looked so boyish, so pleased as he leaned back, arms folded, that she had to get him something else. Moths were swirling in the lighted doorway as she shut the larder with her elbow, carrying in the basin of blancmange. She had the teapot now, clasping it as if warming it with her own body-heat, watching the quivering pink pudding streaked with cream lifted to his lips, the strong neck moving as he swallowed.

'I've never tasted a pudding like that,' he told her as he scraped the plate.

'Then have some more,' she urged. She put a cup of tea beside him, then went to sit at the other end of the table.

'Do you mind if I smoke in here?'

Goodness, nobody had ever asked her that before. Her hand was at her throat as she gave permission with a smile. This one seemed to have a way of making you feel important.

He puffed out the match and dropped it into his waistcoat pocket.

'Where's the laird?'

It wasn't asked in a forward way and anyway everyone knew. 'He's with the Territorials at camp at Dunoon. My brother Hector's with him as his batman. He's a very good piper,' she added proudly.

'A soldier, is he?'

'Who, my brother?'

'No, the laird.'

'He was a soldier, against the Boers, but he got a bad leg. Are you in the Territorials?'

He shook his head.

'Where were you working?'

'On a farm in Buchan.' He saw the change in her eyes and asked eagerly:

'Have you been to that part?'

She was taken aback. 'Were you working with farm horses?'

'Aye, as a ploughman, like my folks.'

'How did you come to hear of this job?' She was beginning to fear there was some mistake.

'I saw it in the papers. Major Macdonald wrote back with the particulars. I'm glad I took it,' he added with a grin.

But the Master wasn't himself, since that terrible end to the young Mistress. That was one of the things about drink; it made them forget. 'But it's coach horses we've got here,' she had to tell him. It was such a shame if there had been a mix-up, but it was only fair to let him know now.

He sat, unconcerned in his fragrant blue cloud. 'Horses are all the same. It's the way you treat them.'

She felt it was going to be all right and rose to take the teapot to him, but he was covering his cup with his palm as he stood up. 'No, thanks. That was a great treat. I'm a bit tired, after the journey. I started out early. Where am I to sleep?'

She had been worrying about that since she'd met him on the avenue. 'There's a place up at the stables, but it hasn't been slept in for ages.'

'I'll manage,' he assured her. 'I'm used to living in a bothy.'

She felt the heat of the lamp against the back of her neck as she stood behind his chair. That made it sound as if he was just by himself, the poor soul, but it was too soon to ask him about his family.

'The mattress needs to be taken out and aired,' she said. 'I'll do that tomorrow and give the place a good clean. You can sleep here tonight, in my brother's room.'

'I don't want to put you to any trouble.'

'It's no trouble,' she assured him. 'It's only for the one night. You sit here and I'll go up and change the bed.'

He had another cigarette, and when she came back down it was with a lamp.

'Don't forget your case,' she told him.

He followed her up the back stairs to the top of the house. There was a candle lit in the little room, and he could see the gleam of fresh linen.

'I'll give you a knock in the morning. Sleep well,' she said as she closed the door behind her.

But she didn't go to her own bed. She went back down to wash his dishes and to lay out the strips of seaweed she'd brought up from the loch on cloths to dry so that she could make *carraigein*. Then she sat with her feet in the brine in the basin, the hem of her dress lifted back beyond her knees. The moonlight was streaming through the scullery window, changing familiar shapes. The coffee mill clamped to the end of the table became an arm activated by memory. Her mother, who had been cook before her, was rolling out the patch of moonlight that had turned into dough. The glitter of the salad colander became a salmon laid on the table by her father the ghillie, the tick of the clock behind her head the drip drip of his oilskins on the flagstoned floor. Her feet were chilling in the basin. There were only herself and Hector left out of the five of them that had crowded into the croft down the road.

She hoped Hector was behaving himself and not being led astray by some of the Invernevis men he was with, especially that MacDougall, who had a very bad name for women about the place. Hector should remember that there was only the two of them left and that they had to stick together. It was a pity he couldn't find himself a nice girl, though there wasn't really anyone suitable at Invernevis. But why shouldn't he be happy as he was, so long as he behaved himself and kept out of the Arms with that MacDougall?

God knows what those women saw in him.

She looked down at the tennis shoes beside the basin. They'd belonged to the young Mistress. She was a queer one. She wasn't suited to the place and would have been happier in London, among all those artistic people. Night after night she sat through there playing the piano, sometimes singing to herself, sad foreign songs that seemed to follow you wherever you went in the house, even up the stairs. But what an end. She had lain on the day-bed in the drawing-room for three days, speaking in a language no one could understand.

There had been times when she'd thought of moving to

another house, but she'd stuck it out — for her mother's sake, because that was what made the sacrifices worthwhile — and for the Master's sake too. He was so good to her, and to Hector, but he was taking too much drink because he was so lonely. There would be plenty of company at the camp, and temptation too, because some of them were heavy drinkers. Hector should remember that they had a good home here.

She would have to get a bone for broth for the weekend so that she could start building up the Master after the camp. The *carraigein* would be ready. She was tired now, and went up to bed with the lamp. When she passed the new man's room she heard him snoring.

2

Harry Lauder's American earnings had bought the automobile his son was driving. The slightly built Lieutenant with dubious eyesight had already demolished a wall in London, which more dollars had rebuilt, because there were plenty where these had come from. But he slowed down along Loch Eck and was turning up a track, parking so that the headlights shone on the building ahead. He took his passenger's hand and led her into the farmhouse which was being renovated.

'Careful,' he cautioned as they walked the planks laid on the joists. 'This will be the sitting-room,' he explained, turning her by the shoulders to the large gap in the wall. 'It's going to have quite a view.'

She looked across the dark glen, down to the lights of Glenbranter House.

'We'll tell your parents first that we want to get engaged, then I'll tell mine when I get out to Australia. We'll get married in the spring. This place should be ready by then.'

'I want you to do something for me, Johnnie. Go back to Cambridge and finish your music degree.'

'But I know as much as I'm ever going to need to know. There's the Steinway grand down in the house that the old man bought for me, brand new. We'll move it up here and I'll play every night for you – your requests.'

'It won't be 'Roamin' in the Gloamin', she said quietly.

'He gives people what they want, Mildred. Isn't that the important thing? If he wasn't such a big success in the States he couldn't have bought this place. There's twenty thousand acres here, and look at the money he's spent on the big house.'

'But for what?'

He looked at her in surprise. 'It's not for himself and mother. A lot of people misunderstand my father. I suppose it's his own fault, because being mean is all part of the act. He's very generous, but he doesn't want to give me everything at the one time. We'll stay here about a year. Then he'll move out to his house in Dunoon and hand this place over to us.'

'That's what worries me, Johnnie. You're trying to be what he wants you to be, instead of being what you want to be.'

'What do you mean?'

'He wants you to be a laird.'

'So do I. I like riding and shooting.'

'But I thought you wanted to be a musician. Wasn't that why you went to Cambridge?'

'I'm a good pianist, Mildred, but not good enough to go on a concert platform. My father accepts that now. I think he's secretly pleased, in case I stole some of his limelight. I want to make a success of running this place. I'm going to buy a lot of sheep.'

'We can't talk to sheep, Johnnie. What's the point in living here in grand isolation?'

'That's why I joined the Territorials, to make friends.'

'They weren't very friendly this afternoon.'

'They'll come round. It's just that I'm new. A year from now you'll be hosting a dinner for them at Glenbranter, you'll see.'

She didn't want to be in their company again. They were so arrogant, so sure of themselves, with their affected voices. They'd all ignored Johnnie, except Mrs Richardson, and nobody seemed to take her seriously. When she was sitting beside the Duke of Argyll, he hadn't even asked her name, but told her between mouthfuls of strawberries some silly story about a galley being seen in the sky above Inverary at the death of his father.

But she didn't want to quarrel with Johnnie when he was going away to the other side of the world. Maybe it would all work out. She put her head on his shoulder and they both admired the moon at the window awaiting glass. He was getting ready to kiss her, but she moved away at the vital moment, and he knocked his spectacles off. He squatted with a match while she retrieved them from underneath the joists.

'Have you messed up your shoes?' he asked.

'That doesn't matter. The main thing is that these aren't

broken,' she said, hooking his spectacles behind his ears. 'Poor darling.' She took his head between her hands and kissed him.

He smoked a cigarette as he sat on the window sill, looking down into the darkness.

'I'd like to plant all these hills, right up to the top,' he said.

'But why?'

'Because I like trees. I find them mysterious.'

'Tomorrow's our last day,' she reminded him. 'Let's go rowing on the loch. We can take a picnic.'

They drove down to Glenbranter House. His father had spent a fortune modernizing it, literally raising the roof. The floors of sprung pine were new; he'd bought the new rugs on his travels; and the sofas had come from Heal of London, along with the rest of the new mahogany furniture. Instead of oil paintings on the walls there were photographs of Harry Lauder on tour, disembarking from another liner, plying his crooked stick on another stage. The Lieutenant had his own room, the slate of the billiard table perfectly true, a lockable cupboard for the guns that had been tailored for his slim shoulder by Holland & Holland.

His own thoroughbred was in the stables.

He watched Mildred as she sipped her malted nightcap. She was very beautiful. He wanted more than to look at her, but didn't know how to go about it. She was his first woman. Once or twice in Cambridge on foggy nights he'd thought of going out and trying to pick up a woman, paying her for the experience of her body, but he didn't have the courage.

She set down her empty cup. 'It's been a long day.'

He followed her upstairs. They were alone in the house, apart from the servants on the top floor under the new skylights. He was going to be separated from Mildred for several months. He should take the initiative tonight. She was standing waiting for him on the landing, and he took the stairs two at a time, but she kissed him on the cheek before turning away to her room.

The old lady made a great effort, lifting her head from the pillow, then used her good hand to wave away the native woman swaddled in a sari squatting by the window. But it was only the white muslin curtain that had been put across the open window to keep out the wasps.

She couldn't even look at herself in a mirror any more. It was a sad thing, to be so old and helpless, but at least she wasn't so bad as Sandy had been. Poor soul. Oh, India had been bliss for a young woman, far more servants than they could ever have afforded here. How proud and thrilled she was, sitting in the stand, watching him, half out of his saddle as he swung the polo stick, the best horseman in the 93rd. When he took off his clothes for a bath black faces appeared at the window. She heard them talking among themselves. They called it the 'elephant's trunk'.

When he started coming home late she thought he'd been in the mess. One night she'd followed him into the bazaar. She was frightened by the indignant looks of the natives, but she was determined. When she arrived the bead curtain was still trembling, and there he was, on top of one of them. She wouldn't have minded so much because he was such a big strong man and it was so hot, especially in uniform. But she was only a girl with sticks for legs under all that heaving weight.

His uncle at Invernevis had taken so long to die. But shooting and fishing weren't enough for Sandy, after the life he'd led in India. She'd gone up the back stairs, looking for one of the maids for something. His sporran was twisted onto his backside, and the girl was on the step above, her skirt bunched up, her hands pressed against the wall, going up and down as if she was doing gymnastics under his direction.

Then he'd wasted away with that horrible disease he'd brought back from India. They'd had to fumigate the room and burn the mattress. Poor, dear Sandy. It had been a weakness, not wickedness. That was the way some men were made. Of course she shouldn't have taken to the bottle, but she missed him so much, and her sister Carlotta was such a tyrant. She'd stopped drinking, only to have the stroke that had left her with a useless hand.

The bed she was lying in had the brocade curtains furled like sails round its four poles. One morning she expected to wake up and find it had sailed into another world. Niall wouldn't miss her. When he did come up to see her, it was only for five minutes.

Alexander had been his father's favourite, but of course he was the younger son and couldn't have inherited the place. What a tragedy. There was nothing worse than losing a child, because it made life and its purpose seem so futile. If only Niall had had the strong personality of his father, things would have worked out differently. One thing for sure: he'd married the wrong woman. That was another tragedy, as if there was a curse on the family.

She wanted her grandchildren with her, but Niall kept putting off bringing them back from Switzerland. They belonged here, and they would be such good company for her. He was drinking; she'd smelt it on his breath. Maybe she was to blame for that. Oh *no*: when she felt the movement her good hand reached for the bell-pull.

When the bell jangled on the board on the wall behind her head, Maggie dusted the flour from her hands. The old lady had always been the same, wanting something at the most awkward time, but at least it wasn't drink any more.

She had to wheel the commode to beside the bed and help her on to it. Then she went to the dressing-table on the other side of the room and tidied it while she waited.

'I'm such a bother to you,' the plaintive voice said.

'No you aren't, ma'am,' Maggie said without much conviction.

'It's a pity I hadn't gone when I took the stroke.'

'Sit quiet and don't upset yourself.'

Maggie glanced into the mirror. It was comical, really, the way she was sitting on the mahogany throne, with the roll of paper like a sceptre in her hand, getting more and more like Queen Victoria.

'There's nothing,' she moaned.

'Just sit quiet,' Maggie advised her. 'Then we'll see if you need a dose of syrup of figs.'

That was enough to make her try. The lid was closed, and she was settled into the bed again, the pillow smoothed behind her snow-white head. The ritual was always the same: her little handkerchief soaked in eau-de-cologne, then dabbed on her forehead for her effort on the commode.

Just as Maggie feared, she wasn't going to let her go back down to her baking. The good hand patted the bed for her to sit. 'Have you heard from camp?'

'I had a postcard from Hector, ma'am,' Maggie said, though she knew that wasn't what the old lady was meaning.

'It wouldn't cost much for Niall to put a stamp on a card to me,' she said sadly. 'His father never went anywhere, even in India, but he sent me a card, and if he could get them to me, flowers. He once sent an Indian on horseback a hundred miles with a bunch of lilies. By the time they got to me they were like rags, and the man was barely hanging on to the horse, but it was the thought, you see.'

'But the Master's got duties at camp, ma'am,' Maggie said. 'There's a lot of men to be looked after.'

'You're always defending him,' his mother said, with more admiration than irritation.

'You should try and have a wee sleep, ma'am.'

But the white head shook defiantly. 'I've been having a wee sleep for years, and much good it's done me. I was thinking, maybe I should get up and sit in the chair by the window.'

Maggie had been waiting for that one coming. 'Doctor MacNiven said you were to be kept in bed in case you got a chill.' It was too much, heaving and hauling her over there. The last time she was at that window, she'd been stung by a wasp, and all hell had broken loose.

'Have you *any* news for me?'

'We've got a new groom, ma'am. A fellow from Buchan.'

'And is he nice?'

The old lady was watching Maggie's face.

She nodded.

'I remember the first day we arrived home, it was Roddy drove us from the station. He was a young man then. I often think it was a mistake, coming.'

But Maggie had heard it all before. 'I have to go down and get on with things, ma'am. I'll send up your tea tray in an hour. Try and have a wee sleep.' She patted the hump in the bed affectionately.

But there was something else. Maggie had to locate the bead bag at the foot of the bed. The old lady's good hand twisted the catches and the contents were tipped out on to the patchwork quilt.

'You have this,' she said to Maggie.

It was a tiny ivory elephant, with a loop on the back for threading through a chain.

'Dear Sandy gave me that long before you were born.'

'I can't take it, ma'am.'

'There's no one deserves it better, for what you've done for me and Niall. If it was not for you he—'

But she stopped, and was now feeling the coins lying in the hollow of the quilt between her wasted knees. She gave Maggie the shilling. It was the same ritual, as if Maggie was renting out the commode to her each time she used it, which was only three times a week now.

'What's for dinner?' she asked.

'A nice salad, ma'am'.

'I'm sick of salads,' the old woman complained. 'I keep thinking of a plate of kedgeree.'

'Kedgeree? But there's no fish in this weather.'

'We had kedgeree for breakfast in India. I can still taste the moist rice.'

Was this the old warrior getting at her cooking?

'If you don't want salad, I could give you an omelette, ma'am.'

'That's not exciting,' she said disdainfully. 'No, I'll take the salad, though it'll give me wind. Have you had a postcard from Dunoon?'

'He's getting on fine. But I'll need to go and get on with things, ma'am, for the Master coming home.'

'I hope he remembers to bring me something this time,' his mother said plaintively. 'I never asked much of my children. Maybe that was the trouble. Now Alexander—'

'Try and have a wee sleep,' Maggie said, already at the door.

* * *

26

From the window on the landing Maggie saw Sam going down the avenue on the gig. It was a good chance to go up to see if he'd settled into his room. The baking could wait. She went up the mossy path, hesitating at the bottom of the steps before going up and pushing the door timidly.

The loft smelled of polish, and some of the dust her brush had stirred up was still drifting in the sunlight streaming through the skylight. She stood on the threshold, looking at the old brown suitcase under the bed she'd made up, the fresh white sheet folded down over the blankets tucked under the mattress she'd taken off her brother's bed. The poor soul, he didn't have much. Then she saw the black Sunday suit hanging from the nail in the rafter. It needed a good press after its journey from Aberdeen in the suitcase. She ran her fingers over it, straightening the lapels.

The top drawer of the chest squeaked as she pulled it open. She felt that she was prying when she saw the little pile of vests and pants, and beside it, the Bible. She lifted it out. The gilt-edged leaves were well used. He was of a different religion to her, but what did that matter? Not that she went to chapel as regularly as she should, but the Master was often late down for breakfast on Sunday morning.

She laid the Bible on the top of the chest and opened the cover. There was an inscription in black ink.

For I am persuaded that neither death, nor life,
nor angels, nor principalities, nor powers,
nor things present, nor things to come,
Nor height, nor depth, nor any other creature,
shall be able to separate us from the love of God,
which is in Christ Jesus our Lord.

She stood there, touched. It added another mystery to him. She laid the Bible back in the drawer, easing it shut with her hip. Then she heard the gig coming into the yard. There wasn't time to go down the steps, so she tried to compose herself before she went out.

'I was just making sure you were comfortable,' she said, embarrassed. 'Do you not need another blanket?'

'No, I'm fine,' he said, unconcerned. He took a match from his waistcoat pocket and struck it on the iron hoop of the big wheel as he leaned against the gig. He smoked like he ate, like he laughed, with relish.

'I'd better be getting back down,' she said awkwardly. But she stayed at the top of the steps, watching the way the smoke was caught by the sunlight as it drifted round his face. She was becoming acute to all his movements.

'They're nice beasts. I'm getting the hang of the gig,' he told her.

'I wouldn't tell the Master you haven't driven a gig before if I were you,' she said earnestly.

'Why is that?' he asked.

'It would just worry him, and he's got plenty worries already. I'm sure you'll manage. Anyway, I'd better get back down, otherwise you'll get no food tonight.'

'That would be a great pity,' he said, grinning as he began to unharness the horses.

Later from the kitchen window she watched him leading the horses with the gig up and down the avenue, running beside them to get them used to him. The ripple of the sunset through the leaves made it look as if their flanks were on fire.

Jura was sitting under the golden sky outside the mess tent, his riding boot slung across the knee of his trews as he smoked a cigarette. The last night was always noisy, with the men drinking round the fires. Somebody was singing a Gaelic song. It rang out, pleading, wistful. You didn't need the language to know it was about love. There was something very satisfying about commanding men. He'd felt the same in India, at the close of day, watching them bedding down − like children, really. He'd always kept a loaded revolver beside his head in case a wild beast came padding into the camp among them.

The singer had finished, and they were clapping him. Now it was the turn of a mouth-organ. He could see the fire flaring on the tin instrument, the fluttering fingers coaxing the tremulous tune out of it. Further away, in the dimly lit frieze of tents, figures stooped, packing. He was always affected by this last night, though there was always next year to look forward to.

Having had his addictive after-dinner pibroch, Kilberry had nodded to sleep in the mess tent, the whisky bottle by his hand. Further down the long table young officers were slapping down cards by the light of a lantern.

'Is there anything you require, sir?' the orderly in his ghostly white jacket asked the Adjutant.

Jura had had enough to drink, but Niall Invernevis, who was sitting beside him, handed over his brandy glass for a refill. This likeable man should remarry instead of brooding at his gloomy place.

'Why don't you come to Jura in August for the shooting? My father would be so pleased, and so would Dorothy.'

'That's very kind of you,' Invernevis said without commitment. It wouldn't be fair, with Jura newly married.

MacDougall and Hector were lying at one of the camp fires. Hector was nodding to sleep with the heat and the amount of whisky he'd had from the bottle that his friend had been passing him in celebration at winning all the heavy events at the sports.

'Oh, *Dhia*,' MacDougall said. 'There must be something in this whisky. Are you sure it wasn't holy water you bought, Eachan?'

Hector sat up. Alanna Richardson was moving among the fires in a long white gown, her sequined bag sparkling in her hand as she stooped to speak to the men.

'I would like to visit the men in the camp,' she had told her husband in their hotel room after dinner.

'It's not the done thing, women going into a camp,' the Brigadier said, a ghost in the haze of cigar smoke in her dressing mirror.

'I don't care what the done thing is, Freddie. I want to thank the men for the entertainment they gave us this afternoon. Ring the porter to arrange transport.'

'I'll get a gig,' he said dutifully.

'You will not, or it'll take all night to get there. Hire a motor car.'

As she was sitting in the back of it, her head bound in a silk scarf against the night breeze, she was thinking of the big handsome man who had tossed the caber that afternoon. She wouldn't be able to sleep unless she saw him again, so she was picking her way among the camp fires, watching for him as she complimented the men on their performances in the sports.

'She won't come over here,' Hector said sadly.

But MacDougall knew she would, from the touch of her hand that afternoon when she had presented him with the medals.

The golden shoes stopped beside him. 'Now aren't you the man that won the caber?'

'I am, ma'am,' he said, getting to his feet.

She put a hand on his shoulder. 'Don't get up. What's your name?'

'Dochie MacDougall, ma'am.'

She knew that already. 'You're from Invernevis. What do you do?'

'I run a croft and work as a ghillie.'

'And you won the piping,' she said to Hector.

She looked so beautiful, towering above him against the moon, that he couldn't say anything.

She turned to Jura. 'Thank you for the tour, Jock. I've enjoyed the visit.'

The night seemed to get chilly after she had gone, and they threw the last of the wood on the fire.

'That's some woman,' Hector said. 'I bet you would like to have a go at her, Dochie.'

But the big man was silent.

The Adjutant was moving among the men, and came to sit on his heels beside MacDougall and Hector, the firelight gleaming on his riding boots.

'Had a good camp?'

'Yes, sir.' They were relaxed and at the same time respectful with him.

'I hope to get up to Invernevis this winter to see how things are going,' Jura said. 'Keep working at your drills.'

'Yes, sir.'

Jura went back up to where Invernevis was sitting, swirling the brandy balloon in his fingers as if it were a dark crystal ball in which he was studying the future.

'I'd better get home to Dorothy. Now you will think about coming to stay?'

'I will, Jock.'

The Adjutant whistled softly and his black charger came trotting from behind the mess tent where it had been grazing. Invernevis watched him enviously as he mounted, sitting up among the stars. Jura had everything, good looks, a first-class soldier, a lovely wife, and he was heir to that mysterious island, with its Paps in the clouds. Some of the men lying at the fires would be leaving very early in the morning, and one suddenly got to his feet.

'Three cheers for Captain Campbell of Jura!'

'Hip Hip!' they shouted as they rose, waving their bonnets.

Their 'Hoorays!' rang out as the Adjutant rode into the darkness, his arm raised.

3

As the gig swayed down into the darkening countryside Invernevis was impressed with the way the new coachman was handling the horses. Hector was sitting beside Sam in the front, telling him about the camp. Invernevis sat back, listening to an owl. The lamps of the house were on across the river, and Maggie was waiting in the porch to light him in.

'Did you have a good journey, sir?'

'Very good, Maggie.'

She helped him off with his Inverness cape. The West Highland terriers were waiting to welcome him in the hall full of the mingled fragrances of the beeswax the housemaids had rubbed into the woodwork and the roses that Maggie had arranged in the vase on the table. Eight servants inside and out ran the house and garden for the comfort of this one man, who had never questioned his right to it. The long-case clock had stopped. He wouldn't allow anyone else to touch it, and he rewound it, setting the hands by his watch before he went into the library.

Everything was in the same place as he had left it, though the room had been spring-cleaned in his absence. It was a gentleman's den. His fishing books had been dusted and replaced on the shelves in their correct order. The silver-capped inkwells on his leather-topped desk had been refilled with the blue ink he favoured. The anemone trapped inside the paperweight seemed to burst into a star of blossom in the silver fluted lamp that Maggie had lit for him. The ivory paper knife with its serrated edge was on top of the pile of a fortnight's post, with a bundle of copies of the Times in their wrappers from London.

He was going to sit down to go through the mail, but Maggie was at his back to tell him that his dinner was in. There was a candelabrum at his place at the long mahogany table, his crested King's Pattern cutlery set out, a white starched napkin sheathed in a silver ring with his arms. Jessie the tablemaid served his broth from the sideboard with a ladle, and then held the hot dish in a napkin so that he could help himself to new potatoes and vegetables with his lamb chops, accompanied by wine. When the bowl of *carraigein* was brought to him he took two helpings to please Maggie. He went through to the library, lighting a cigarette. The silver coffee pot and the large Spode cup painted with fruit with the matching bowl of brown crystals of sugar were waiting on the little table by his arm chair. He poured himself coffee and he sat at his desk, shuffling through the letters. There was one from Switzerland.

I am sorry to keep bothering you about money, but our situation is becoming very serious. The Fräulein in our pensione is getting most unpleasant about the six months' rent we are due, though I keep telling her that a cheque will be coming from Scotland any day. I have been saying that for weeks now. I am afraid that one day when we return from our walk by the lake we will find our luggage out in the courtyard.

The children are well, and the air here certainly suits them, but the tension in the pensione is disturbing their lessons. The little boy is particularly sensitive to the Fräulein's eruptions. Last night I asked for a cup of cocoa for him so that he would sleep. She shook her head and rubbed her fingers together to show that she had to have money first. She is a very vulgar woman, but we cannot move until we have settled her account.

I am not worried about the six months' money I am owed myself, but there is a limit to how far my own savings will stretch, when Switzerland is such an expensive place. I came out here on the understanding that it would only be for a year until you decided what was to be done after your wife's tragic death, but we have been here four years

now, and the children need the love and supervision
of a parent. I am most willing to return with them to
Invernevis to be their governess there, and I
anxiously await your instructions.
Yours obediently,
Sarah Fraser.

He'd got used to being by himself, and three young children
about the house would mean more servants. Maggie wouldn't
be able to cope, when she had his mother to look after as
well. He would have to get money from somewhere to send
to Switzerland, but he wasn't going to worry about that tonight.
He opened the new bottle of Mackinlay's that Maggie had put
on the tray beside the crystal glass and turned his swivel desk
chair to the window on the west. It was as if a lamp was being
turned down slowly in the countryside. This had been his view
since coming home from South Africa at the turn of the century,
but many lairds before him had also seen it. It had taken so
much spilt blood to put a window round this scene, to allow
that old plough-horse to settle for the night among the daisies
in the meadow on the other side of the river.

He would love to take a hat from the hall stand and start
walking, down the avenue, along the estate roads, for the sheer
pleasure of the summer night with its peace, its fragrances. But
there were regrets. What a tragedy that Alexander had got mixed
up with that tribe up at the Home Farm, because it could all have
turned out so different. His brother could have married someone
from his own class and been factor of the place. They would have
worked well together. But of course so many things might not
have been: a few more seconds, and these two vehicles would
have been round the blind bend safely. He could hear Mary
Rose at the piano across in the drawing-room. But where
did brooding get you? It was evenings like this that made it
worthwhile to go on.

He took the bottle of whisky and the present he'd bought for
Maggie in Dunoon through to the kitchen where Hector was
showing his piping medals to Maggie and Sam.

'He did very well,' Invernevis said. 'Colonel Campbell says he's a very fine piper.'

He sat at the end of the table, the signal for Hector and Sam to go. He gave her the present, chosen not for the contents but because he knew she liked nice boxes. It was a gold box of *marrons glacés*.

'Oh, you shouldn't have, sir,' she said, coy as a girl.

'I'm so sorry I forgot to tell you about the new coachman. How's he getting on?'

'He likes it here, sir.'

'I'm glad. He seems to handle horses well. How's my mother?'

'She's fine, sir.'

The cat came on to his knee and he caressed it as he told Maggie about the camp. She listened eagerly to the news about Princess Louise and the Duke of Argyll.

'The Duke's a very clever man, and so is his sister Lady Elspeth. I must invite them to stay.'

She nodded, but knew it was the whisky speaking. There were eight surplus bedrooms whose mattresses hadn't been slept on for years but which she still dragged downstairs to air every summer.

'We've got a new lieutenant. John Lauder, Harry Lauder's son.'

'Fancy that, sir. An officer.'

'Yes, they have the Glenbranter estate near Dunoon. They say he's made a lot of money in America. The son seems very quiet.'

He tilted the bottle again. She was tired, but she never sat down in his presence. She stood by his chair, nodding and listening because she was glad to have him home, to see that the camp hadn't tired him too much.

A good hour before the train was due the old man was sitting on the big stone by the roadside, waiting. But the train was late and he nodded to sleep. MacDougall saw him as he came round the corner, looking like a benign gnome with his white whiskers, the toecaps of his big boots polished. He swung down the kitbag from his shoulder to stoop to kiss the top of the white head.

' *'S ciamar a tha mhàthair?* ' ('And how is mother?')

'Mar a dh' fhàg thu i,' ('The same as when you left her,') the old man said.

She had the pot of potatoes on the range. She was even smaller than the old man. MacDougall lifted her off her feet to kiss her and she gave her high cackling laugh as he swung her round, her head touching the ceiling. She always wore a small peaked hat, even indoors. They called her *Peigi bheag na biorraide* (wee Peggy of the hat). The language of the house was always Gaelic. When the old woman tried English she called her husband 'it' and the dog 'he', though it was a bitch. But her Gaelic included words that no one else in the district had.

'Tapadh leibh a mhàthair,' ('Thank you mother,') he said as she put the plate of golden broth in front of him.

But she wasn't his mother. She and the old man sitting on the opposite side of the fire had brought him up after his mother had died, without revealing the name of his father.

'Did you behave yourself at camp?' she asked.

'Oh, aye,' he said. 'By God, this is good soup. We didn't get anything like this at Dunoon.'

She kept reaching over to touch him, cackling because she couldn't believe that *Mairi Peigi bheag na biorraide* (Mairi, daughter of wee Peggy of the hat) could have produced a man like this.

'I think you met someone,' she said accusingly.

'No, no. Not when there's you.'

She cackled with sheer pleasure as she busied herself, giving him the white breast of the chicken. The last winter when she hadn't been well he'd carried her in his arms like a child to the *taigh beag* at the top of the garden, waiting in the rain till she knocked the door, signalling that she was ready to go back in her nightdress and hat, her hands clasped round his neck.

The old man was sitting beaming, seeing his own shoulders in the boy at the table. He was full of *sgeulachdan*, the old tales, and was sure that his grandson was a reincarnation of the warrior Fionn Mac Cumhail who'd vanquished many men with his sword Mac a' Luin and broken many a woman's heart.

'Will you take curds and whey?' the old woman cackled, knowing she needn't ask. She sat watching him spooning it into his mouth.

'Was the laird at camp?' the old man asked.

'Yes, and taking a big drink.'

'That's a pity if he's going to go the same way as his mother. A finer lady you couldn't meet. I remember the old laird well. *Pheigi bheag*, away into the scullery for a moment, till I tell the boy something.'

She shuffled away, cackling at men's crudeness.

'He was a big man, like yourself, with a birthmark his beard couldn't hide.' He touched his cheek with the stem of his pipe. 'Some folks said it was the mark of the devil, and others said that a woman threw a lamp at him. He used to come up to the village to play quoits behind the smithy. What you did was to hammer pegs in the ground and throw the horseshoes at them. I never saw him in anything but the kilt. He had a way of swinging the shoe between his legs before he threw it. It wasn't the peg the women were watching behind his back.' The old man put the pipe into his mouth and made curves with his hands as if giving his grandson a lesson in geometry. 'He had balls on him like a ram.'

But he wasn't ready to call the old woman back yet.

'You're not going to join the army?'

'Hell, no,' MacDougall said, helping himself to more curds and whey.

'Because it would only upset the old woman,' the old man said confidentially. 'You keep her going, you see. I'll tell you – sometimes she wakes up laughing beside me in the middle of the night. What's wrong, *Pheigi bheag*? I say. That boy's the limit, she says. I think she must dream about you. It's not a life that would suit you.'

'What isn't?' he asked.

'The army.'

'I'm not going to join the army, but I'll stay with the Territorials.'

'That's good. Oh, go and enjoy yourself at camp for the fortnight. That's what I used to do, in the time when the old laird was in charge. My God, I never saw a man drink so much with so little effect. You would think he had hollow legs. That was before he went down with that disease he got in India.'

'What disease was that?' MacDougall asked.

'No one put a name to it, but they say he got it from black women.'

MacDougall was wondering if this was a warning to himself, but the old man was calling:

'*Pheigi bheag*, the boy's ready for his cup of tea!'

But when she came through she made a fuss. The old man had left the window to the west open. It wasn't the wasps of that summer she was frightened of; after sunset the *Sluagh*, the host of the dead, passed with a whistling noise like *sgaoth fheadag*, a flock of plovers, and if they got in through an open window they left a deathly chill in the house. Once as a young woman she'd been caught up by them and whirled away across the mountain to a cemetery in a strange glen where they'd left her all night among the ancient stones with no names before returning her to her own doorstep in the morning. She was too old for that kind of trip now, but they would take the boy, and they wouldn't bring him back.

She was full of superstitions and old cures. They brought animals to her from miles around and she muttered Gaelic incantations as she plucked the figwort and other plants from the ditch to make medicines, applying them to the black toadstools of cancers on the lips of horses which dropped off after two days. Once a ballooned cow was brought to her on a cart, near to death because the vet could do nothing about the calf stuck inside it. She had whispered to the cow in Gaelic, then pushed her arm up its vulva. The calf and its mother went home on their feet together.

MacDougall managed to get the window shut before the *Sluagh* passed. It was time to give them their presents. The old woman got a little brass shoe, the old man a bar of thick black tobacco in gold paper.

'Are you going out tonight?' she asked, putting the teapot in front of him. It was always the same question, and the answer was always the same. He would 'take a wee turn round the place' on his bicycle. She peeked round the door at him, like a girl seeing her first naked man as he washed in the scullery, and when he came through she had his shirt warming in the oven, as she did when he was a boy going to school on winter mornings.

He wouldn't stop growing. At the age of one he was far too big for her to carry about the room when he got gripe at night, and at two she walked him up to the village to the doctor's surgery on his sturdy legs.

'He's a fine big boy,' Doctor MacNiven said, remembering the tiny mother he'd also delivered.

But *Peigi bheag* was unbuttoning his trousers and pointing to his *bod*.

'*Nach urrain dhuibh a thimcheall-ghearradh feuch an sguir e dh'fhàs?*' ('Can't you circumcize him so that it stops growing?')

'*Chan urrainn, chan urrainn. Chan eil e ach nàdarrach, ach tha amharas agam gun adhbhraich e dragh fhathast,*' (I can't, I can't. It's perfectly natural, but I suspect it will cause a bit of bother in the future,') Doctor MacNiven said with a smile.

The day he started school he was bigger than any of the boys in the senior class. He carried pockets of coloured marbles and his aim was always deadly accurate as he knocked the others out of the circle. The old man delivered the mails, and at eleven o' clock, when he rode past the school, the boy stood up in class and waved, though he was caned every day for it.

At the age of eight he'd crossed the wall into the girls' shed. The MacPhee twins stood with their tartan skirts hoisted to their chins, their long bloomers round their boots while MacDougall inspected them. But when they saw what he had they began to cry. The teacher had seen from the window, and told him he was 'for the bad fire' before she broke the cane on his backside.

He was too big for his desk, and had to sit sideways with his knees out. He pushed his fingers up through the hole where the inkwell should have been. The teacher from the south caned them if they answered in Gaelic, but he held out his hand every time. Hector Macdonald sat at the desk in front, but there was no use copying off him, because there was no sense in both of them getting beaten for the same mistakes. One day the old man didn't ride past the school at eleven. MacDougall stayed standing, though the teacher threw the duster at him and then laid about his back with the blackboard ruler. At noon the old woman appeared in the classroom, frightening the children because of her pointed hat and the noise her boots made on the boards as she went up to his desk and led him out by the hand.

The old man had fallen off the horse and broken his leg.

From the age of nine MacDougall was doing most of the work on the croft, and he kept growing and growing. Women coming down from the village rested their baskets on the hedge to watch him scything. He came across to make liaisons with them as he sharpened the blade while the old man sat smiling to himself in the porch and the old woman cackled as she bundled up the hay he'd cut.

The old woman was sitting by the fire, fondling the brass shoe when he went out. He lifted his bicycle from the byre and cycled along the hedges, taking his hands off the bars to roll a cigarette. He rode up the brae to the Arms, standing on the pedals to get purchase. He dominated the bar as he stood, even bigger than mine host behind the counter. When MacDougall was speaking in Gaelic the dominoes stopped clicking and old men sitting with half pints saw themselves in him and nodded to Carmichael behind the counter to give him a libation.

He drained the glasses of whisky that had been lined up for him as if they were water. The customers looked at each other, wondering if it was their wife or daughter he was going to bestow his favours on, but none of them made a move to go home, as if it was an honour for their women to have a visit from him. He put his boots up on the handlebars and freewheeled down into the evening countryside for an assignation he would never speak about. As far as the old woman was concerned, he could do anything except eat and sleep in another house.

He took off his boots and went upstairs quietly, opening the door to make sure the old folks were asleep. The old woman's hat was hung over the bedpost, and the brass shoe was on the pillow by her face, the mouth puckered in a dream. They lay together like two little people under a spell in a ballad. He stooped over to kiss them both on the forehead before going across the landing to his room, leaving the door open. He lay in bed in the tiny room, his head and feet almost touching walls, looking at the glint of the medals on the dresser in the moonlight as he thought of Alanna Richardson. Her hand had been hot as she'd given him the medals.

4

Hector Macdonald marked time on the gravel under the big bay window at the front of Invernevis House as he played 'Hey, Johnnie Cope, are ye wakened yet?' Then he took the tray of tea upstairs and opened the curtains. The big kettles which had sat overnight on the stove were being lugged up the back stairs by the maids to the bathroom which had been put in after Invernevis's marriage, though the money had run out before a hot-water supply could be installed.

When Invernevis went through the big iron tub on its claw feet was steaming fragrantly with the essences Maggie made the maids put in. He lay for ten minutes, immersed to his shoulders, then rose for the voluminous white towel. He went back through to his bedroom. The jug of shaving water with the white cloth over it like a Mass chalice had been brought up by Hector, who had also stropped the cut-throat razor and laid it open on the mottled marble slab of the wash-stand.

'What clothes do you want today, sir?' Hector asked.

As Invernevis shaved with measured strokes it seemed that the same blackbird on the bush below had been singing to him each morning since he'd moved into the master bedroom after his father's death. It was spacious, a sitting-room as well, with a desk and sofa, sporting magazines on the round table and paintings with sporting themes on the walls.

He cleaned the blade before folding it into its ivory handle and laid it back in the case with its twin, then took the soap from his face with the small white towel which had been warmed by the steam of the jug it had covered. While he was snipping his moustache he heard the woodpecker beginning on the tree at the bottom of the lawn. He shook bay rum into his palm and massaged it into his tingling skin.

He loved these hot summer mornings of open windows because they reminded him of his boyhood when he would be down at the river early with a rod, practising his casting while the house was still sleeping. He went through to his dressing-room where Hector had laid out the chosen clothes: lightweight trousers and a summer jacket, a shirt from the cabinet of long shallow drawers pungent with camphor, the sleeves folded over by Maggie in an attitude of supplication after she had ironed them herself.

He knotted on his Royal Company of Archers tie, though he had not been to Edinburgh for years in attendance on a visiting monarch with bow and quiver. Hector had already sprung the trees from a pair of brown brogues from the row made for him by Lobb of London on his own last. He replenished his silver cigarette case from the sandalwood box before going down to the dining-room to a breakfast of porridge made with oatmeal, followed by a brown egg from the Home Farm boiled to soft perfection by Maggie without a timer. He spread Gentleman's Relish on toast from the white porcelain jar that had come from Fortnum & Mason with the speciality teas for breakfast and afternoon.

He was lighting his first cigarette of the day as he went through to the library. A stamp album lay open on the desk, from the shelf of red-bound books, the colourful history of Empire arranged alphabetically: a subservient tribe in a canoe in the 2d blue of the British Solomon Islands; a Malayan tapir on the 1901 one–cent black-and-brown of North Borneo; the annas and rupees of Victoria's ageing profile in the issues of loyal India, mounted on their flimsy hinges by his mother while his father was forcing himself on thin, ill-fed native minors in the bazaar.

William Tell's face was wrinkled by the Lausanne postmark in the stamps of Helvetia lying on the open album, doubles from the letters from the governess, pleading for money. Invernevis was getting anxious about the children because of the worsening international situation which he had been following intently in the newspapers since the assassination of the Archduke Francis Ferdinand and his wife by the Serbian fanatics, shots that were ricocheting round Europe.

As he stood at the window looking up the avenue he was

43

already having his first drink of the day from the new bottle of Mackinlay's. When he saw the gig coming round the bend he went out to the front to get the papers.

Sam was no sooner in the kitchen than the bell rang. Maggie came back through to give him his orders.

'He wants you to take him up to the village right away.'

He didn't like forcing the horses like this on such a hot day, when they'd just come down from the village, but he was under orders to hurry, so he plucked the whip from the socket. The gig swayed between the hedges, the hub-caps strumming briars, the two heads in harness well back. Invernevis was sitting silent and serious-looking beside him. They ran along main street, a child's iron hoop wobbling out of the way.

'Left, up the cemetery road,' Invernevis directed. 'Wait here,' he ordered at the first gate, though Sam wanted to take the team down to the water trough at the smithy after their dusty run.

The rhododendrons on the short curving driveway had been hacked back, and the speckled gravel from the quarry was clear of weeds. Invernevis pulled the knob in the polished brass plate, bringing a dark shape to the stained glass. The thin housekeeper with her hair bunched tight behind was deferential, showing him into a sitting-room of severe chairs with antimacassars, and in a corner, a plant that looked as if it had never flowered. While he was waiting he smoked nervously.

When Father Macdonald eventually came in, Invernevis rose to shake hands. The contact was cold and weak.

Invernevis spread the newspaper on the desk.

AUSTRO-SERBIAN CRISIS
SHADOW OF EUROPEAN WAR
MOBILISATION IN
AUSTRIA-HUNGARY AND SERBIA.

The priest, who was senior trustee of the estate, glanced at the headlines, then resumed watching him over gold spectacles which seemed too sparing for his face.

44

In the silence the visitor heard a measured pendulum.

'I must bring my children home from Switzerland.'

But there was going to be no encouragement from this expressionless face.

'I need funds today, for their fares.'

The priest went to his bookshelves. He was a scholar who had come to Invernevis with a considerable library as a young man. He brought back a folio volume which he opened and laid on the desk in front of his visitor. 'That is Switzerland.' A finger stubbed on the map of Europe. 'And Serbia.' The callipers of two fingers stretched for the connection. 'Even if a war involving Switzerland were to break out tomorrow – which is absurd, of course – I can't authorize any money to be paid to you from the estate. There would have to be a special meeting of the trustees, and I think we both know what the answer would be.'

'But this is an emergency,' Invernevis said despairingly.

'Like all the other emergencies,' the priest said cynically, replacing the atlas in its slot on the shelf before going back to his swivel chair behind the desk. 'We've given you a great deal of money lately, to keep your house going because you won't cut back on your expenses.'

'I *have* been careful, but the international situation is affecting the stock market.'

The priest folded his spectacles on the blotter, his eyes even fiercer without them. The light seemed to concentrate on the slope of his bald head. He spoke as if he hadn't heard Invernevis.

'You've had warning after warning from the lawyers, which you've chosen to ignore. You're spending money which you're not entitled to spend.'

'I have a large house to keep going.'

'Then let it out and move into a smaller one. You could rent your brother's place.'

After his marriage to the daughter of the Home Farm tenant, because she was expecting by him, Alexander had built a house by the river, but his widow had left the district, and the garden was so overgrown that the residence was disappearing in the rhododendrons.

Invernevis ignored the provocation. 'My house is the centre of the estate, and the tenants expect the laird to live in it.'

'They also expect the laird to be responsible. If you continue as you're doing you'll leave the trustees no choice but to sell part of the place.'

'You can't do that,' Invernevis said, appalled. 'I would fight you through the courts.'

'We *could* do it, by showing that the estate couldn't survive unless part of it went. There are enough powers if we need to use them. It's in your hands; you know the terms and conditions of your father's will — which you persist in not keeping to.'

'But damn it, it's my place,' Invernevis said angrily.

The priest ignored the blasphemy. 'It isn't your place. It's being held in trust for your son to inherit when he's twenty-one. Those were the terms of your father's will.'

'All the more reason for bringing my son home now, so that he's safe.'

'Unless you cut back, there won't be a place for your son to inherit. What about your late wife's money?'

'The little she had she left in trust to the children,' he told the priest, though it was none of his business. Mary Rose couldn't stand having him in the house.

'And another thing,' Father Macdonald said as he rose to show that the interview was over. 'I haven't seen you in chapel for years. It's a bad example to set the tenants. You'll only keep an estate going if the people respect you.'

As he followed the priest to the door Invernevis would dearly love to have said: *then I shall hold you responsible if anything happens to my children.* But this was a dangerous man, even though he was wearing clerical cloth; perhaps even more dangerous because of it, since he believed himself to be the most powerful person in the place. He had been Aunt Carlotta's ally and had caused so much trouble down at the house as well as in the district. He blamed this man for his mother's heavy drinking. But he could make a lot of trouble with the trustees.

How was he going to solve this crisis? he asked himself helplessly as the gig hurried him down again. A man had stepped on to the verge and was lifting his cap as the vehicle passed, but Invernevis was too preoccupied to acknowledge the greeting. The bank had written to warn him that unless he brought his overdraft down to the agreed limit, his cheques would be returned. He needed to find some way of raising money quickly, and he also needed a drink.

Maggie had baking to do, but had put the stuff away after two burst yolks. Everything was changing: she felt the chill of it in her bones, the feeling her mother had reported when going into a haunted room.

Sam came in with two pails. 'There isn't a trickle in the stable tap,' he complained.

'I'm sick of all the coming and going. Where was he this time?' she asked.

'We went up to see the priest.'

Now what on earth was he wanting with Father MacDonald, when they disliked one another so much?

'He looked very angry when he came out of the house, and he didn't say a word to me all the way down.'

She didn't like encouraging him to gossip, but she was intrigued. It must be to do with money, seeing the priest was one of the trustees. There were more and more reminders for bills on his desk, and she was getting anxious about ordering things.

'It'll take you ages to fill these pails in the scullery,' she warned him.

'The horses need water, in case we have to go up to the village again,' Sam called back to her as he went through with the pails. He left the tap trickling and leaned in the doorway, his ankles crossed as he made a cigarette, the membrane of the paper stretched between his hands in the strong light. She watched him nipping off the ends of the tobacco and putting the surplus strands back into the tin.

'Have you seen today's papers?' he asked as he struck a match on the lintel. 'I had a look when I brought them down.'

'You had no business,' she rounded on him.

'Where's the harm in it?' he asked, surprised by a side of her nature he hadn't seen before.

'He doesn't like anyone else reading them before he sees them.'

'Shadow of European war. Mobilization in Austria-Hungary and Serbia.' He'd been repeating it all morning to himself, like one of the poems, 'The Charge of the Light Brigade', he'd had to learn at school.

'What are you talking about?'

'That's what it says in the paper.'

But she'd never heard of Serbia.

'Go and get that pail and get back to your work. If he comes through and finds you hanging about you're for it.'

'It's not nearly filled,' he said casually.'Do you fancy a walk tonight?'

'I've too much to do,' she said brusquely. 'Everything's at sixes and sevens.'

'Can I do anything for you?'

'Can you bake scones and prepare for tomorrow?' she asked scornfully.

'Look,' Jura said, holding the stalking glass against his knee as she went down beside him on the shoulder of the ben. In the circle of the lens she saw the velvet of the stag's antlers swinging like ribbons. Jura counted the points on the antlers: sixteen, a royal animal. He moved the glass back to her and she could have shouted with joy when she saw the calf feeding by its mother.

'I think shooting's so cruel,' she said.

But he didn't want to ruin this day with an argument over his favourite sport, so he shut the glass and they began climbing the ben again. The last few hundred yards were hard going, but it was worth it for the view. As she rested in the heather, her back to the cairn, he identified the panorama of the islands; the white strands of Colonsay across the sound, and north, the channel separating Jura from Scarba that boiled up into the whirlpool of Corryvreckan.

'Let's take a sailing holiday next summer,' he said eagerly.

'But you'd be jumping ashore, wanting to recruit for the Territorials,' she teased him as she lay back in the heather. The heat was making her want to sleep. Jura, who seemed always to be such a restrained man, had an intense desire to make love to her there, on the high top, but he'd brought a ghillie to carry the picnic. While the man unstrapped the basket, Jura weighed down the white cloth at the corners with stones from the cairn. There was cold chicken and wine which was warm. The ghillie had beer and sandwiches, sitting some distance away, his back to them.

'You must leave the army, Jock, and take over this place. That's what your father wants, and you love it so much.'

It was a beautiful island, but it was uneconomic, with so much high ground only good for stalking. If they were going to hold on to the place, they would have to rent out the shootings for as much as they could get. He could still keep up his interest in the Argylls by running the Territorial company on the island. The only worry was that Dorothy wouldn't like the winter. Some nights, lying in bed, you thought the sea was going to tear the house from the land. It didn't just affect the landscape; it also affected your mind. How had those Viking conquerors stayed sane as they voyaged among the islands in all weathers, he often wondered?

The ghillie was gathering together the remains of the picnic. Before leaving, Jura replaced the stones he'd taken from the cairn. There was a cooling breeze going down. Dorothy had a hand-lens, and kept stopping to examine the flowers.

'I shall write a book about the flora and fauna of Jura,' she announced. 'I don't think you realize what gems you have here.'

'I know the rarest one,' he said, taking her hand.

They went down through a glen filled with a light like a blue mist, where the fragrances made it feel as if they were walking in sleep.

'This is Kilearnadil,' he explained when they came to a cemetery. 'It's named after Saint Ernan. The tradition is that he died outside Jura but his body was brought back here for burial.'

'It's a beautiful place,' she said.

'I'd love a small house here,' he said. 'Imagine going to

sleep to the sound of the burn, then waking early and climbing the ben.'

'But not with a gun?'

'Not with a gun.'

He was lying on his stomach, drinking from the pure water that came down from the bens.

'This is where my family are buried,' he said.

But she didn't like graveyards.

They went down the track hand-in-hand, towards the hamlet of Keils with its thatched roofs. The people had come out of their houses to see the couple from the big house, as if they were royalty. An old woman was sitting in a plain chair, her back to the wall, a clay pipe clamped in her jaws as she watched them coming down. Then the pipe fell, breaking on the stones at her boots. She began to shake and call out in Gaelic in a wailing voice.

'What's wrong with her?' Dorothy asked, frightened, clutching his arm.

'She's probably had too much sun,' Jura said.

Two men were now carrying the old woman inside on the chair. The door had closed, but the wailing followed them down the track.

'Shouldn't we get a doctor?' Dorothy asked.

'Best to leave her. She'll be all right.'

A gig was waiting for them at the bottom of the track, and Dorothy sat silent as they jolted back to Jura House. The laird was eager for his son's company.

'Did you have a good day?'

'It was wonderful,' Dorothy said.

'Now go and get some tea, and Jock and I will have something stronger.'

He followed his father into the library. The two day old newspapers which had come across by boat that morning were lying on the desk.

THE FEARS OF EUROPE

'Will it mean war?' his father asked anxiously as he poured generous measures of malt whisky from Islay across the sound.

'I don't know,' Jura said. But he felt strangely elated.

'I hope it won't involve you,' his father voiced his fears. 'This place needs proper management if we're going to hold on to it, and I'm getting too old to get about as I should.'

'I promise you, if I'm not called upon, I'll leave the service next year, and come and live here. It's what Dorothy wants too, so I'm outnumbered.'

'Then I think we should have a special bottle at dinner,' the delighted old man said.

On his way down to dress for dinner Lieutenant Lauder put his head into the ship's wireless room.

'Nothing for you, sir.'

Because of his kilt and doublet with the lace at his throat the diners in the first class saloon stood up and clapped him to his place. The Captain's braided cuff went up in a salute, and the select company at his table laughed.

'I don't need to introduce Lieutenant Lauder. You've all had the pleasure of hearing his recital last night.'

'Charming. Exquisite,' the old diamonded dames said, fur stoles round their frail shoulders even in that mild latitude.

'But of course, we all know to whom he owes his talents,' the Captain said. 'You'll be looking forward to seeing your father in two days time,' he added, signalling to a waiter. 'He'll be keeping Australia singing. I heard him once, in London. I've never forgotten his performance with that knobbly stick. It's the way he leans on it, you think he's going to fall over. He's got such a fine voice. Was he trained?'

But the Lieutenant didn't want to discuss his father's abilities.

'Is there any news of the international situation?' he asked.

'Apparently Austria has declared war on Serbia,' the Captain said. 'Not that that affects this voyage,' he added, seeing the ancient faces becoming anxious around him.

'I may not be very long in Australia,' Lauder muttered, spreading his napkin on his lap.

'How is that?' the woman at his left elbow asked.

'If we get involved in war, I'll be recalled to my regiment,' he said enthusiastically.

'There won't be a war involving England,' a man with a foreign accent said across the democratically round table. 'This will blow over.' He was a merchant from Vienna, still trading on the high seas, using the medium of wireless. 'There have been alarms before. Bosnia, Agadir, the Balkans. Who remembers them now?'

'I'm not so sure,' Lieutenant Lauder said.

But the Captain didn't want his dinner spoilt by gloom. The waiter arrived with the hors d'oeuvres, and napkins were spread on frail knees.

'Now who saw the porpoises this morning?' asked the Captain.

Several shrivelled hands, well endowed with gold, went up obediently.

'There's a couple want to go fishing for a few days,' Carmichael told MacDougall in the bar of the Arms.

'I can't. I've got hay to make, and anyway the river's too low,' the big man explained.

'If you don't go with them it's the last time you'll be asked,' Carmichael warned him. 'If they want to pay good money to fish a river that's too low, that's their affair.'

MacDougall was at the door of the Arms next morning at nine, carrying a gaff with a cork on its barb and a landing net. He took off his cap as the fishing couple emerged.

We met at the camp sports,' Alanna Richardson said, holding out a hand.

She was wearing a long skirt totally unsuitable for fishing, and she handed him a parasol to hold as she put her dainty boot into the iron step of the gig. The Brigadier in plus fours was snorting snuff from a little silver box as the gig jolted down. As they rumbled across the humpbacked bridge MacDougall said nothing about the river being too low to fish.

'Don't let me hold you back, darling,' Alanna told her husband blithely, kissing his cheek. 'The ghillie here can teach me how to cast.'

The Brigadier went up to a pool he had fished before, his hat festooned with flies. After he had assembled the rod, threading the line through the eyes, MacDougall showed her how to cast, but her first attempt tangled in the bushes behind.

Will you teach me?' she asked in the plaintive voice of a girl to whom it was all a mystery.

MacDougall stood behind her, trying not to press into her skirt because the perfume on the back of her neck was giving him a hard-on as he put his arms round her waist and held the rod with her.

'It's too heavy for you, ma'am. A little trout rod to get the feel of it would be better before you go on to a bigger one.'

'I can manage,' she told him stubbornly.

'You'll have to keep the point up,' he demonstrated. She stood back to watch his strong arms whipping the greenheart rod, the fly drifting over his head as if it was alive. He looked so handsome, so vital, with his arm muscles rippling and a smile on his face, something she rarely saw on her husband's. She knew she was in love for the first time in her life, and that the attraction wasn't only physical.

It was her turn, but the hook caught in her skirt. 'You'll have to cut this,' she said, tugging at the catgut.

'You never cut a line,' he told her, trying to work the hook out of the silk at her thigh.

He had such gentle hands for such a big man. She lifted up her skirt. 'Surely you can work it out now.'

He had to ease his fingers between the material and her thigh to push out the barb. She lifted her skirt up to the thigh. She wasn't wearing anything underneath.

'Night after night I see you coming towards me in my dream, carrying the caber,' she told him in a faint voice. She clasped the back of his head and held his face against her thigh.

He had been with many women in Invernevis. He had taken

them standing up with the hems of their skirts in their fists while they watched over his heaving shoulder for their husbands coming up from the fields. But he had never been with a woman like this one. As she wriggled under him the tip of the rod snapped. They were laughing as they came.

'The mark of it's across your arse,' MacDougall told her.

'It's one of his best,' she said, giggling. We're going to have to think up a good story.' She sat up, pulling down her skirt. 'Give me a cigarette to steady my nerves.'

'They're only Woodbine,' MacDougall said dubiously.

'Whatever you have.'

'Any luck?' the Brigadier called an hour later as he came down the bank with an empty basket.

'I had a big one on, darling, but the tip of the rod broke. Isn't that true, ghillie?'

'It was one of the biggest I've seen for ages, sir,' MacDougall told him.

'Then I'll try this pool myself,' the Brigadier said eagerly.

He whipped lure after lure out over it for the rest of the week while his wife and the ghillie moved upriver, to a pool screened by alders, where MacDougall didn't tie one cast. They removed their clothes and lay on the bank, going into the river to wash off the sweat of their exertions.

'I don't want to go tomorrow,' Alanna told the big man. 'I can't stand the thought of the season in London, with all those boring parties and absurd hats. It's so different here. And you've made me find myself, as a woman.'

'You'll have to go,' he said apprehensively, seeing the complications.

'I know, I know. But promise me you'll come to London to see me.'

He laughed. 'When will I ever be anywhere near London? Dunoon's the limit of my travels.'

'Promise me you'll come for a holiday.'

'I couldn't afford a holiday,' he told her factually.

'Then I'll send money and you'll come to a comfortable hotel in London. No, better still: we'll go across to France for a holiday. They're not so stuffy about protocol. Mr and Mrs MacDougall,' she said wistfully.

'France?' he said uncomprehendingly. It was no more than a name in a school atlas.

'Promise me you'll come,' she pleaded.

It was the easiest thing in the world to promise.

5

Shortly after three in the sultry August afternoon the rachet-wheeled mechanism began to move, letter by fretful letter, as if someone trying to communicate from the spirit world had forgotten how to spell. The postmistress sat in the shaft of sunlight by the machine, the pencil moistened on the tip of her sharp tongue poised for the next word.

The bang of the date stamp scattered the pigeons from the corrugated iron roof of the post office. She came out, using her boot to rouse the boy dozing on the step.

'You'd better get down to the big house quicker than you've ever gone in your life,' she warned him in her abrasive Gaelic.

He put the envelope into the pouch at his waist and mounted the bicycle, becoming a winged messenger pursued by the *Sluagh*. But bouncing on the hard saddle was loosening his bowels, so he left the bicycle with wheels spinning in the middle of the road while he did a *cac* in the ditch among the murmurous insects. As he was wiping himself with the docken leaves he saw a newt in the bottom of the parched ditch. *Dearc-luachrach bheag*; the little lizard of the rushes. Its Gaelic name was longer than the creature itself. They lay trying to outstare each other among the flowers, and when the boy caught it he took the telegram out of the pouch and put the newt in, with a few leaves of grass.

He rested his boot on the parapet at Wade's Bridge, leaning over to see if there were any fish in the river before swerving between the trees on the avenue to the big house, pulling on the handlebars as if he was reining a horse. He took the blind bend too fast but the rhododendrons cushioned his fall and he remounted.

From the library window Invernevis saw him coming. He was expecting the telegram, after reading the newspapers Sam had brought down earlier. He went out and gave the boy threepence.

'Will I wait for a reply, sir?'

'No. I'll attend to it myself.'

He rang for Maggie, and she saw by his expression that it was bad news.

'The Territorials will have to go on the late train, Maggie, because of the war.'

'Where are they going, sir?' she asked, frightened.

'To Dunoon. They have to stand in for the regular army if it's sent abroad. But it probably won't come to that. It's a precaution till the Kaiser comes to his senses.'

'How long will they be away for, sir?'

'That depends on the War Office, Maggie. Where's Raeburn? I have to go up to the village right away. Would you tell Hector that he'll be going?'

He went up to the smithy. A horse was being shod, and the blacksmith's son, the sergeant of the local company of 8th Argylls, was rummaging with the pincers in the fiery basket of charcoal.

'You'll have to leave for Dunoon on the late train,' Invernevis told him. 'We'll hold it if necessary.'

The sergeant left the glowing shoe on the anvil for his father to finish and pushed his motor bicycle outside, to go round the doors to muster the men. Sam was sitting self-consciously on the gig outside the post office, where a small crowd of anxious-looking women had gathered. The horses' heads were down, eyes heavy in the heat, and the white-aproned boy from the store was sent across with lumps of sugar for them. Sam felt the strangeness of the afternoon.

The postmistress came out to hand him a shovel for the steaming heap of horse dung.

'Put it on my vegetables round the back,' she ordered.

Invernevis was trying to get up on the gig, but the women had surrounded him.

'Is it true they have to go away tonight, sir?'

'I'm afraid so,' he said, his brogue in the iron step. 'But it probably won't be for long.'

'For God's sake stop all this noise!' Maggie shouted as she came into the servants' hall, the clothes for her brother folded over her arm. The maids were making a fuss of Hector as he laid out his kit on the table.

'I'll press the brave boy's kilt,' one of them offered, lifting it from the chair.

'Leave it, it's fine,' Hector told her.

The maid from Barra had pulled his bonnet down over her ears and was striding about, arms swinging.

'Come on, you lot, you've got plenty to do,' Maggie warned them, holding open the door.

Hector was going round, checking from the list: braces, shaving brush, clothes. 'What about the housewife, with buttons, needles and threads?'

'What's the use of you taking that when you've never sewed on a button in your life?' his sister said scornfully.

'I'll manage,' he said stoically. 'One spoon.' He pulled open the table drawer.

'Make sure it's an old one,' she warned.

'Don't worry, you'll get it back soon.'

'Will I?' She was about to say what she felt, when Invernevis came through to speak to Hector.

'I expect they'll have special boats crossing to Dunoon tonight because the other companies will be arriving too.'

Then Maggie saw what he was carrying. He put the scarred black box on the table and sprang the catches. Hector lifted out the set of pipes, the ebony drones circled with yellowed ivory and tarnished silver, the bag of Macdonald tartan.

'Take good care of them,' Invernevis warned. 'They were played at Culloden. I don't want anything to happen to them after all this time.'

She'd heard him say that before, to their other brother Donald before he'd gone out with him to South Africa. Donald had played these pipes in the dawn advance on Magersfontein Hill, but they'd been brought back by someone else, with a bullet hole in the bag. Hector was dismantling them to clean them. Suddenly she hated history, tradition – everything about bagpipes and uniforms.

'We're meeting in an hour,' Invernevis warned Hector before he went upstairs to change into his uniform. He felt self-conscious in the kilt because of his game leg, but this was a special occasion. As he lifted it from the rail in the mahogany wardrobe the mothballs which Maggie had pushed into the pleats clattered on the boards at his feet. Buckling the dark tartan on in front of the long pier-glass, he was a young captain getting ready to go to the South African war with the First Battalion of Princess Louise's Argylls.

'I need some honey and hot water,' Hector told Maggie.

'If you've got a sore throat you're not going,' she told him, so glad to find an excuse to keep him.

'It's not for my throat. It's for the pipes.'

'You're not wasting my good honey on them,' she said, but she gave him the jar and heated up the kettle for him. He mixed the warm water and honey in a jug and took it through to the servants' hall. One of the maids held open the tartan bag while he poured the mixture into it to seal the inside.

Sam was still hanging about the step, irritating her. A bell rang at her back.

'That's him wanting you,' she told Sam.

MacDougall was scything the nettles round the *taigh beag* when he saw the old man coming along the path. He knew by the way he was walking that there was something wrong, so he threw down the scythe and ran towards him. The old woman must have taken a turn.

'It's someone for you,' the old man said.

'Who is it?'

'MacPhee the Territorial sergeant. You're to go away to the war.'

'What war?' MacDougall asked. He didn't bother with news-papers.

'MacPhee says that there's war with Germany and the company has to leave for Dunoon on the late train.' His lower lip was trembling.

MacDougall ran into the house, but the sergeant had gone on

to knock more doors. The old woman was sitting, staring into the fire.

'It's nothing to worry about, *mhàthair*,' he told her.

'I knew it couldn't last,' she said in a faraway voice. This time there was no cackle.

'Damn it, he doesn't have to go,' the old man said. 'You didn't sign anything, did you, boy?'

But he'd put his name on the piece of paper the laird had given him, asking him if he'd read it and understood it fully. The thought of war excited him. 'It'll only be for a few days, till they sort things out,' he told them.

'MacPhee left you this list of the things you've got to take with you,' the old man said, handing him a paper.

When he was going to the camp she got his clothes together, ironing the pleats of his kilt with a wet cloth. It took her an hour as she folded each one so carefully, so lovingly, and afterwards she put the garment to dry round a chair in front of the fire, touching it and cackling every time she passed it, as if he was already inside it.

She remained sitting by the fire. 'Who'll look after the croft?' she asked in a voice that seemed to belong to another person.

'I will, *Pheigi bheag*, till the boy gets back,' the old man said.

'You.' She turned on him. 'You that can't even hold a cup without spilling it. If you were to have a scythe in your hands there would be no legs left on you.'

'There's no scything to be done,' MacDougall told them. 'I've cut all the hay, and Archie next door will stack it. I'll probably be back within the week,' he reassured them. 'I'd better go up and get my stuff together.'

But she stared as if he was no longer there.

The gig was parked on the sandy plateau by the loch where the company was drawn up. Invernevis inspected them before addressing them. He hadn't had time to prepare a speech, but he'd had an inspirational whisky.

'I don't know how long you'll be at Dunoon, nor do I know where you'll be sent to from there, if anywhere, because everything's so unclear at the moment. But I do know this: wherever you're sent, whatever you're called upon to do for your country, you'll do it well, and be a credit to the Argylls as well as to Invernevis.'

The Sergeant-Major gave the signal, and Hector struck up the heirloom pipes. The big drummer began twirling the padded sticks in his fingers. They were on the march, tramping up the slope, turning for the village in a cloud of dust. More and more people left their crofts to follow, except the old men who'd been out in India and South Africa. The Territorials turned down to the station where Father Macdonald was waiting in his black cloak and wheel of a hat. His hand hushed the crowd as he addressed the men.

'Some of you have not bothered to come to chapel, and now, in your hour of need, you have deprived yourself of the comfort of Jesus Christ. Nevertheless I will give you my blessing.'

The ranked volunteers stood at ease, the butts of their rifles between their boots as the priest said a short prayer.

'Amen.'

Hands were removed from weapons to cross themselves before they turned to the train. Some of the women were crying, pulling at the soldiers' arms as they boarded. The old man had toiled up the brae to see MacDougall off, and had hardly any breath left. The big man leaned out of the window, taking the white head between his hands to kiss it.

'*Màthair* will be all right,' the old man said. 'I've only got one piece of advice for you. *Leig do cheann far am faigh thu sa mhadainn e*' ('Lay your head where you'll find it in the morning').

As the train began to move a woman ran forward. Her husband was going, but it was the handle of MacDougall's carriage she was hanging on to, her feet braced against the door. Two men had to break her grip before she was carried up the line.

Brigadier Richardson had spent most of the morning impatiently tapping the telephone, trying to get through to the War

Office. Alanna was sitting in the drawing-room, leafing through magazines.

'I shan't be in for lunch,' he came through to tell her.

'But you wouldn't be involved in the war, surely,' she said. 'You're on the retired list.' She had married a man more than twice her own age, and told her friends blatantly that it was for his money because of the freedom it had brought her. Handling him in bed was no problem, and there were other advantages. Several times he'd come home from his club to find the drawing-room filled with suffragettes, some of them sprawled on the floor, studying maps of their next bombing campaign, no doubt.

He'd seen action in India with the old 91st Highlanders. Sometimes he started up in bed, hearing that cry he'd heard at Ginginhlovo in '79 when the Zulus had appeared over the ridge, with their long shields and spears to strike in horn formation. He'd been sent with the Mounted Troops and the Native Contingent. They'd lost one man, but there were at least 500 of the painted savages strewn within a radius of 400 yards of the laager, their long doings hanging out for the vultures.

'The War Office says there should be some work for me,' he told his wife.

'Damn the war, I was wanting to go abroad,' she said, lighting a cigarette.

'I'm afraid there won't be a chance of that now.'

'Will it be a long war?' It was one of the few subjects on which she would accept his opinion — because of his well-placed friends.

'I shouldn't think so. The Kaiser will make a show, then back down.'

'I wonder if I shouldn't take a few days fishing at Invernevis?' she pondered. 'I learnt so much from that ghillie.'

'I shouldn't think Niall Invernevis will be at home, seeing his company has to report to the Dunoon depot.'

She absorbed this information silently, trying to find an excuse for another visit so soon.

'Shouldn't you be going up, seeing you're the Brigadier?'

'I don't think so. Kilberry will be there, and he's got a first-class Adjutant in Jura. I'd better go for this meeting.' He stopped at the door. 'Your campaign is going to have to be suspended.'

'What campaign?'

'The suffragettes' campaign. It can hardly go on when we're at war with Germany. We're all going to have to pull together, and that includes the women.'

'Did you get that from the War Office?' she asked suspiciously.

'I got it myself. It's an easy conclusion to reach, given the facts.'

'But you say the war will be over soon.'

'We'll all have to wait and see – and that includes the Pankhurst women.'

After the sound of the pipe band had faded, Maggie felt remorse at not going to see Hector off, but it was too late to get up to the village. She looked at the clock, then threw her overall over the back of a chair and hurried down the avenue. There wasn't time to go up the track by the Home Farm, on to the moor to wave to the train, so she turned left, taking the road south above the river. It was humid, and her clothes were sticking to her back, but she was running now. She heard the train approaching. There was a stitch in her side as she tried to get more speed out of her legs, but as she came round the bend the train had already crossed the river, and she saw the lamp on the guard's van disappearing into the pass.

She sat on the wayside dyke, getting her breath back, tasting the bitter smoke left by the engine as it dispersed over the fading countryside. Hector would have been watching out for her. A few more seconds and he would have seen her waving. But he was away now, and he would think that she didn't care about him. If anything happened to him she would never forgive herself. She was sobbing as she made her way home slowly, the road fading rapidly in front of her. She stopped when she heard the owl. It seemed far away tonight, its tremulous call passing through her like a pain, as if this was the last evening of the old world.

As she crossed Wade's Bridge the gig came clattering at her back, its lamps lit. Sam got down to help her up, and she sat behind Invernevis on the way up the avenue.

'They got a good send-off,' he said to her, but that only made her feel worse.

'I'll put your dinner through in five minutes, sir,' she promised as Sam helped her down.

'I'd better go up and see my mother first, Maggie,' Invernevis said.

'You'll need to light the lamp, sir. It's by her bed.'

When she heard the pipes starting up she was back in the insufferable heat of India, hearing the same tune as the battalion drawn up in the dusty square under dear Sandy prepared to march against the natives who were making more trouble in the hills. She wished she had the strength to get out of her bed to shut the window because she couldn't bear another war in her lifetime. It was like the day Niall had gone off to South Africa, and his father lying dying. If Niall hadn't come back, then Alexander would have inherited the place. He was Sandy's favourite, but it would probably have had to be sold by now because he wasn't interested and had got in among that crowd at the Home Farm.

The pipes were stimulating another memory: she was holding a dinner party. She'd had a row with Alexander about going about in ploughman's clothes, his leggings bound with twine. He'd gone shooting on the mountain behind the house. The candelabra were lit, and twenty guests were enjoying salmon from the river when the door burst open. Her son was staggering under the weight of the stag slung round his shoulders, like a horse's halter. It was trailing blood from its cut throat, and some of the women began screaming.

'This is for the feast,' he announced, slinging the carcass across the table. Its antlers knocked over the candles and sent the silver cutlery skidding. She'd had to make the excuse that he'd been drinking, though she knew it was more serious than that.

'Is that you, Sandy?' she called out anxiously.

'It's Niall, Mama.'

'I never thought I would hear the pipes of war again.'

As he lowered the globe on to the wick he had lit he saw her small white face almost absorbed by the pillow.

'It's only a precaution,' he told her. 'You mustn't start upsetting yourself.' He took up her hand to reassure her.

'I remember the day you went to South Africa. It was a beautiful day, just like this. Your father was alive then, and so was Alexander.'

She was using his hand to pull herself up.

'You'll need to go for the children,' she told him, agitated.

'I can't go to Switzerland, Mama.'

'And why not?' she demanded.

'Because it's too expensive. I'm going to send a telegram to the lawyers, asking them to send money to the governess.'

'I'll give you money,' she said.

She was wandering again.

'It's all right, Mama. Try to sleep, and don't worry about a war. There probably won't be one.'

'I wouldn't trust the Kaiser. Over there,' she said, waving her hand as if there was a ghost at her desk.

'There's nothing over there, Mama.' Her mind must be going.

'My bank book. In the top drawer.'

He carried the lamp across and found the small blue book, turning to the last entry. £693. 15/-. It must be an old one, the money used up long ago on drink.

'I've got the annuity from the estate,' she was explaining from the bed. 'But I don't spend much nowadays. I get Maggie to post away the book from time to time to get the interest made up. It must be due to go away again. Take what you need out of it to get the children home.'

'I'll borrow a hundred from you for a few months,' he said, immensely relieved. 'This is so good of you.' He went back to the bed to hug her.

'It's the least I can do,' she said. 'I want to see my grandchildren again before I die.' Then the tears came.

* * *

The train was noisy, but MacDougall was sitting drinking the half bottle by himself, thinking of the old woman by the fire in the croft. But this was a chance to see Alanna again. She would probably come up to Dunoon with the Brigadier. If he could get a few nights with her before being sent home, that would suit him fine.

Hector had been disappointed that Maggie hadn't come up to the station. He sat smoking by the dark window while Invernevis men slapped down cards around him, using one of the drums as a table. They would have to change to another train in Glasgow, then cross by the steamer from Gourock to Dunoon.

After Sam had put the horses away he stood smoking in the night air. He would miss Hector's company. Maybe he should have joined up himself, to see more of the world. But Maggie needed someone, she was so nervous. He hadn't eaten all day, what with being up and down to the village. He went down the dark mossy path to the house, but through the lighted kitchen window he saw Invernevis sitting talking to Maggie, so he went back, going hungry to bed.

Captain Campbell the Adjutant was riding his black charger along the lane in the twilight. He'd spent the morning sending out telegrams ordering the companies of the 8th Argylls to the Dunoon depot, and the afternoon requisitioning all the available halls for accommodation for the men till it was decided where they'd be moved to. But he still didn't know if he had enough space, so he was going out to see Major Pender at Dunloskin Farm to ask if men could camp there if necessary.

'Most certainly. I'll give you an extra field if you like.'

'The one we had for the camp will do, thank you,' Jura said. He rode down it, taking another way home in the fading light. The hooves stirred up the black circles of ash from the camp fires that seemed to him to have burned so long ago, though it was only a matter of weeks. How quickly the world moved on. His horse splashed through the burn and he rode along the edge of the field, the corn in stooks now, turning down by the

Lorne Bar, trotting to his home at Hunter's Quay, an hour late for dinner. Dorothy was sitting on the window seat of the drawing room, staring out over the water.

'It's so sad,' she said. 'The Holy Loch was full of yachts this morning, and that's the last one going now.'

He sat beside her watching it. In the windless evening it was using its engine, its poles bare, its crew like ghosts in their whites.

'I expect some of them are Territorial officers, going to join their units,' he said.

'Have you had a busy day?'

'Very. But I think we're ready for them. They'll start arriving tonight, so I'll need to go out again. I may be very late.'

It had been Harry's birthday party in a private room in the Sydney hotel the night before, but one of the staff must have been bribed because there were cameras in the corridor and reporters shouting questions through the door as Harry cut his cake, its icing softening in the antipodean night. They'd had to return to their rooms by the fire escape, but his father was laughing.

'It all helps to sell tickets, laddie.'

His father wanted him to wear his kilt in public, but it was far too hot. The Lieutenant was in white flannels and shirt, smoking as he paced his room, and every time he heard the jolt of the lift he stopped and waited. He'd never felt so keyed up, not even when he accompanied his father on stage.

At three o' clock a bell-boy arrived with the cable on a silver tray.

6

'Onward 8th Battalion,
Marching as to war;
Campbell of Kilberry,
Leading as of yore.
Jura Jock the Adjutant,
Twice as stiff as starch,
On his Irish charger
Regulates the march.'

The Argyll Territorials were singing in the last stage of their twenty-mile march through the market garden of England in the clammy autumn day that made kilts stick to legs. They had been sent from Dunoon to Bedford for training. The roofline of Bedford Camp was in sight, cobbles under their brogues now. The Adjutant turned in his saddle, stopping the singing with a raised hand. On the pavement women were holding up their children to watch the Highlanders passing, and Hector Macdonald winked at a little girl in a grubby frock.

She started to cry.

The Adjutant called for the band. Hector Macdonald took his time from the Pipe-Major, the drums rattling arrogantly as the battalion wheeled through the gates of the camp. The thousands of men of the Highland Division were billeted in the camp and in houses throughout the town. After fall-out Hector and MacDougall went back to the place they were sharing with other men of the Invernevis company. It was a shambles. When the gas mantles broke they bought candles, and two of the kitchen chairs had been chopped up for kindlings for the fire in the front room where they slept on the floor. One night Hector had come home to find MacDougall washing his kilt hose in the toilet bowl.

Tonight the big man was stretched out on the sofa while Hector sat cleaning his pipes.

'I'm sick of these bloody marches,' MacDougall complained. 'What good are they?'

'They're supposed to get you ready.'

'Ready for what?'

'For the war.'

'I'll tell you this, it'll be over before I get a go at these Germans. I'm as well at home, helping the old folks.'

'Have you heard from them?' Hector asked.

'Aye, I had a letter yesterday from the old man. He says the old woman's gone very quiet, with me being away. They won't be able to manage much longer by themselves.'

'Then why did you sign up to go to France?'

'Because I thought we were going right away, not hanging about here, and that the war would be over.'

'We'll go soon enough,' Hector said, testing the reed of his chanter by blowing mournfully through it. It was over a week since Maggie had written, but he couldn't bring himself to tell her that he'd signed up. Like MacDougall he wanted to see what like it was over there, but unlike the big fellow, he didn't want a fight. That was Dochie's trouble; the big fellow had too much energy. He'd had another argument with Lauder, and it had looked as if MacDougall was going to hit him.

'We're going up to London for the night,' MacDougall announced.

'You know we're not allowed outside the camp limits.'

'To hell with the camp limits.' He swung down his legs. 'Come on.'

'The Brigadier's giving us a pep talk tonight, and everyone's got to attend.'

'They won't miss me,' MacDougall said. 'You'll cover for me — say I'm ill.'

'*You* ill? They won't believe it. Anyway, you can't go to London in your uniform.'

'I'm not daft,' MacDougall said. 'All I need's the loan of a suit.' He opened a cupboard. 'Willie's should fit me.'

'You'll have to ask him,' Hector warned.

But MacDougall had lifted out the black suit and was holding the trousers against himself. 'They're a wee bit short, but they'll do.'

He put the suit on, but it was too tight to get the buttons of the fly closed.

'It'll do fine, if I keep the jacket closed,' he said, studying himself in the mirror.

'You'd better not get a hard-on,' Hector warned him.

'Now all I need is a shirt and tie,' MacDougall said. He was opening a drawer.

'You'd better ask Willie,' Hector said. 'You know what like he is about his things.'

'Willie won't mind.' He was buttoning up the shirt, then putting the collar round his neck.

'Do you know how to work this thing?' he asked helplessly, holding out the black tie.

'You look like an undertaker,' Hector said as he knotted it for him.

'It's fine. Now all I need is for you to lend me five bob and I'm away.'

Sam reined the gig by the smithy and went into the post office, pushing the poster under the grille. The postmistress studied Kitchener's face behind the pointing finger.

'The laird wants it up in the window straight away.'

'I heard you the first time. One hundred thousand wanted. Ah well, it's your chance this time.'

The eyes hardened by the glinting spectacles were waiting for his answer, but he wasn't going to give her the satisfaction, so he turned and went out. She called out something but he banged the door behind him.

He left the horses and walked the hundred yards to the Arms. Carmichael was drying a glass as Sam laid the poster on the counter, explaining that the laird wanted it put up in a prominent place.

'Oh, aye,' Carmichael said. 'He's already sent the Territorials away, and I'm to lose more customers, is that the way of it?' He picked up the poster and ripped it carefully in two.

The last poster was for the village store, but he didn't go in straight away. He stood with his back to the big wheel of the gig, but the three women weren't coming out of the store, though the baskets on their arms were full. They were watching him as he struck a match on the iron rim of the wheel for the cigarette end he took from his waistcoat pocket. He seriously considered putting the flame to the poster, but the laird would find out about the one empty window.

He couldn't wait any longer, but the women weren't going to go away till they heard what he wanted. Even a bag of sugar for the big house was worth its weight in gossip. He dropped the cigarette into the dust as he crossed the road, walking as casually as he could. The three turned heads were together, waiting for him.

Sam didn't look at Munro's face as he put down the poster between the grocer's white knuckles on the worn counter. The three heads inclined, taking in the big print before the storekeeper swivelled the poster. Now the women were complaining loudly in Gaelic at Sam's back, and he knew instinctively that they were miscalling the laird. He should walk out, but Maggie had asked him to get salt.

'Rock or sea?' the grocer asked.

Sam showed his ignorance of the difference.

'Whatever the big house usually gets.'

'The big house doesn't usually get salt here,' Munro said.

The women had gone quiet, and Sam knew that what he said would be carried away with their baskets.

'Whatever you think they would use.'

The fist slid off the poster, under the counter, and a packet was dumped down.

'It's to be charged,' Sam said.

'I know that.'

The hand went down again, into a drawer, producing a book. He wet a finger, flicking through the pages, then took the pencil from behind his ear.

Maggie kept the top copies on a nail, but Sam wasn't going to ask for this one.

'The salt,' Munro called after him, holding out the packet when he was at the door.

'And you can tell the laird from me, my man's not going for Kitchener or nobody,' one of the women said.

He swung up on to the gig, aware that four pairs of eyes were following him. He glanced at the post office as he passed and saw Chrissie MacSween using stamp perforations to put Kitchener's face and finger up in the window.

MacDougall sat on the top of the omnibus, looking down on London by night. He'd read out the address on the letter to the conductor before he'd given his fare.

'Going there for a job, mate?' he asked.

'That's right.'

'That's a posh address,' the conductor said knowledgeably. 'You can have your pick of vacancies now. There's crowds outside the recruiting office, pushing to get in, as if they're giving away something free. You won't catch me doing that. Glory's one thing, coming home in a box another. I'll call up when it's your stop.'

MacDougall got off and asked directions, then went up the imposing steps, pulling at his borrowed suit to make himself presentable before he lifted the gleaming brass knocker in the shape of a lion's head. Just when he was thinking that nobody was coming, the door opened.

'Dochie! I'm so glad you got my letter!' Alanna Richardson said as she put her arms round him. 'I gave the servants the evening off.'

The staircase she was leading him up was even bigger than the one at Invernevis House. The hem of her dressing-gown rustled as they went along the corridor, past rows of portraits, their gilt frames held up by chains. He was conscious of the noise his boots were making on the polished boards and tried to walk on his toes. The bedroom she led him into was twice the size of the croft house at home, and the canopied bed looked as if it could take half a dozen people comfortably.

Her foot was up on the stool as she rolled down the silk

stocking. He could see her buttocks in the mirror and put his hand between her legs, but she pushed him away. She removed his jacket and hung it across the back of a chair. She loosened his tie. The brass stud clinked into the dish on the dressing-table, and she made him sit on the bed while she unlaced his boots.

'My God, you'll do yourself an injury, wearing such tight trousers,' she said as she pulled them off.

Next moment they were on the bed. It rocked like a boat in a swell, as if the canopy was going to come down on top of them.

'I thought you'd like some whisky,' she said when she had recovered her breath, pouring him a bumper from the decanter by the bedside.

'I haven't tasted anything like this since I left home, he told her appreciatively. 'The beer down here's like water, and you can't get a dram.'

'It's Islay malt. My husband drinks it. Help yourself to more.

'Will he not miss it?' MacDougall asked, tilting the decanter.

'He's got a cellar full of bottles.'

She gave him a cigarette from a silver box. It had a gold band round it and was strong and satisfying. He blew the smoke to the ornate ceiling from which a winged cherub was suspended, aiming an arrow at the bed.

'When I think of the time I've wasted,' she sighed, snuggling into him, her fingers spread through the hair on his chest. 'I should have stayed at Invernevis instead of coming back here.'

'The Arms isn't a cheap place,' he told her. 'That Carmichael's a robber.'

'I'd have taken a house, and you could have visited me every night.'

He smiled because the thought of it appealed to him. He would even have given up his other assignations.

'I'm serious, Dochie. I hate this way of living, all these meaningless receptions and parties. I've always wanted something else, but I've never known what.'

'Aye, but Invernevis can be a very quiet place.'

'Not with you around,' she murmured. 'I'm sure all the women are chasing you.'

But he never discussed one woman with another, because he knew how jealous they could get.

'You've got the most adorable cock.'

He was shocked. Where did she learn language like that? He lay looking at the silver-backed brushes on the dressing-table, her dressing-gown in a gleaming heap on the floor. In the Invernevis houses he went into for his assignations he never bothered with his surroundings. This was the first time in his life that he felt inadequate.

'I'll need to get back to camp,' he told her.

But she was pulling him on top of her again. Then she went through a door and he heard water running.

'You're going to have a bath,' she said when she came back.

He hadn't had a bath since he was a wee boy, sitting in the tub in front of the fire while the old woman washed him before wrapping him tenderly in the warm towel. The old man had carried him up to bed.

'I don't need a bath,' he protested. The one at the house in Bedford was full of the coal he'd stolen off a cart.

'Come on,' she ordered.

The bath was so big you could have drowned a cow in it. As the water gushed through the brass faucet the foam rose like the froth on milk hitting the pail from the udder. He stepped in gingerly.

'It's hot.'

'It's meant to be. That's why it does you good.'

As he sat down he was sure it was going to burn his balls off. She began to rub his back with a brush on a long handle. He lay back, his head between the brass taps. It was good.

'I could do with another dram,' he said.

She held the glass to his mouth, then let the gown slip from her shoulders on to the tiles as she stepped in beside him.

'It's your turn to soap me.'

He'd never smelt soap like it. It went into sparkling white froth between his hands while he smeared it on her tits. Then she was reaching underwater. As she bobbed on top of him the water washed over the sides and when she came he thought she was going to drown him.

'I'll need to get back to the camp.'

'You don't have to go so soon.'

'If I'm caught they'll put me on a charge. Lieutenant Lauder's got it in for me.'

'I met him at Dunoon. He doesn't have much to say for himself.'

As he climbed out of the bath she was holding open a large white towel to rub him down. She wrapped another towel round herself and left a trail of wet prints as she went through to her dressing-table.

'That's for your fare,' she said, stuffing a note into the breast pocket of his jacket.

He'd never seen a five-pound note before.

'I can't take this,' he said apprehensively.

'Keep it. When will you come again?'

'It depends,' he said evasively.

'Then I'll just have to come to the camp,' she said blithely.

'You wouldn't.'

'I could come and inspect you, but it's far safer for you to come here and inspect me. What about next Wednesday evening? It's Freddie's night at his club.'

'I suppose I could make it.'

'Take a cab from the station. Every minute with you is important to me.' As she buttoned up his jacket she was filling his pockets with cigarettes.

It was raining hard, but Sam came in at nine as usual, putting the hissing lantern on the dresser beside the oil lamp. She put the tray of tablet near him.

Even the slow drip of his oilskins on the stone floor soothed her after another busy day.

'You'll hear from Hector soon,' he said, reading her face.

She looked forward to seeing him every night, and he understood that if the boss came through he would go immediately. He sat opposite her, eating the sweet tablet she'd made for him.

'Why don't they send the Territorials home, instead of keeping them down there, that's what I want to know,' she said.

'Maybe they need to keep them down there because of the numbers that are being lost in France,' he suggested gently. 'I mean, they don't want the Germans to think that we don't have an army at home.'

'I don't know what the Germans are thinking, but it's an awful loss of life,' she said.

She watched the way he slid open the packet of Woodbines, tapping the end of the cigarette on the match box before lighting up.

'What's doing up in the village?' she asked.

'Not much.' He didn't want to tell her about the way the women were whispering about him in the store.

'I see you got a letter this morning,' she said.

'Aye, from my mother.'

'And what was her news?'

'There's only herself and George on the farm now.'

'What's happened to the other two?' she asked, surprised.

'They've joined up.'

'And what does she want you to do?' She was watching him.

'I'm staying here, when I get tablet like this,' he said, putting another piece in his mouth.

It was after midnight when MacDougall got in. Hector was lying awake for him.

MacDougall lit two cigarettes.

'Where did you get them?' Hector asked. 'They smell as if they're made from *cac*.'

'They're Turkish or something. The woman I was with gave them to me.'

'Was she a foreigner?' Hector asked eagerly, sitting up. He'd heard that foreign women did special things.

'No, no. An Englishwoman born and bred.' He trusted Hector, but didn't want to tell him too much.

'You took a chance,' Hector said. 'What's that funny smell?'

'It's the cigarettes,' MacDougall said. 'I told you, they're Turkish.'

'Not that smell, a smell like perfume. It wasn't in the room before you came in.'

'Oh, that. I had a bath.'

'A bath? Where?'

But MacDougall wasn't saying. He sat there, drawing on the cigarette with the gold band, feeling very satisfied. He would have a bath with her again next Wednesday, with more of that Islay malt.

'I didn't say anything to Willie about you having his suit,' Hector said. 'You'd better get it off, and the shirt too.'

'I had a wee accident,' MacDougall said, turning to show him.

The trousers were split, his bare arse showing.

'How did that happen?'

'That happens when you're with a woman that won't wait,' MacDougall said.

'Willie's going to go bloody mad,' Hector warned him. 'He's very proud of that suit. He got it made for him in Glasgow for his mother's funeral.'

'Are you any good with a needle?' MacDougall asked.

'That's a job for a tailor.'

'I'll find one in the morning.'

'And what are you going to tell Willie?'

'I'll pay him for the hire of it,' MacDougall said.

'What with? You owe me five bob first.'

MacDougall felt in his top pocket and took out the five-pound note which he spread on the bed.

'Where the hell did you get that?'

'I didn't steal it, if that's what you mean. I got it as a present from the woman – the lady, I mean. So I'll give Willie ten bob for the hire of the suit, and ten bob to you for the loan. How will that do?'

'You'd better get rest,' Hector warned him. 'We'll be marching again in the morning.'

'If that bastard Lauder gets in my way again I'll break his

77

neck,' MacDougall vowed as he unlaced his boots. 'What did the Brigadier say in his talk?'

'He said our time would come.'

'He didn't need to come all the way down from London to tell us that,' MacDougall said as he settled down for the night on the floor. With the smell of the perfumed soap it was as if Alanna was with him in the blanket.

She heard the discreet knock on her door.

'Come in!' she called.

The Brigadier opened the door. 'Is your head better?' he asked gently.

'Much better.' She was sitting at the dressing-table, in the glow of the lamp. There was also a glow inside her. She felt she could float away in her silk nightdress.

'I'm so glad. I was anxious about you all evening. I blame myself, for all this talk about war.'

'Did you have a good meeting?'

'The Division's in very good heart.'

'What about the Argylls?'

'I spoke to Jura. He says they've improved a lot with all the training. They're ready for France, when the call comes.'

She turned on the stool. 'But the 8th Argylls are Territorials. They can't be sent abroad. You told me that in the summer at Dunoon.'

'They signed up themselves.'

All her euphoria was vanishing at the thought of Dochie going away from her.

'It's not fair,' she said bitterly.

'What isn't fair? I don't understand,' he said, watching her in the mirror, wondering if she was well.

'Taking men like that away from their homes just to send them to France. What a waste it would be.'

'Plenty other units have gone,' he reminded her.

'And how many have come back?'

'We need to win.'

'Would you have to go to France with them?' she asked.

'I don't know. But don't start worrying about that now. It may not happen. Probably by the time the Highland Division gets its orders, the Germans will have surrendered. They can't win.'

'If you go, I go,' she said firmly.

He was overcome by her loyalty, and began to open his dinner jacket as he sat down on her bed.

'I'm tired,' she told him.

7

The nurse held Hector to her starched apron as he was racked by another spasm of coughing. She was frightened that the thermometer she was withdrawing from his oxter had been broken.

'One hundred and three, sir.'

'Bronchopneumonia,' the doctor said. 'You'd better send for the padre.'

'He's an RC, sir.'

But the doctor had turned away to another critical case. The room was crowded with beds because of the epidemic of measles among the Highland Division in camp at Bedford. The young nurse found it eerie. The lights were dim because of the damage that could be done to the men's eyes, but as she went to fetch the priest, blotched red faces followed her as if they knew they were next.

The priest set the vessel of holy water, with cotton wool and bread on the bedside cabinet. He put a wooden crucifix into Hector's hands.

'*Exaudi nos Domine sancte* . . .

The nurse stood at the foot of the small man's bed, her head bent at the murmured Latin. He'd been so nice, so grateful to her as she sat bathing his eyes with saline solution, the little kidney-shaped enamel dish balanced on her lap. When he'd put out his hand she'd held it, though the matron was doing the rounds.

'Is the box under the bed still all right?' he'd kept asking.

'It's safe,' she assured him.

Hector had insisted on bringing the case of Invernevis pipes in with him.

'Will you give me a tune when you get better?'

'I'll play you a reel you can dance to,' he'd promised.

'*In nomine Patris et Filii et Spiritus* . . . '

He made the sign of the cross over Hector and dipped the

thumb of his right hand into the stock of oil for the sick. Since it was a contagious disease he used separate pieces of cotton wool to anoint the dying man's body in case the infection returned to the vessel of oil. As he touched the closed eyes, the ears, nostrils and closed lips with the moistened cotton wool, he said the prayer for each sense.

'You can't stand there all day, Nurse Finney,' the matron said. 'Nothing more can be done for him, and there are plenty of others who need attention. That man in the corner is in distress because he's so itchy. Make him comfortable.'

As the nurse turned she saw the big man standing in the doorway. He'd been visiting the dying man every day.

'You can't come in here,' she warned him as she hurried across. 'It's not visiting time. There are some very ill men here.'

'How is my friend?'

She could smell drink off him.

'He's passing on. Show some respect by going.'

'Passing on?' The brown paper bag he was carrying burst at her shoes, a peach spattering the linoleum. 'Passing on!' he roared, pushing her aside as he made for the bed in the corner.

'Have you gone mad?' she shouted, pursuing him.

But he was knocking her away with his arm. He lifted Hector up in bed, holding him as if he was a child, his other hand slipping the half bottle of whisky from his tunic.

'You're not dead yet, Eachann,' MacDougall said gently.

The whisky was running down the patient's chin as he lolled in the big man's arm like a child. The nurse was half across the bed as she struggled with the intruder.

'He's my friend,' MacDougall said, pushing her away.

'I'll show you!' she shouted as she ran for matron.

He was laying Hector back down gently on the pillow when the two military policeman came running in. Weak men in the beds turned their heads to watch as MacDougall was dragged away, shouting, overturning a trolley, enamel dishes clattering and spinning across the floor.

When the nurse had covered Hector's face with the sheet she

went and sat at the table in the centre of the ward. Some of the men wouldn't make the morning now. She was shaking, as if there was now a malevolent presence in her ward. What a terrible thing to do, breaking the seal the priest had put on the patient's lips with a prayer to signify that he was finished with life. She should go and tell them to take the body away, but she was frightened to leave in case that awful man came back. Drink caused so much trouble.

MacDougall was manacled between the military policemen as he stood in front of the desk where Colonel Campbell of Kilberry was sitting, angry at having his dinner in the mess disturbed.

'Look at his record, sir,' Lieutenant Lauder said, bending over his commanding officer as he pointed to the book. 'One offence after another.'

'I don't understand why you did such a thing,' Kilberry said, shaking his head. He always tried to see the good in his men.

'He's my friend, sir. I have to look after him.'

'You chose a strange way to do it.' The Colonel turned to Lauder. 'What's the news from the hospital, Lieutenant?'

'I spoke to the doctor, sir. He confirmed that the patient was on the point of death when this man interfered with that natural process and forced whisky down his throat. It could turn out to be manslaughter.'

'He's not dead,' MacDougall said.

'Oh, he's dead all right,' Lauder said. 'He couldn't be anything else, the way you manhandled him.'

There was silence. The Colonel was uncomfortable because he could see tears in the big man's eyes.

'He was a damned good piper,' MacDougall said. 'There was only one better, his brother that was killed by the Boers.' The strength of his grief strained against the handcuffs on the wrists of his keepers.

'What was this man's name?' the Colonel asked, turning to Lauder.

'Macdonald, sir. Hector Macdonald of Invernevis Company.'

'Is that the chap who took the march, and strathspey and reel at Dunoon?' Kilberry asked, attentive now. 'It's a great shame, losing a man like that.'

'For a wee fellow he could put a hell of a lot of wind into the bag,' MacDougall added earnestly.

'Remarkable how piping runs in families,' the Colonel mused, tapping the end of his pencil on the desk as if the wail of a lament was running through his fingers.

'Well it's gone with him, sir. There's only a sister,' MacDougall said.

'It's getting late, sir,' Lauder reminded the commanding officer.

Kilberry closed the book and stood up, wanting back to his dinner. 'I'll sleep on it and see this man in the morning. Keep him in the guard-room overnight.'

'It would be better to deal with it tonight, sir,' Lauder urged.

But the Colonel was taking MacDougall's salute before he was led out.

Invernevis came through to the kitchen when Maggie was clearing up after breakfast.

'Where's Raeburn?'

'He'll be at the stables, sir. It's too early for the papers,' she said, glancing at the clock.

'I'll get them later. I want him to find me a small table.'

'A table, sir?'

'Yes, about this size.' He measured with his arms. 'Tell him to put it out at the front door — and a chair.'

She was pleased that he was going to sit out and get some sun while he wrote letters. It meant that she could get on with baking, instead of keeping an eye on the new bottle of Mackinlay's which she'd put through in the library.

'There's the small table in the servants' hall, sir. I could cover it with a cloth.'

'No, no, it'll do as it is. Get Raeburn to take it through when he comes in.'

When Sam came in she gave him his instructions. The post was past, and she took her annoyance out on the dough in the bowl at Hector's selfishness in not writing. It would be a different matter if he needed money.

Invernevis's game leg was thrust under the table on the gravel at the front of the house as he tried to draw inspiration from his surroundings to compose a reply to Jura's letter which had been days on his desk.

I must say that I am not surprised by your news.
At this very moment I'm making my own war effort
in a small way by—

When Maggie brought out his morning coffee she saw the sovereigns glittering in the black cashbox by the Bible. She slid the tray on to the table, reading the form over his shoulder. Then she hurried through to the kitchen and up to the stables.

Sam was sitting on a stool on the cobbles when her shadow dulled the horse-brass he was polishing.

'What was it he sent you up to the village with the other day?' she demanded angrily.

He hesitated, but she was hovering for an answer.

'Posters,' he said. 'They need more recruits.'

'And he told you not to let Maggie see them,' she said in a sad voice.

'He didn't say anything like that.'

'I would advise you to keep out of his way for the rest of the day because he's going to be in a bad mood after I've finished with him,' she vowed.

She went back down to collect his tray.

'Are you waiting for recruits, sir?'

'Yes, Maggie, but nobody's come so far.'

'But I thought there was enough Territorials at Bedford, sir.'

'It's not the Territorials the new men will be signing up for, Maggie.'

She was confused. 'But how can that be, sir, when they've got all these Territorials at Bedford?'

He saw now what she was getting at, and he stood up.

'I thought Hector would have told you in a letter.'

'Tell me what, sir?' She was determined that she wasn't going to let him off.

'That most of the Territorials have signed up to go and fight abroad.'

'*You* should have told me, sir.'

He saw how upset she was. 'I'm sorry, Maggie, but I only got the news myself the other day from Captain Campbell.'

The sun seemed to lose its warmth as she stood on the step, so disappointed in this man, after all the work she'd put in for him over the years since he'd come back from South Africa. As for her brother, that explained why she hadn't had a letter. Well, if he didn't have the courage to put pen to paper, what was he going to do when he was sent across to France?

'Don't worry, Maggie, the news is good.'

'Is it?' she said, biting her lip. 'You're forgetting he's the only one I've got left.'

'I mean the news in the paper.'

'I wouldn't know, sir.'

'We're across the Marne, Maggie. The war will be over by Christmas.'

'Then why do they need more men?'

'It's just a precaution,' he answered without conviction.

The peat stack which MacDougall had built up against the wall of the croft was going down rapidly because the old woman sat at the fire most of the day, even though it was mild outside. As he was filling the pail the old man was thinking that he would have to get more fuel.

He put a turf on the fire and the kettle on top of it.

'I'll make you a cup of tea, *Pheigi bheag.*'

But she didn't hear him. She was thinking of the time she'd taken *Mairi Peigidh bheag na biorraide* (Mairi, daughter of wee Peggy of the hat) to the shows which came to the common grazing every year. She herself was too small to be any good at throwing the little white balls into clustered bowls with their narrow necks, but her daughter had won a golden fish before they wandered across to the two tents set up on the edge of the field.

85

'You wait here,' she ordered the girl, paying the threepence to the man standing at the first tent. There was another man inside the tent, squatting on a table with his trousers down, a candle guttering in a bottle beside him. A pack of running hounds was tattooed across his buttocks, chasing a fox whose fine bush was disappearing down into his *toll tòine*. The other people in the tent were laughing, but *Peigi bheag na biorraide* had pulled the pin from her hat.

The next tent was sixpence, and *Mairi Peigidh bheag na biorraide* was already inside it. *Peigi bheag* stood beside her daughter. The tall man in the blue cloak had a flaming stick in his hand and a black mask over his eyes, but the old woman knew who he was. On a frosty night she would suddenly get up from the fire and lift the latch, but neither the old man nor MacDougall followed her because they knew where she was going.

She stood waiting in the garden. The sky brightened, and then the *Fir-chlis*, the men of the tricks, came over the mountains from the north. They were immensely tall and thin, in white, green and red costumes, and they darted about the sky, leaping, somersaulting, dancing from peak to peak as she raised her dazzled face. At the end of the performance they stood in line and bowed to her before they sank out of sight behind the mountain, and she went back inside to warm her hands.

This was one of them in the tent. His blue cloak swirled around him as he swallowed the fire from the stick, breathing it out again against the newspaper he held up between his two hands, but there wasn't a mark on the paper. The tent was like a furnace and *Peigi bheag* went to stand outside, waiting for her daughter. When she wasn't coming she pulled back the flap. But it was too late: *Mairi Peigidh bheag na biorraide* was smoothing down her skirt. He had put his fire into her *pit*, and when he went away back over the mountain again he'd left her with a *tacharan*, a changeling. He was no ordinary baby, the way he had to be lifted off her daughter's breasts, otherwise there wouldn't have been a drop left, and his eyes were never still in his head. His mother had died of TB when he was two, and she'd brought him up herself. He'd grow up into the big strong man who would turn the heads of all the women in the place, but the *Fir-chlis* had come back for him and spirited him away over the mountains to the other world.

She would never see him again.

The two cups and saucers rattled in the scullery as the old man set them out. Because her gums were bare she liked to dip a biscuit into her tea, but the tin was empty. He would have to try to remember biscuits when he went up to the village, but he kept forgetting things. As he lifted the kettle water tipped from the spout on to his leg, burning through his trousers. She didn't move.

'You're taking it too badly. He'll be back soon. You can kill a chicken for him, and he'll build up the peat stack,' he reassured her.

But she was glaring as she thought of the fire-eater who had put his *bod* into her daughter. That was their trick, to leave a *tacharan* to be brought up among mortals, then come back to claim him.

'Here's your tea,' he said, putting it beside her.

But she ignored it. The old man had an idea. He opened the drawer in the table, and took out the paper, the pen and bottle of ink. Then he sat down, putting on his spectacles, writing in the elegant hand that he owed to the fact that MacCallum his headmaster had been a calligrapher.

'The only way she's going to get her strength up and eat is if you get your picture taken,' he wrote to his grandson. 'Get it done in your uniform. That'll please her. And write something on it. We're managing fine. It's her birthday on Friday; she'll be 80, or so she says. She says she was born in the year of the big flood, but that was 1832, because I was three then and I can remember the bridge over the river going, so she must be eighty-two.'

As he sealed the letter he looked at her, but she had fallen asleep.

Invernevis had to stop himself from nodding to sleep in the sun. He was watching the avenue, but there was no sign of anyone coming. Perhaps the posters hadn't been up long enough. He should give it a few more days. But he knew how fast word travelled. They weren't coming because they would be sworn in as soldiers, not Territorials, and they would be sent overseas. Changed days. When he'd gone off to fight the Boers, local men had come up to the house, desperate to enlist, but his father was lying dying in bed, and Aunt Carlotta had threatened to set the dogs on them. He would sit out again in the afternoon. If nobody came he might have to go up to the hall, to give them a pep talk. He closed the cash box and went inside.

Sam was sitting on the kitchen step.

'I want you to do something for me,' Maggie said. 'You'll go up to the post office and send a telegram for me.'

She sat at the table, taking her time before writing.

'Can you read it?' she asked, giving Sam the paper.

'Are you all right, Hector? Send word back at once. Love, Maggie. ' He put it carefully into his waistcoat pocket. 'I'll go right away.'

'But you can't send it without money. I'll go upstairs for some. There's something else I want you to do later: go up to the late train and see if there's a sack of flour for me. I need it for baking in the morning.'

'Why don't you come up with me?' he suggested.

'Who'll give him his dinner?'

'He gets it at seven. The train's not till half past eight.'

'Now wouldn't that give them something to talk about in the village?' She'd said it without thinking, and she saw that she'd offended him. She couldn't get out of it now.

'All right, I'll come up for the drive.'

He had the gig at the back door at eight. She tidied her black dress and sorted her hair before she came out, and he helped her up as if she was the lady of the house.

'It's a lot of fuss for a sack of flour,' she said.

But he knew that she said it because it was a new stage in their relationship. There was no hurry. The gig went slowly down the avenue. She was enjoying the evening, looking at the fields with their hay stacks, appreciating the wayside fragrances. Suddenly he reined and dismounted. She thought there was a stone in a shoe of one of the horses, but he was picking flowers from the verge. She held the small blue bunch self-consciously as they rode up the brae to the village, turning down to the station.

They sat on the gig on the platform, waiting. Word was spreading that the housekeeper from the big house was making a rare visit to the village, so there must be someone special coming off the train. People began to gather on the bridge above the line. She didn't care; once they saw the sack of flour they wouldn't have much to talk about.

The train was twenty minutes late. The guard swung off before it had stopped and went into conversation with the station master. They slid open the doors of the guard's van and lifted out a coffin.

Maggie looked in alarm at Sam as the train pulled away, leaving the coffin lying on the platform. There was no name plate on it. Sam had taken up the reins, but she restrained his arm.

'Someone's going to need help to lift it. It can't lie there all night.'

They sat waiting on the gig while the crowd on the bridge got bigger as oldtimers left their dominoes in the Arms. The last blackbird had stopped singing and the light was going quickly when Doctor MacNiven's gig arrived on the platform. He helped down his passenger.

'Now steady,' he cautioned.

But she was running, throwing herself across the coffin, crying out in Gaelic against the unfairness of life.

'My God, it's Annie MacPhail,' Maggie said to Sam. She was one of the few people in the village she liked. 'Get me down from this thing.'

She hurried across, helping the doctor to lift her off the coffin while the frightened crowd watched from the bridge.

'It's Alasdair,' the distraught woman said. 'He never had a day's illness in his life, but he got measles at the camp. We all had measles when we were young, but none of us died.' She started pounding the box with her fists, shouting in Gaelic to waken him.

Maggie remembered lying in the darkened room with her blotched skin. But Hector had escaped.

'You'd better take her home,' Dr MacNiven told Sam, and helped him to get Maggie up on to the gig.

He took his jacket off and put it round her shoulders for the run home because she was shaking so much. He was making her tea in the kitchen when Invernevis came through for his usual conversation.

'Maggie's not feeling well, sir. She's had a shock.'

She looked at him standing there with his cigarette, the glow of whisky in his face and a glass in his fist.

'That's Alasdair MacPhail home from the camp, sir,' she said in a quiet voice.

'Home on leave?' he queried.

'In a coffin. There's been an outbreak of measles. You didn't tell me that, sir,' she said, shaking her head at the lack of trust.

'Captain Campbell mentioned it, but I didn't want to worry you.' He signalled for Sam to go before he sat down. 'I'll send a telegram first thing in the morning to make sure that Hector's all right.'

What was the use, when a big strong fellow like Alasdair MacPhail could be taken? She'd nursed Hector herself as a boy when their mother was sick, rubbing butter melted in her own hands into the swollen glands in his neck, sitting up with him, keeping peats on the fire to sweat out his fever, then holding him in her arms when he saw the beasts on the flickering wall he couldn't even put names to in English. His chest had got stronger, and he'd been able to play the pipes, but what had it all been worth?

MacPhail's crying children were taken upstairs to their beds before his coffin was brought in and rested between two chairs.

'I want it open,' the widow demanded.

'That wouldn't be wise,' Dr MacNiven cautioned. 'It's several days since he passed away.'

'I want him washed,' she said. 'I've asked old Annie to come at eleven.'

'The military authorities will have washed him,' the doctor said. 'Everything will have been done for him. Would you like somebody to stay with you?'

'I'll be all right.'

When they'd gone she lit the lamp and put a shawl round her shoulders, then carried the light out into the night to the byre, setting it down on the bench. The last he'd repaired the family shoes on looked like a black horn, and the scythe handle he'd been shaping with the adze when he was called away was lying among its shavings. She searched his tools till she found a screwdriver.

She went back into the house and put the lamp on top of the coffin. The screws were tight, but she was a strong woman from working the croft. The last screw wouldn't shift, though she put all her strength on it. It was just as well because it was wicked to disturb the dead.

But this was her man. She had borne five children by him and had loved him dearly. He'd always been faithful to her, a good father, and he had such tender Gaelic. She found more strength and the screw began to turn. She pushed the lid aside, but it wasn't the smell that made her cry out. This mess wasn't her Alasdair; he'd had such fine skin and when she woke in summer dawns she liked to run her fingers over his back. There had been a terrible mistake, and she felt like dancing round the kitchen with relief.

Then she noticed the little blackened fingernail and remembered the night long ago he'd hit it with a hammer when he was putting a mirror up on the wall for her.

Old Annie knocked at eleven.

'I'm afraid he's in a bit of a mess,' the widow said.

But the old woman was a professional washer of the dead. She had been rowed across to the quarry to sponge the granite dust off men whose bones had been broken in a blast. She had washed the breasts of young women who had perished from cancer. She busied about the croft kitchen, filling the enamel basin she had brought with her from the big kettle, taking the water temperature with her hand as if it was a baby she was about to bath.

The old woman asked for scissors and cut off the shroud the military authorities had put on him. The widow had torn up one of her nightdresses to use as cloths. Old Annie rubbed the skin gently, squeezing the water from the cloth, washing every part of him, under his armpits, between his legs.

The widow had his nightgown warming in the oven, and both women moved him to put it on him. Then the widow took the scissors and went out to the porch, feeling for the honeysuckle he'd trained up the wall. She put the fragrant ropes in with him.

'You're not to say to anyone that you washed him,' the widow warned.

Old Annie nodded. Her trade was secrecy, and she had seen some peculiar things. She put the half crown into her apron pocket, and, basin under her arm, went home to sleep soundly.

But the widow didn't put the lid back on. She didn't know how she was going to manage to work the croft and look after five children who were all clever and needed to get a chance. She built up the fire and sat by it, singing Gaelic songs, lullabies she sang to her children. It seemed to her that the man lying beside her in the sweet blossom was smiling as he slept, his skin unblemished.

8

The doctor was standing by Hector's bed as dawn brightened the window. He was watching the nurse withdrawing the thermometer.

'Ninety-nine, and his coughing's so much better.'

The doctor nodded. 'You'll put nothing about the administration of whisky on his records, nurse. Just show his temperature falling.'

When the doctor went away she sat on Hector's bed, holding his hand. From what she had seen in that ward there was no reason to believe in miracles.

'There's a telegram for you. Will I read it out?'

He nodded.

'Are you all right, Hector? Send word back at once. Love, Maggie.'

'It's my sister,' he said weakly.

'That's nice of her. Would you like me to send a reply?'

'Aye, say I'm fine. Don't say I've had the measles. It'll just worry her.'

'That's very considerate of you,' the nurse said, even more taken with him.

'There's money in my locker there,' he said, embarrassed.

'I'll send it when I go off duty,' she promised. 'Ah, here's Father Ryan.'

The priest looked in astonishment at the man to whom he'd given the Last Sacrament the night before.

'It was a miracle, Father,' the nurse told him. 'It must have been the power of your prayer.'

'But it was you that gave me the medicine,' Hector said to her.

'What medicine?' She was worried now that she was going to be caught out in a lie in front of the priest.

'Someone lifted me up and gave me medicine,' Hector said.

'It wasn't me,' she said. 'You were in a fever.'

'But I was lifted up,' he insisted.

'You were lifted up in the strong arms of the Lord,' the priest told him. 'He laid you back in this world because your time had not yet come. I'm going to say a prayer, and I'll write to the Bishop.'

The nurse winked at Hector behind the priest's back as she went to put on her coat. But instead of going to send his telegram she hurried to the guard-room to tell them that Private Macdonald was on the road to recovery – because she now felt sorry for the big man who'd given him the whisky, though it had been a terribly risky thing to do that could have cost her her job.

'It's no thanks to you,' the Colonel told MacDougall. 'You did a very reckless thing, and Lieutenant Lauder's got quite a few complaints of insubordination against you, going back to the camp at Dunoon. You've signed up for France with the others, but do you really think you're a fit person to go?'

'I'm as fit to go as anyone else, sir,' MacDougall told him. He'd spent the night trying to sleep on a stone shelf in the guard room. 'And Eachann's not going without me. I'm not going to let these German bastards kill the best bloody piper in the Division.'

'How dare you use such language to the Colonel,' Lauder cautioned him.

'I'm sorry for putting it that way, sir, but Eachann's been my friend since he was that high.' He held his hand level with his knee. 'And I promised his sister I would look after him.'

Kilberry was studying MacDougall's papers.

'You're the fellow from Invernevis who won the caber at the battalion sports?'

'Aye, and the hammer too, sir, and putting the weight.'

'Major Macdonald of Invernevis is a very fine man, with a long association with the 8th Argylls. He would be very disappointed if I wrote to tell him how you'd misbehaved. What do you do for a living?'

'I have a croft, sir, and I do a bit of ghillieing.' He wasn't going to tell him about the two old people.

94

This fine big fellow was far too valuable to lose.

'I'm not going to be as severe as I could be, because I can't think you would have done such a thing unless you cared deeply for your friend. You'll move into camp and be confined to barracks for fourteen days.'

MacDougall smiled as he saluted, bringing his heels together. Then he saluted Lauder, who was furious at the outcome. Kilberry was far too soft: this man should be dismissed from the battalion for what he'd done.

'Can I have permission to visit my friend, sir?' he asked Kilberry.

'If you don't cause any more trouble.'

MacDougall went straight across to the hospital.

'You've had a bad time, Eachainn,' he said, putting the bag of peaches on the bedside table. 'Yesterday you were the colour of a boiled lobster.'

'What's the news?' Hector asked weakly.

'Captain Campbell's been transferred to the Gordons. That's the way it is, the best bloody ones are always taken, and we're left with weeds like Lauder.'

'Who are we getting as Adjutant?'

MacDougall shrugged. 'They don't tell us much.'

'That fellow in the next bed told me what you did for me last night. He said he never got such a fright in his life. It made him better too.'

The man held out his hand from under the covers to shake it with MacDougall.

'I did bugger-all expect bring you a wee dram,' MacDougall said dismissively. 'I haven't got one on me today, because the bloody nurse frisked me before she would let me in to see you. But she says you should be up and about in a week. I was thinking we should go up to London for the day.'

'What for?' Hector asked suspiciously.

'The woman I go to see's got a lot of maids. You could attend to one of them while I'm upstairs.'

'You're going to a house with maids?' Hector asked, intrigued. 'Who the hell are you mixed up with now?'

MacDougall leaned confidentially over the bed. This was the only man he could trust. Besides, he needed something to take his mind off his sickness.

'Do you remember the fine-looking woman that gave me the medals at the sports and came to the camp that night?'

'Christ, you don't mean Mrs Richardson?' Hector said, trying to sit up on an elbow.

'The very one. I go up to London to see her.'

'You're not shagging the Brigadier's wife? If you're caught—'

'I won't get caught,' MacDougall said confidently. 'You'll need to come up with me.'

'Time's up!' the nurse called.

'Now *she*'s a good-looker,' MacDougall said appreciatively as he watched her coming across. 'You should try and get a leg over her when you're stronger. Give her one of these peaches.'

Maggie was very relieved to get Hector's telegram, but she was worried about Sam. He'd lost his cheery outlook and seemed nervous and short-tempered every time he came down from the village.

'Somebody's been saying something to you,' she said as she stood at the table, baking.

He was sitting on the step, his back to her, smoking a cigarette as he played with the dog between his boots. 'It's just when I go into the store.'

She gave him time, her whisk clicking rhythmically against the side of the bowl.

'It's the women. They talk in Gaelic behind my back, but I know what they're saying, all right. They're saying that I should be away at the war.' He tried to make it sound as if he wasn't concerned.

The whisk stopped in the thickened whites of the eggs.

'What has it got to do with them?' she asked indignantly. 'Anyway, *their* men aren't away at the war.'

'Some are back,' he said.

'Back? Don't tell me more of them have died from measles?' Her fear for Hector was returning.

'No, no. The ones who're too old have been sent home.'

'Why should these women take it out on you?'

'Maybe I should leave,' he said.

'And let them get the better of you, just like that?' she said scornfully. 'These bitches have been at it for years, war or no war. Pay no attention to them.' This war was getting on everyone's nerves.

'I'd better go up and see to the horses,' he said evasively, nicking his smoke and pushing the dog away.

But she didn't want him going away in that mood, so she said:

'We'll go for a walk tonight, after dinner.'

'That would be grand,' he said as he went away.

But Invernevis came through after dinner, with a good drink in him as usual. He sat in her chair, smoking as she tidied up.

'That was good news about Hector.'

'Yes, sir. Just as long as he doesn't go and catch the measles now.'

'I had a letter from Colonel Campbell. They think the epidemic's almost over, thank God. It certainly took its toll.' He still couldn't believe that some of the strong men who'd lain round the fires at the Dunoon camp had gone.

'What I don't understand, sir: why have they kept all those men in the camp for so long?'

He shrugged. 'Who knows the ways of the War Office? It depends on what moves the Germans make.'

She'd seen the pictures in the magazines of men crowding round the recruiting offices in London and other places, some looking desperate, as if they weren't going to be taken, so many of them only boys.

'But why are all those men who're joining up getting sent overseas, sir?'

'They're different from the Territorials. They're part of Kitchener's New Army.' These were the recruits the posters he'd had put up in the village were supposed to attract, but so far not one man had come down to sign on.

Sam was smoking another cigarette at the corner of the house. It was getting so late that he could barely read the watch he took from his waistcoat. He knew what would be keeping her: the boss would be through in the kitchen, talking, no doubt with a good drink in him as usual. Maggie shouldn't encourage him by talking to him; she should make it clear that she had to have time off.

He was beginning not to like the place. He trod out another cigarette. What was keeping her? Maybe it had been a mistake, leaving Buchan.

'I'm sorry,' Maggie said at his elbow, startling him.

'I know what kept you,' he said tersely.

She didn't like the tone. It implied that there was something between herself and the Master, but she was tired and she didn't want a row.

'It's getting too dark to go down the avenue,' she said, thinking about the blind bend.

'You could come up to my place,' he suggested.

'I don't think I should.'

'Why not?' He looked at her small earnest face in the last of the light.

'All right,' she said, following him up the mossy track.

'I'll go first,' he said at the bottom of the steps.

As she waited she heard the horses shifting in their stalls. A head came out and she touched it. Then Sam appeared at the top of the steps. The lamp he was carrying made it look as if he was surrounded by a halo.

'I bought it in the store,' he explained as he closed the door behind her.

It was a small paraffin lamp, the silvered shield in the shape of a shell.

'It's very nice,' she said appreciatively. She watched him setting it down on the dresser. It seemed to flood the coombed room with warmth as well as light.

'My, but you have made changes,' she said, looking around.

He stood there proudly. He'd washed the skylight and painted the frame white. He'd seen the linoleum advertised in a magazine and sent away a postal order for a roll which he'd laid carefully with tacks.

She picked up the ram's horn from the bed. He'd begun carving it for a walking stick and it was almost finished.

'You've made a very good job of it.'

'There's more in the corner there,' he said, pointing. 'I was thinking of trying to sell them up in the village, but they're not very friendly in the store.'

'I'm sure the Master would like one,' she said.

He looked at her as she laid the horn back on the pillow. Then she picked up the book lying on the wooden chair.

'*A Manual of Agriculture.*' She turned the pages to pictures of tractors and feeding troughs.

'I'd like to have a wee farm of my own sometime,' he said. 'Things are changing, though. You've got to have knowledge as well as strength, with all the new machines. The first time my father saw a tractor he took a kick at it.'

'I'm sure you'll get your own place,' she said, laying the book back.

'Sit on the bed,' he urged. 'It's more comfortable.'

But she stood where she was. 'I really should be getting back down.'

'But you've only arrived. Sit down. I was thinking of getting a wee primus stove, to make a cup of tea, but I like going down to your kitchen so I won't bother.'

She blushed as she sat on the edge of the bed. He'd turned round the wooden chair and was sitting opposite her, his bare arms over the back.

He'd never been very good with words. Ploughing the flat landscape of Buchan day after day, the few words he'd had were for the horses, and he'd been alone in the bothy at nights. God, but she was a good-looking woman. He wished he had a photograph of her. He looked at the way her neat white hands lay on her lap, her small shoes together on the linoleum. A moth had come in with them and was flickering round the lamp on top of the dresser. He leaned over and kissed her.

She was taken by surprise. He was going to do it again, but she stood up.

'I have to get back down.'

'Why?' he asked, frustrated.

'Because I've work to do in the morning – and so have you,' she said with a hint of rebuke.

'I'll see you down.'

'I can manage.' But when she was at the bottom of the steps in the darkness she lingered, looking at the movement of his shadow on the bright slab of the skylight.

MacDougall was sitting on the top of the omnibus in the thick fog, thinking of Alanna's hands rolling down the stocking, exposing the white thigh. He hadn't heard from her for too long. He had to pull his jacket down over his erection as he went down the winding stair of the bus.

He could barely see the streets, far less find the way. The looming figure turned into a policeman in a cape.

'Eaton Square?' he asked suspiciously. 'What are you wanting there?'

Because he was supposed to be confined to camp, MacDougall had his story ready:

'I've got a friend who's a coachman. I'm going to talk to him about joining up. He's frightened.'

'But you've joined, Jock?'

'Oh, aye.'

'I'm going that way,' the officer said. 'Well, you'll be in France soon.'

'I'm not complaining,' MacDougall said.

The policeman left him at the steps. The windows were dark, but there was a light behind the bars in the basement. The maid who answered was alarmed by the big man.

'I need to see your mistress,' he said. 'I've got an urgent message for her.'

'Who sent you?'

'Never you mind that. Tell her that Mr MacDougall's here.'

'I can't,' the maid said.

'Why can't you?' he asked, feeling in his pocket for a shilling for her.

'Because she isn't here.'

'Oh, I see. She's out for the evening,' he said, disappointed.

'Look, if you're wanting a job here, you're wasting your time.'

'Who said anything about a job?' he asked truculently. This woman wasn't his type, with her lace cap and prim mouth.

'I suppose this is a social call,' she said sarcastically.

'You could put it like that.'

'Clear off before I call the police!' she said, shutting the door.

He was going to use his boot on it, but he heard the chain being put up, then her footsteps going away along the flagged passage. As he followed the railings in the foggy street he was angry that there hadn't even been a note. She'd been using him and had got tired of him. That was the way with these society women: he should never have got involved with her.

The looming figure turned into a woman.

'Interested, mister?' she drawled in Cockney, angling her body against the wall to show him her wares in the gas lamp.

He took her hand and put it down his trousers.

'My God, I'm going to have to charge you double,' she said.

Invernevis had sent another £50 borrowed from his mother, together with a telegram warning the governess not to attempt to bring home the children by any route whatsoever. If they came by land they could get caught up in the fighting, and if they came by sea they could get torpedoed. He hadn't had a reply, and didn't even know if the money had got through safely.

He had had to settle the Home Farm milk bill before MacPherson wrote to the trustees, and under the paperweight there was still the pile of accounts which he couldn't pay. There was no point in going back up to Father Macdonald. He was going to have to do something drastic soon, like selling something, even though the contents of the house were under the trustees, and there was an inventory.

Because of the worries that the war had brought, his room – with its log fire, its shelves of books and gleaming silver on the desk – had lost its intimacy, its atmosphere of security and comfort, and he was still supposed to go recruiting up in the village, where he could detect hostility, with the Highland Division about to leave for France. It was becoming impossible to run an estate in these conditions. For all his womanizing, his father had never had to contend with these problems.

He was trapped. Even if the trustees would agree to the sale of the estate, who would buy it at a time like this? What had been a position of privilege was now a feeling of imprisonment. Maybe his brother had been right to make the break by marrying out of his class, though he hadn't lived to enjoy his revolt.

He went to the bottle of Mackinlay's, but it was empty. Damn it: there wasn't another bottle of whisky in the place. He lit a cigarette and went through to Maggie.

She was apprehensive because she could see he had a good drink in him.

'I've been doing some thinking, Maggie. We're going to have to cut back on the staff.'

Here it comes, she thought. *This is his way of getting Sam to go and join up.*

'We'll have to get rid of two of the maids.'

'Which ones, sir?'

'I'll leave that to you. They're all paid the same. It'll save some money when things are so tight.'

It wasn't fair, leaving her with this responsibility. Obviously she would have to hold on to Jessie, who'd been the longest there. She would have to wait at table as well as doing the cleaning, and there was the old lady upstairs to look after. She wasn't worried so much about the extra burden that would fall on herself, because she'd never been afraid of hard work. It was the two girls. They wouldn't get a job locally, and would have to go away to the city to work, where the one from Barra would just get into trouble, the way she looked at men.

'When do you want them to finish, sir?' she asked quietly, keeping her thoughts to herself because he looked so worried.

'At the end of next month. I'll give them first-class references, of course.'

'I'm having a job getting things from Liptons in Glasgow, sir. They used to be very good at putting anything on the train, but I've been waiting days for a sack of flour. I can't do any real baking without it.'

It was her way of saying that the account hadn't been paid.

He nodded. 'I must send them a cheque tomorrow.'

There was silence. She was wishing he would go to bed, so that she could go up herself.

'It's becoming very difficult, isn't it, Maggie?'

It was the first time she'd heard him acknowledge this, and it moved her.

'Things will get better, sir,' she said, but with no conviction in her voice.

'If I didn't have you, I don't know what I would do.'

'You mustn't let things get you down, sir.'

'I mean it. You've been so good to my family since you came here to work. How long is it?' he mused through his cigarette smoke.

'It was the day you went out to South Africa, sir.'

He nodded. 'Sixteen years. That's a long time.' He was watching her. She didn't look any different from the day she'd arrived. In fact he thought she was even prettier, and that her fuller figure suited her better. He was having a vision: following her up the back stairs, then watching her removing her clothing, pulling the pins from her piled-up hair till it tumbled down her back. His urge was so strong that he would have gone if there had been the slightest encouragement, but she was sitting smiling at him.

'I think you should get to bed, sir. You look tired.'

9

The bombardment opened in the dawn, as the 6th Gordons were being brought up to the old German front line. Where shells left gaps, men soon moved up. Captain Campbell of Jura the new Adjutant was standing in the orchard beside his commanding officer, Colonel McLean of Breda. They were watching the mist rising to reveal the shell-ploughed countryside up to the Aubers Ridge, that near yet so distant prize.

The shells made even shouting impossible. Not that the Adjutant wanted conversation. He was worried because this Territorial battalion wasn't ready for an attack like this. They were even rawer than the 8th Argylls had been in the Dunoon camp that seemed now to have taken place in another world of light and intact fences. Jura had never yearned so much for summer, for unbruised fruit he could reach up to, for the warmth of his wife's body.

The commanding officer signalled to his officers to gather round him as the map was spread out and weighed down with stones. The ferrule of the Colonel's cane went straight to the Moulin du Pietre, where trenches and a few houses were to be captured. Jura shielded his eyes, but there was only rubble up that way. He looked left, to where the 2nd battalion was also waiting. Now the pipes and drums were tuning up. Surely to God they weren't going to march into the heavy fire that had held up the general attack. But even if he could have made himself understood above the stupendous din of the shells he wouldn't have said anything. This was what the years of training, the long service in Nigeria and other lands were supposed to be about. He was a professional soldier, so he knew the risks. He was also a Campbell heir, and Highland history was littered with their corpses.

He composed himself by thinking of Dorothy cutting flowers in the gardens at Hunter's Quay, where he himself had planted the lilies. She laid the stalks, side by side, in her trug. The shells were breaking up the tune of the pipes but he recognised the 'Haughs of Cromdale', the regimental charge of the Gordons. For once the sound of the pipes, which Jura had grown up with, didn't raise his heart. Pipe-Major Howarth gave the signal for the band to lead the advance, the officers following. Jura saw a piper swaying like a tree in a storm, then going over, collapsing in wailing drones into the mud. He began to run. He knew that the revolver in his fist was useless against what they were facing, but there was a certain reassurance in its feel.

Machine gun bullets were spattering the mud as they went up the slope. Colonel McLean was trying to establish contact with the 2nd Gordons on his battalion's right front when he was hit.

'Go about your duty,' was his last order to the officers trying to lift him.

Captain Cooke was in command now and ordered the advance to be carried out on a four-platoon front. Jura was running on, wishing he had his Irish charger. But there was no room to manoeuvre himself, never mind an animal among these wire entanglements, bullets splintering the wooden rests. They had come to a halt on a line a little in advance of the 2nd battalion. The confusion was making the Adjutant angry, because the men were such easy targets. The band had broken up, otherwise it would have ceased to exist, with pipers acting as stretcher-bearers. Then a runner came veering with a message for Captain Cooke.

'They're going to send over howitzers to give us support!' he yelled to Jura as his arm signalled the advance on.

As Jura ran on bodies rolled back to meet him because the Germans had fortified the ruins that had been farmhouses. In the thunder of the howitzers he was a boy again, running down to the sea boiling in the channel below Jura House on a day of storm, the spume rising to meet him.

The mud sucked the brogues from his feet, but he ran on in his stocking soles. Then something tugged at his kilt. He thought it was an officer wanting assistance as he fell, but he'd become snagged on a bundle of barbed wire. He tried to tear the thick tartan away, but as he twisted it more pleats became caught.

When he saw the blade he thought it was one of his men coming to cut him free.

But the bayonet passed into his side.

When the letter from Hector came Maggie read it and then sat staring at her lap for a long time. Invernevis came through to see why his mail was still lying on the kitchen table.

'Is something the matter, Maggie?'

'Hector's going overseas, sir.' She had been praying it wouldn't happen.

'I'm sorry, Maggie.'

'Not half as sorry as I am, sir.'

'He did sign up.'

'That was because he was tricked it into it,' she said wearily.

'I don't think that's true,' he said gently. 'The army is very careful about that sort of thing. It would all have been explained to him before he signed. I understand that most of the 8th Argylls signed.'

'But what could the fellows from Invernevis do, if all the others signed? It would have made them look like cowards.'

'You're not to worry, Maggie. I've told you before, pipers have a better chance than others. They aren't sent into the fighting, but they're just as important as the infantry, maybe more so because they raise morale. The pipes have helped armies to win wars for centuries. Hector and the others will play the Argylls into battle, then he'll have some first-aid duty.'

But it still didn't reassure her. The war had changed everything, even the man sitting at the opposite end of the table, his hand trembling because he hadn't yet had a drink. The war was supposed to be far away, in foreign countries, but it had arrived at Invernevis, and it was doing such damage.

'There'll be a lot of talk up in the village, sir,' she warned him.

He knew she was speaking the truth, and he didn't know how he was going to deal with the Territorial wives. It was an impossible situation: they couldn't work the crofts with their husbands away, yet the estate needed the rents, and he needed more money to keep this house going.

'I'll have to have a public meeting to explain things,' he said.

Sam came in with the newspapers, and Invernevis took them through to the library.

'You mustn't allow it to get you down,' Sam said, standing behind Maggie's chair, his hands on her shoulders. 'We could ask for a few days off and go to Glasgow.'

She turned her head. 'Oh, aye. And what would we do there?'

'I think we should get engaged.'

He could feel her stiffening under his fingers.

'It's not the time to speak of such things,' she rebuked him.

'Why not?'

'I can't think about such things just now,' she said, rising to move about restlessly. 'I've got too much to do about here.'

'I know why you won't come to Glasgow: because you're frightened to leave him.' He had said it impulsively and immediately regretted it, but he was on edge because there had been more talk behind his back in the store that morning.

'What do you mean by that?' she confronted him.

'The way he's drinking.'

'That's none of your business.'

He shrugged. 'All right. Then I won't tell you what I've got out on the gig.'

'What do you mean?' she asked, alarmed.

'There's a case of whisky.'

'Take it straight back up to the station,' she ordered him.

'It didn't come off the train. I got it from the Arms.'

'Who told you to do that?'

'The boss did.'

'And what did you use to pay for it?'

'Nothing. He told me to tell Carmichael to put it on the account.'

'But he's never had an account at the Arms.'

'He has now. Carmichael says that he's not worried: if he doesn't get paid for it he'll keep it off the rent he pays to the trustees at the half year.'

'God, what a mess.' She was close to tears as she sank down

on the chair, her head in her hands. 'I can't cope with this place any more. Did the sack of flour come off the train?'

'There wasn't anything for us on it.'

'How am I supposed to feed people if I can't get the stuff to make the food with?' She turned to him. 'I'm telling you these things, but you've never to speak of them to anyone, inside or outside this house.'

He felt privileged by her confidence because he knew that she needed someone she could trust to talk to. It was a big responsibility, however, and he had to be very careful what he said.

'A walk tonight will do us good.'

'If I can get through till then,' she said.

'It will be seven shillings for three,' said the photographer with the waxed moustache and floral waistcoat.

'How much for one?' MacDougall asked.

'It's not worth my while doing one,' the photographer told him. 'I've had hundreds of Scotch in here, and they all took three, for parents and sweethearts.'

But MacDougall wanted to consult Hector. 'If we get taken together that will be three and sixpence each,' he said in Gaelic, while the photographer hovered on the supple toes of his fashionable boots.

'It's not a good idea,' Hector told him. 'If I send one with you in it to Maggie she'll just write back to say that I'm keeping bad company. I'll lend you the money till pay day.'

'All right, I'll take three,' MacDougall told the photographer.

But he didn't think that it was going to take such time.

'What background do you want?' the photographer asked. He jerked a cord and a scene rolled down. 'I can do you this.' It was grey, indistinct. He gave another jerk. This one had bushes on it, and a road wending away into the distance, a little house with a smoking chimney on the hill.

'Are they both the same price?' the client asked.

The photographer nodded.

'I'll take the first.'

Now the photographer was fussing round him, making him place a brogue up on the rustic bench, adjusting the pleats of his kilt and the hang of his badger-hair sporran. MacDougall didn't like the way he was being touched.

'You want to look like a soldier ready to go overseas to fight for his country,' the photographer said, adjusting the slope of his subject's bonnet. MacDougall could smell perfume off him. He had no time for that sort of thing, and if there was any more nonsense, he would have to deal with him.

But the photographer had crossed to the other side of the studio to put his head under a black cloth.

'Smile at me, but not too much.'

MacDougall had never seen a camera before. How was he supposed to smile at the bugger when his face was hidden?

'Stay still,' the muffled voice warned.

MacDougall watched the hand rising, holding something. He was getting cramp in the thigh, but the old man had said that a photograph would mean the world to the old woman.

The sudden flash made him lose his balance.

'If you keep moving and they're ruined, I'll have to charge you,' the muffled voice warned.

MacDougall only blinked at the second and third flash because they were each worth two-and-sixpence.

'Can I see myself?' MacDougall asked, ready to put his head under the black cloth.

The photographer started to laugh, rocking on his toes.

'What's so funny?' MacDougall demanded.

'Nothing,' the photographer assured him. 'Come and collect them tomorrow morning, but send your friend through now.'

Hector wanted to be photographed with his pipes under his arm, which meant a lot of arranging, making sure the tartan bag was hanging correctly, and that the drones were lying right. Very likely Maggie would give a copy to the boss, so he'd better look serious.

'You look very nice,' the photographer said, standing back to admire him, one eye shut.

'It's only my photograph I want taken,' Hector warned him while MacDougall stood by watching.

Jura opened his eyes. He was being rocked gently from side to side. With great effort he raised his head from the pillow. At the end of the dim corridor he could see a figure standing in white from head to foot. It was so peaceful, far from the pain of his wound.

'Nanny,' he said.

The figure was coming towards him. She was a beautiful woman, her head swathed in white. When she came closer he recognised Alanna Richardson.

'Jock,' she said, holding him.

She'd waited three Wednesdays for MacDougall, sitting on the stairs in her silk nightdress. Something must have happened to him. She'd quizzed her husband carefully about the 8th Argylls. How were they behaving at Bedford? Reasonably. But she wanted more, so she put her arms round his neck as he sat stiff, smoking his cigar, his eyeglass in place. No fights? Very few. Then everyone should be very proud of them, she told him.

She put the back of her hand against his precisely trimmed moustache. Ah, but there was something. Did she remember that big fellow who'd acted as her ghillie at Invernevis and who'd thrown the caber at the Dunoon camp? Vaguely, she said, adjusting his tie knot. Well, Kilberry had told him how the man had forced his way into the measles ward and brought round his friend by pouring whisky down his throat. Bloody dangerous thing to do. The big fellow had been confined to camp. If it wasn't that his kind were needed in France to show the Germans he should have been dismissed.

Then he'd told her what he'd been trying to tell her all night, but didn't have the courage, because women's tears terrified him. The Highland Division was under orders for abroad, in a month or so. He would have to go, but he would be out of danger, at Divisional Headquarters, and he would try to get as many leaves as possible, since it wasn't so far.

As a young wife she'd kept him quiet by joining the other officers' wives in the St John's Ambulance Brigade, going to meetings to apply tourniquets. When she went up the stairs that night she had her maid search the cupboards for the certificates she'd received. They were turned up at the bottom of a trunk at 2 a.m.

By next evening she was in Calais, knocking on the door of the office in the Duchess of Sutherland's Hospital. The woman who hurried to greet her from behind the desk with a hug was already a legend.

'What are you doing here, Alanna darling?'

'I want to work for you.' She put her St John's certificates on the desk. 'Freddie's coming over here with the Highland Division and I want to play my part.'

'There's a part for us all, especially those of us who've been privileged in life,' the Duchess said. 'And I admire persistence.' She opened a drawer and put a revolver on the desk. 'That was my calling card in Belgium.'

Alanna couldn't stand the woman. She found her insufferably arrogant, but next day she was helping in a ward in the Duchess's hospital. She'd only stayed a fortnight, because she wanted to get near the front, ahead of the Highland Division, and the only way to do that was to join a hospital train.

Tonight the train was nearly a third of a mile long, crowded with the wounded from Neuve Chapelle loaded at the railhead at Merville. She should have been in the next carriage with the sitting-up cases, but when she saw Jock Campbell, she'd asked another nurse to swop.

'Where am I?' Jura asked, agitated.

'You've been wounded, but you'll be in base hospital in Boulogne in a few hours. Try to rest.'

The bandage was like a tight belt round his midriff.

'What are you doing here, Alanna?'

'As you know, I adore soldiers.'

His wound wouldn't allow him to laugh, so he lay there, admiring her. She became a white sail. He was sitting at the tiller of his boat, sailing in the Sound of Jura on an evening of gentle breeze.

'It was a terrible slaughter, wasn't it?' he said.

'You mean Neuve Chapelle? Yes, it was a bad battle.'

'Will Dorothy know I've been wounded?'

'I'm sure the War Office will have sent a telegram,' Alanna said.

He was looking around the other beds. The face in the covers of the next one had a bandage round the eyes, and there were screens round the next one. He was a child again, in the nursery at Jura House, his mother coming to say good night, bending over him, her pearls touching his face.

Alanna was arranging his head on the pillows.

'I've got something to make you sleep.'

When she came back from her berth she had a bottle and glass with her.

'It isn't Islay malt, but at least it's whisky.'

She poured him a large one and held it to his mouth.

'Have you any news of the 8th Argylls?' he asked.

'They're due in France within weeks.'

He wished he'd been allowed to stay with them, but not because he would have been safe. As he lay there he was thinking fondly of that last camp at Dunoon.

'You must rest, Jock.'

'There'll be plenty of time for that. Stay and talk to me.'

'I must go and attend to the others,' she told him gently.

He watched her swaying away, stooping to talk to a man in a bunk. He was a French officer. His legs were mangled, but his hand was active as he sketched, as if there wasn't much time left.

'*Qu'est-ce que c'est?*' she asked, bending over him as if he was a child.

He showed her. The ground was cut up with trenches, and a deranged bearded man was standing in one, holding up the stump of an arm. At first she thought it was a self-portrait, but he was printing the title in wavering letters:

Le Christ aux Tranchées de Neuve Chapelle.

10

The 8th Battalion of the Argylls was paraded so that the Colonel could read out the news about their late Adjutant. He could see how affected the men were, so he got the Sergeant-Major to dismiss them.

MacDougall saw Hector going round the corner of a hut with his pipes, but instead of following him he went to sit in one of the huts. He desperately needed a woman and couldn't understand what had happened to Alanna Richardson. He would like nothing better than to be lying right now with her in a foaming bath. He'd sent one of the photographs of himself to the old woman, which should keep her happy. He'd also put in ten shillings. He was keeping another photograph for Alanna, when she came back from wherever she was. He had to admit it: he'd never felt like this about a woman before, and he'd had plenty of them, so it must be love. By God it made you restless.

There was no one else in the enclosure reserved for pipers to practise in. Hector walked about, a chanter in his hand. He fingered the instrument, playing faltering snatches as he tried to put music to the images in his head: Jura sitting up against the sun on his black charger on a dusty road outside Dunoon; Jura standing talking to another officer against the fading sky, the ribbons on his bonnet being lifted by the breeze; Jura squatting by the camp fire, the glow reflected in his riding boots. Hector's fingers speeded along the chanter as he tried to imagine Jura going in for the charge, fearlessly. Was it a sword he'd had in his hand?

He felt as if he were drunk, yet he hadn't had a drop that day. The snatches were coming together into a tune as he picked up the full set of pipes. He paced the enclosure as if he were measuring out the music, slowly and carefully, toe to heel, with his brogues. He didn't care that the light was going; he couldn't go for his supper until this was finished.

The officers of the 8th Argylls were dining in the hut that

was their mess. There was no conversation because they were still shocked by the death of Jura, and when Lieutenant Lauder started to speak about how the war was going, Kilberry frowned. He was particularly affected, because Jura had been a friend for a long time, sometimes crossing in his skiff to Kilberry Castle for the day, then going home with his sail spread against the sunset.

Pipes were being tuned.

'I'll go and stop him,' Lauder said, pushing back his chair.

'Never stop a piper,' the Colonel warned him, motioning him to sit again.

Then the tune came. It was slow, it was stately, and every man at that table knew instinctively who it was for. Kilberry had laid down his cutlery and was sitting, listening, his head inclined. As the music surged and fell, like the swell of the sea, tears streamed down his face. Lauder was awed by the occasion, by the respectful silence of the other officers who kept their hands crossed as they looked at their plates, each with his own memory of the Adjutant. The Lieutenant hadn't understood the force of the pipes before.

The tune seemed to go on for a long time, and then it stopped abruptly. But the silence continued at the table, and even the orderlies remained standing behind the chairs, their napkins over their white sleeves as if they were statues.

'Bring him here,' Kilberry ordered Lauder.

Hector saluted and stood at the end of the table, his pipes folded under his arm.

'What's your name?' Kilberry asked him from the other end.

'Macdonald, sir. Hector Macdonald.'

'Where are you from?'

'I'm an Invernevis man, sir.'

'Ah, you are the one your friend saved from the measles.'

'Yes, sir. Big Dochie MacDougall brought me a dram.'

'And you were the one who took the march, and strath-spey and reel medals at Dunoon. I recognize your finger-ing.'

Hector was flattered by Kilberry's recollection. He looked along the table, at the full glasses, the silver cutlery.

'And what name are you giving to the tune you were playing just now?'

'The 8th Argylls' Farewell to Captain Campbell of Jura, sir.'

'It's too formal,' Kilberry said.

'What – the tune, sir?' Hector said, confused.

'No, the title. What about the 8th Argylls' Farewell to Jock of Jura?'

'That's fine by me, sir.'

'You must write it down, in case anything happens,' Kilberry urged him.

Hector hesitated. 'I can't write it, sir.'

'That's no problem,' Kilberry said. 'Many of the best pipers can't write music. You'll come tomorrow at eleven and play it, and I'll write it down. And then you'll play it at parade for the battalion.'

'Yes, sir.'

'Give Macdonald a dram – a good one,' Kilberry told an orderly.

'To Jock's memory, and the piper,' Kilberry said, proposing the toast when all the officers had got to their feet.

'To Jock's memory, and the piper,' they repeated, raising their glasses.

'And while you're here, you may as well give us a tune,' the Colonel said to Hector.

Lauder was angry. He wanted to leave the table, so that he could take a run up to London to see Mildred, but he was forced to sit out the racket, and the bloody piper wouldn't move away from behind his chair.

When the muffled drums began playing 'The Flowers of the Forest' she knew that the steamer with her husband's body was approaching Dunoon Pier, but she was strangely calm as she lay in bed in the villa at Hunter's Quay, the bay window propped open with one of his Gaelic grammars, because he'd been so eager to learn to speak the language of his people when he took over the island. How strange; she could smell the flowers he'd picked for her on her first visit to Jura in the big sloping walled garden, with the stream running through it. She was sitting on the little bridge, in the sun, when he came with the blue flowers, holding them to her face.

'One day this will be our garden,' he'd said.

Now the pipes of the company of the 8th Argylls were playing 'Lochaber No More' and she knew the steamer was sailing away. She threw aside the covers and went to the window. Its flags at half-mast, the boat was passing the Gantocks. That was when she began screaming, when the maid rushed in and had to get help to lift Mrs Campbell from the floor because the child she was carrying was due in a few weeks.

Invernevis was attending the funeral on behalf of his company of the battalion, though Maggie hadn't wanted him to go because she knew he would drink once he got in amongst the Argylls again. He'd had to go up to his mother to borrow ten pounds for the fare, but didn't tell her what it was for. He'd got the train to Gourock, and was quite drunk by the time he boarded the ferry for Dunoon – because he dreaded the experience.

He'd stood on the pier, listening to the pipe band bringing the steamer in with the cortège. Invernevis went aboard and was met by Jura's brother Ronald, who was serving with the Royal Fusiliers.

'You've brought him a great distance,' Invernevis said, shaking hands.

'He doesn't belong over there.'

A soldier was standing by the railings, clearly in some distress.

'Who's that?' Invernevis asked Jura's brother.

'Peter MacGregor, Jock's batman.'

Invernevis went across to speak to him.

'I'm pleased to see you again, Major. Captain Campbell always spoke about you with great affection.'

'And I felt the same about him. We all did.'

The batman was fighting back tears. 'You know what happened at Neuve Chapelle, sir?'

'No, I don't.'

'He was put on a stretcher, but insisted that a private who was wounded was to get attention first. That was Captain Campbell, sir. If a man can love another man, sir, I'm not ashamed to say that I loved him. He should never have been taken away from the Argylls.'

The remains were carried from the steamer at Inverary, where the Duke of Argyll paid his respects, and then the coffin was driven to West Loch Tarbert, where Brigadier Richardson was waiting.

'I couldn't let Jock go without saying farewell. Alanna was on the hospital train with him, you know.'

'No, I didn't know,' Invernevis said, surprised.

'Oh, yes,' he said proudly. 'She was so worried about me going to France that she got there before me. She's a clever woman, with so much energy.'

'How long is this war going to last?' Invernevis asked.

The Brigadier wanted to show that he was in close touch with the War Office. 'It's proving trickier than we thought at first. The Kaiser's ruthless and clever – there's no doubt about that. I'm going to say something to you in confidence because I know I can trust you as an Argyll and as a friend of Alanna's. Kitchener doesn't have any confidence in John French and neither do his staff. He didn't know what was going on at Mons because he didn't keep in touch with his command. He lost his nerve at Le Cateau and got Douglas Haig out of his bed at two o' clock in the morning to order an immediate retreat. Then he wanted to withdraw from France, and Kitchener had to persuade him to remain.'

'So you reckon victory's a long way away?' Invernevis asked.

'I think it could go another two years.'

'But there'll be no army left,' Invernevis said in despair.

'They'll have to conscript, sooner or later.'

'But they've got the Highland Division and the other Territorials.'

'Kitchener despises the Territorials. He says they're amateurs who can't replace well trained soldiers, though some of the Territorial battalions that have been sent out, like Jock's, have shown they're just as good as the regulars.'

'Will the Highland Division be going?'

'We'll be there by the first week of May. The men are well trained and keen: that's as much as one can hope for at present. I'll do my best to see that they're wisely used, but I can't overrule French, of course. But there's a movement at the War Office to get Haig to take over from French. Kitchener's keen. But as I said, all this is strictly confidential.'

They dined together in the steamer's saloon. Invernevis was very drunk as he groped his way along the deck to his berth in the starlit night. He couldn't sleep and lay smoking, thinking about Maggie back at Invernevis. She needed to take a holiday, but he had come to depend too much on her. She really was a splendid woman.

He was on deck to see the Paps of Jura emerging from the morning mist, asking the steward to open up the bar before breakfast. The tenants were waiting at Craighouse to shoulder the remains up the stony track through the thatched hamlet of Keils, where a young woman stepped forward and threw a posy on the coffin.

The Laird of Jura carried his son's sword and cap. He saw the old woman sitting on the plain chair against the wall of the croft, her arms folded, a clay pipe in her jaws. That summer afternoon when she'd watched young Jura, his wife and the ghillie coming down from the cemetery he'd been barefooted, and the blood from the wound at his side was spurting through his fingers. She'd taken to her bed for five days after the vision, as she'd done when she saw the boat capsized by a harpooned whale in icebergs as tall as mountains, drowning a son of Keils who came home two months later in a coffin that stank like a fish box.

'*Ach chan fhaic mi mo bhàs fhèin*,' ('But I will not see my own death,') she said.

It seemed as if James Lochnell Campbell of Jura was going to be buried among the bens, the way the mourners were climbing. Round the corner was the churchyard of Kilearnadil, the warm hollow of Saint Ernan. A clear cold burn comes straight from the Paps.

Invernevis found the climb hard going with his game leg,

and wished he had his hip-flask with him. The iron gate to the Campbell mausoleum had been opened, and the piper from Jura House was now playing a lament that the hills took up and circulated. The minister said a prayer as the body of the younger of Jura was laid among his ancestors. The flagstones were levered back, and the many floral tributes placed on them, from the estate tenants, the 8th Argylls, the 6th Gordons. There was a bunch of flowers that had been cut from an embankment in France, with a black-bordered card:

'To my brave Jock of Jura, once an Argyll, always an Argyll. Alanna.'

The teapot by Maggie's hand was cold as she sat at the kitchen table in the fading light. He shouldn't have gone to Jura, even though Captain Campbell had been a friend. He would take too much drink and fall from the steamer with that game leg. She could see his body laid out, the rings glittering on his wet fingers. Oh, what a terrible world this was turning out to be; all those names of the dead in the newspapers, and now Hector going to France. It was all very well to say that because he was a piper he would be all right, but pipers made a lot of noise and drew attention to themselves.

Sam didn't want to go up to the village, because they were speaking about him in English now in the store. She was sure that the Master had been dropping big hints about enlisting, but she daren't ask Sam because he was getting so touchy. She noticed that he was smoking two packets of Woodbine a day now. It was getting on her nerves. Maybe Sam was right; maybe they should just go through to Glasgow and get engaged. She was very fond of him, and she would be alone if anything happened to Hector. They could get married and have a wee place of their own. Sam could get a job, maybe in a factory; he was so good with his hands.

But she couldn't leave that poor soul alone in this house. Everything was getting into such a mess: his face was showing the drink, and there were all those unpaid bills on his desk. She was frightened to order anything from Glasgow now, and Munro up in the store was complaining about the size of the account. Maybe the world would be a better place if it was run by women, though she'd no time for the suffragettes.

'Penny for your thoughts,' Sam said from the door.

'They're not worth that,' she said earnestly.

'The boss will be all right,' he said. 'He's a survivor.'

'What do you mean by that?'

'All his kind are.'

'Captain Campbell wasn't,' she reminded him.

'Are you coming for a walk?'

'Not tonight.'

'But you haven't got a dinner, with him away.'

'There's a lot more to be done than just cooking,' she told him.

Harry Lauder had become the champion of the Highland Division, going down to Bedford to give them concerts. Tonight was the last one before the Division left for France, and he and his wife were dining with the officers beforehand. The comedian was regaling them with stories of the success of his recent American tour. He'd travelled thousands of miles by train and sung in dozens of cities. He used his hands to describe the splendour of the Golden Gate at San Francisco. Negroes had made him huge hamburgers, and mayors had turned out to welcome him.

'I always gave the audiences a pep talk,' he explained as the orderlies came round with more coffee and a choice of liqueurs. 'I told them they should be in the war with us.'

'They'll come in in time,' Brigadier Richardson assured him.

'It would save a lot of lives if they came in now,' the comedian said.

His son was squirming in his seat. His father seemed out of place in his kilt and jacket among these men who wore their doublets and trews so naturally. He remembered the visits to Jesus College when the door would burst open, interrupting his piano playing, and his father would insist on trying out his latest song on him, marching up and down the room in his loud brogues. He looked to Mildred for reassurance that the evening was not a disaster, but she was uncomfortable as she sat beside Kilberry, who was well away with drink.

'And how's my laddie shaping up?' Harry Lauder asked.

The Brigadier indicated with the movement of his eyebrows that the Colonel should take the question, which had to be repeated to the old soldier, who was thinking about the peace of his castle on the coast.

'Very well.'

Lieutenant Lauder could feel the shame on his face. Why the hell did the old man do this to him?

'Once he's done his bit in the war he'll be laird of Glenbranter – twenty thousand acres. They've cost me a lot, I can tell you, but we're proud of our boy – aren't we, Nance?' He turned to his wife.

'I think we should get the concert started,' the Brigadier said, rising and offering his arm to Mrs Lauder. The hall was packed, and when Harry Lauder came on the stage there was a great cheer.

'Here's a man who's going to remind you of your hills and bens,' Brigadier Richardson told them in his introduction.

Lieutenant Lauder sat down at the piano, his back to the audience. It had been a mistake, agreeing to accompany his father, but he had insisted, though he could have brought a professional player from London.

His elbows going as he strutted the stage, Harry Lauder was singing 'I Love a Lassie', and even the Brigadier in the front row had joined in the chorus. But near the back Hector Macdonald wasn't singing. He would have dearly liked to have got up on the stage with his pipes to show that bugger with the crooked stick what it was really like to be Highland.

But it was Lauder's concert, and as he sang number after number, strutting about the stage the men almost brought the roof down. Their boots tramped the boards as if they were already in France, and some of them were swaying as they sang.

'Aye, you're braw lads,' he said. 'You'll give the Huns something to think about when you get over there.' And he took a swing with his brogue. 'I'd better finish with something special tae send you on your way.'

He sang 'When I Get Back Again to Bonnie Scotland'. They sat subdued, and when he went off they called him back with one voice: 'Give us "Roamin' in the Gloamin'" Harry!'

He gave it to them. They were on their feet, clapping and swaying as they sang the chorus with him. His son had turned round on the piano stool. What was the point in an accompaniment? He saw the power of his father's performance, and he saw what he was doing: raising them to a pitch for the battle to come in France.

'You were wonderful,' he told his father when they were backstage in the quiet.

'I did it tae give you a good send-off too, laddie.' He hugged his son. 'It won't be long before we're together again at Glenbranter.'

His parents went to bed in the hotel, but he stayed in the lounge with Mildred. The place was crowded with officers who were talking in loud excited voices about going to France.

'I just wish we'd been over for Neuve Chapelle!'

Lauder ordered coffee. He was nervous and kept smoking.

'I think you should leave London,' he said suddenly.

'But why?' Mildred asked, taken aback.

'Because there's going to be raids by zeppelins. They've already bombed King's Lynn and Yarmouth.'

'London's defended,' she said. 'I can see the searchlights from my bedroom window. My parents are there. It's our home.'

'Go up to Glenbranter for a bit, with my parents,' he urged. 'It'll please them a lot, before they go to America.'

'Johnnie, I want to stay here and do something for the war,' she told him earnestly. ' All my friends are doing something.'

'Like what?'

'I could join the Voluntary Aid Detachment and learn to drive an ambulance. They need drivers to take the wounded off the trains to the stations.'

'You've never expressed any interest in driving before.'

'This is different.'

'I don't think you should.'

'But why?'

He couldn't give a rational answer. He was jumpy, annoyed by the loud conversations going on around them. He was apprehensive about going overseas himself, not because he was frightened, but because there had been difficulties with the battalion, particularly with that lout MacDougall, who seemed to be making trouble for him with the other men. He was beginning to regret that he'd joined the Territorials, though he'd probably have signed up by now anyway, because most of his friends at Cambridge had. Jura's death had had a strange effect on the 8th Argylls. They'd been shocked that someone who seemed to have been invincible had been killed, but now they were taking it as a personal insult and were desperate to get out there and get to grips with the Germans. His father had given them their marching tune tonight, and perhaps that would make things easier for him.

'A penny for your thoughts, Johnnie.'

'We should get married tomorrow, before I go.'

She was astonished. 'But we're not even engaged.'

'What does that matter? It's just a social convention.'

'It means a lot to my parents. They like to see things done properly.'

He knew that his parents were the same: his father would want a big wedding in London, probably at the Savoy, with his friends from society as well as his theatrical friends.

'Then at least let's get engaged. We've been talking about it for so long.'

'I'll tell my parents we would like to get engaged on your next leave, and you can tell yours.'

They went up in the lift, along the carpeted corridor to the rooms his father was paying for, as he'd paid for everything with his comic songs. He'd even taken his son to get measured for a new Argylls kilt and had kept talking about 'the braw Highland laddies going to France' while the kneeling tailor marked the pleats with chalk.

The Lieutenant stopped outside his room, his key in his

hand. Mildred's room was further along, round the bend of the corridor. She could see the look in his eyes behind his spectacles in the corridor of subdued lighting, because it was late, and most of the guests were sleeping, including the Lauder parents in their suite, with the bouquet of roses presented to Mrs Lauder by the Highland Division in water in the elegant sink.

Mildred Thomson went through the door the Lieutenant was holding open for her. She took off her expensive dress and flung it across the chair, over his trews. She unhooked the pearls from her throat in the sombre mirror, then stepped out of her silk pants before climbing into that high bed of snowy linen warmed by the stone bottle the chambermaid had put in because it was still only April.

But it would not be love: it would be a surrender to fate, to the belief that she was never going to see this man again. Her breasts would smother him.

She had her own key in her hand now, and she kissed him on the cheek before saying good night.

11

The little girl was dancing along beside Hector, holding her grubby frock in her pinched fingers as she spun round, her clogs keeping time to the drums and pipes playing 'The Wedding'. All afternoon units of the 51st Highland Division had been passing through the French village after disembarkation. Women who had men at the front blew kisses and clapped their hands above their heads. Boys held out bunches of grass to the horses the officers were riding. The 8th Argylls were wearing Inverneil bonnets sloped on their heads, khaki side out. A woman ran forward, slipping a bonbon into MacDougall's mouth. He put his hand between her legs in thanks and as she shrieked the Sergeant-Major turned balefully.

The little dancer curtseyed to Hector and spun away as the 8th Argylls left the village, marching along the undulating road between the tall poplars. As Hector Macdonald blew and fingered in harmony with the rest of the band his eyes were taking in the countryside. It wasn't unlike Invernevis, except it was less hilly and the roofs were red. The tune changed and he almost lost it. The Pipe-Major would have heard the falter and would speak to him later. He was wishing that he still had the little girl for company on the long road.

After another hour's marching they turned into a huge field where the tents had to be set up. Hector knelt, holding a peg while MacDougall swung the big hammer.

'You could feel the heat coming off these women. Some of them won't have had it for months, with their men away,' the big man said.

'Concentrate on what you're doing with that hammer,' Hector pleaded as MacDougall swung it. As he closed his eyes he felt the shock going through his body, as if he himself were being driven into the French soil.

'If we don't get out of here tonight I'm bloody well breaking out,' the big man vowed. 'I haven't had a ride for weeks.'

'This is different from Bedford,' Hector warned him. 'If you get caught it could go badly for you. Anyway, you don't know the language. How are you going to make the women understand?'

'Oh, I'll make them understand. Don't you worry about that,' MacDougall assured him. 'I've got the very thing to get across to them. It's the way you use it, not what you call it.'

His friend's boasts about his virility frustrated Hector, who had still to experience a woman.

'You'll have to be quick – we'll be getting moved up to the line.'

'That suits me too,' MacDougall said. 'But you won't be seeing much action, by the looks of it.'

'What's that supposed to mean?'

'Kilberry's here for the piping, not the fighting. You're his blue-eyed boy. He's not going to risk you in the line when he needs a tune to help his drams down in the mess at night.'

'That's Lawrie's job,' Hector said. 'He's the Pipe-Major.'

'Aye, and he's exhausted already, with all the playing he did at Bedford. Have you seen him trying to light a cigarette? He'll set his kilt on fire yet, the shake that's in his hands.'

'I'm not frightened of fighting,' Hector said defensively, though that wasn't strictly true. It was only after seeing the number of soldiers and ships crossing the channel that he'd realized what a big war it was. It had made him feel insignificant, among all those men on the crowded deck of the steamer. They had guns and he had a box of pipes.

'I'm not accusing you of that. I'm only saying that you'll get no peace now from Kilberry, after that tune you composed for Captain Campbell. They say that the Colonel goes about humming it. Hedrum hodrum,' he began to sing as he swung the hammer.

'I heard something interesting in the mess the other night,' Hector said.

'Oh, aye,' MacDougall said warily, resting the hammer.

'It was about the Brigadier's wife.'

'What about her?'

But Hector was going to take his time because it wasn't often he had the better of the big man.

'I was waiting behind Kilberry's chair to hear what tune he was wanting, and Major Lockie leaned over and said something to him about Mrs Richardson.'

MacDougall was getting ready to swing the hammer again, a sullen look on his face.

'He said she's in France.'

The hammer thudded into the turf.

'Your arse. What would she be doing here?'

'She's working as a nurse.'

So that explained why he hadn't heard from her.

'Did you hear what part of the country she's in?' he asked eagerly.

'She's not in any particular part,' Hector said.

'What the hell's this, a puzzle?' MacDougall said. 'She has to be somewhere.'

'She's on a hospital train.'

MacDougall absorbed this information over a Woodbine. 'Aye, but did you hear where it runs?'

'You're taking too long,' Lieutenant Lauder came over to warn them. 'The rest of the men have got their tents up. Get a move on.'

'These pegs are rotten – sir,' MacDougall said, throwing another splintered one away.

'It's not the pegs. It's you. You don't know your own strength.'

MacDougall leaned on the shaft of the hammer. 'Oh, I know that all right, sir.'

But Lauder didn't want another confrontation with this man. 'Hurry up,' he told them as he turned away.

MacDougall made to throw the hammer after him.

Invernevis wasn't down yet because he'd had too much to drink the night before, so Maggie was taking the chance to tidy up his desk. The pile of unpaid accounts was still under the paperweight, but with a form on top.

5 Questions to those who employ male servants.

1. Have you a Butler, Groom, Chauffeur, Gardener, or Gamekeeper serving you who at this moment should be serving your King and Country?

2. Have you a man serving at your table who should be serving a gun?

3. Have you a man digging your garden who should be digging trenches?

4. Have you a man driving your car who should be driving a transport waggon?

5. Have you a man preserving your game who should be helping to preserve your Country?

A great responsibility rests on you.
Will you sacrifice your personal convenience for your Country's need?

Ask your man to enlist TO-DAY.

The address of the nearest Recruiting Office can be obtained at any Post Office.

GOD SAVE THE KING.

Maggie was frightened and wanted to tear up the form. It was as if he'd left it there for her to see. She covered it with the paperweight again and put the morning's papers on the blotter before going back through to the kitchen. There was baking to be done, though she was very short of ingredients. She was thinking about the 8th Argylls as she measured out the flour from the sack that had come at last, using her cupped hand and years of experience instead of scales. She hadn't had a letter for a week from Hector. They were probably in France by now. He could have sent a postcard; he didn't even need to write anything on it. The Master had tried to get more men to go from the village, but they wouldn't, and now he had his eye on Sam.

When anything upset her, the baking went wrong; usually burst yolks. She put the bowl of ruined mixture aside and made herself a pot of strong tea. She'd been having bad dreams. There was an advertisement in one of the magazines up in her bedroom. If you sent away a shilling you got a book back, telling you what your dreams meant. She must get Sam to get her a postal order.

She was still sitting at her tea when he came in, the strike of his boots on the flagstones setting her nerves alight.

'You're certainly looking pleased with yourself,' she said accusingly.

'Is there some news about Hector?' he asked anxiously, setting down the pail on the floor. He'd learned to read her moods.

'News from Hector?' She laughed sarcastically. 'He could be dead for all I know. I'm the last to be told things about here.'

'What's the matter?' he asked, pulling a chair beside her.

But she was moving about now, her hands working at the sideboard as she kept her back to him.

'What's he been saying to you?'

'What's who been saying?'

'Oh, don't act so simple,' she said, turning to have it out with him. 'If he's asked them up the village to go, then he's asked you too.'

'Not this again,' he said despairingly.

'I know he's asked you.'

He shrugged. 'He drops hints, but I just give the reins a shake and that shuts him up.'

'He's not the kind you shut up, as you put it. Swear to me that you won't go.'

She knew that she was showing her feelings too much, but she didn't care. She was too fond of this man to let him go.

'How many times do I have to tell you, I'm not going.'

She was rummaging in the drawer of the dresser. The Bible with her parents' names on the flyleaf had been one of the few

things worth saving from the croft. She put it on the table beside
the bowl of aborted baking.

'Swear on it that you won't go if he asks you to.'

He saw her knuckles whitening as she gripped the back of the
chair. He knew that he was in love with this woman, but he also
knew that he was going to have to make things clear.

'On the night I arrived here you warned me that I had to do
everything the boss told me to.'

'That was different, then.' The match that he'd flared to show
her the letter from the Master no longer glowed in her memory.
'There's a war on now.'

'So if he tells me to go I'm to refuse, is that it?'

She nodded. 'Now swear it, and that'll be the end of it.'

'But it's not as simple as that,' he told her patiently. 'If I refuse
he can sack me.'

'He wouldn't do that,' she said scornfully. 'He needs someone to drive him about. He's never away from the village
nowadays.'

'Yes, but he could bring Roddy out of retirement.'

As soon as he'd said it he saw that that hadn't occurred to
her.

'So he *has* been speaking to you about it.'

'Where are you getting this daft idea from?'

But she wasn't going to say anything about the form she'd
just read through on his desk. 'I don't want to hear any more.
I'm waiting for you to swear it, otherwise that's you and me
finished.'

'I'll swear it, if it'll settle your mind,' he said with a shrug.
'But I could be sent away because of it.'

'Then I'll come too.'

It had slipped out, but he was thrilled to hear her say it. His
hand was moving towards the Bible when Invernevis came
through to ask for a late breakfast.

Lieutenant Lauder was sitting at the card table in his tent,
writing. Ten miles away hands slammed shut the cover on the
gun breech, and fingers plugged ears.

My Darling Mildred,
I'm fine! but I can't tell you where I am. I *can* tell
you though how much I love you.

The whistling sound like an oncoming train broke his con-
centration. As it turned into a roaring the canvas beside him
bulged with mud and stones. He crushed the blotted sheet in
his fist because that seemed to give him courage. It must be
a rogue shell, a gunner getting it wrong somewhere. He tilted
the earth from the table and took a fresh sheet, retrieving his
fountain pen from the turf where it had stuck by the nib, but
with no damage.

Ten miles away another shell was being hoisted, the hot
breech slammed shut by the man with the blackened face.

I'm hoping they'll make me a Captain soon. But
enough about me. What about—

The whistling was coming again, but this time there was a
flight of them turning into a deafening roar. This time the
canvas split as it bulged, throwing earth over his letter. He
looked at his hand which had stopped in the act of writing her
name, like a spirit suddenly breaking off communication. The
nib was splayed on the letter M. It was as if he could rise up and
leave his arm behind him, still trying to complete the name of
his sweetheart. He wasn't frightened, he was very calm. In fact
he started to laugh and couldn't stop.

In their billets at Richebourg l'Avonne the 8th Argylls were
having their first encounter with war. Neuve Chapelle, where
Captain Campbell of Jura had been killed, was nearby. But
Hector Macdonald wasn't thinking of the former Adjutant. He
was bent over his pipe box, not because Invernevis had ordered
him to take care of the heirloom instrument, but because it
gave him something to hold on to in his sick fear as the
screaming came nearer and nearer. As he was propelled forward
MacDougall's hand was out to save him.

'Steady, Eachann.' The big man shook the rubble from the lap of his kilt. 'Nearly a direct hit on my balls. Now think of the crying among the women that would have caused.'

But Hector knew that the joke was to steady him. He gripped the edge of the box again, waiting for the next flight, but nothing was coming.

'Stretchers!' someone shouted, throwing open the flap of the tent. They crawled outside to a different world. Tents had disappeared into craters, bodies were tangled in guy-ropes as if an observation balloon had been brought to earth by the bombardment. Hector and the other man carried the stretcher to the crater where MacDougall was on his knees. Only the man's face was showing in the soil, and his teeth were clenched. MacDougall's movements were delicate, like an archaeologist's as he dug out the outline of the man with his fingertips, exposing an arm, then moving down the right side, scraping away the soil. Hector felt he was going to faint when he came to the bloody stump. He turned his face away as he took the man's shoulders to lift him on to the stretcher.

The man was moaning.

'Leave him,' MacDougall said, lifting him himself, an arm behind his neck, the other behind his knees, and lowering him gently on to the stretcher. Hector helped to carry him the hundred yards to the tent the medical officer had commandeered. Rows of stretchers were laid on the grass, awaiting attention, and the padre was kneeling beside one man.

As Hector went back for another casualty, he passed Lauder being helped along by a soldier. The Lieutenant's arm was round the man's neck, the other dangling, bloody.

'He's going home, the lazy bugger,' Hector said.

'I hope that keeps the bastard at home for good,' MacDougall said. 'Come on: there are others that need help.'

Alanna Richardson raised her face from the folding canvas sink to the window in the cramped cabin. It looked a beautiful evening, but those streaks of red beyond the poplar trees weren't sunset. They were the flash of guns on the western front. She laid down her last piece of Floris soap and put on her starched cuffs for the night's duty. Wasn't it eerie to think that men who would occupy the bunks in the train before nightfall were still fighting out there in the red flicker?

She sat on her own bunk, composing herself. There was one thing she dreaded above all else, and that was that Dochie would be brought on to her hospital train. She couldn't bear that; what kept her going was the conviction that she would meet him again soon.

The fire in the sky was brightening as the Germans sent across another barrage, the boom of the guns like heavy portmanteaux being dropped on the roof of the train. It had been specially built, paid for by a rich man in England. There were nine vehicles with a pharmacy, an operating theatre, treatment rooms, stores, wards for sitting-up and lying-down cases, staff compartments, a kitchen and lavatories.

As the locomotive hauled the hospital on wheels to the casualty clearing station the door of the firebox was shut in case the glare attracted enemy shells. But that day's battle was at an end, and the train shuddered to a halt. The night's duty was beginning.

Alanna was over her ankles in the mud by the track as she helped to raise the first stretcher to the sliding doors. Oh, God, he was a Highlander. She didn't know where the 8th Argylls were fighting on the immense front.

'A light here, please!' she shouted, and when the lantern arrived she lifted the sodden folds of tartan and saw he was a Seaforth. She'd become used to wounds that would never heal. She lit a cigarette and put it in the soldier's mouth, and he used his other arm to draw on it, slowly, as if it was a kiss he wanted to last.

There were more lying-down than sitting-up cases because of the ferocity of the battle, and it was her night with the lying-downs. The bunks were filling fast.

'Where are you from?' she asked the kilted soldier as she made him as comfortable as she could in the top bunk.

He spoke urgently in Gaelic. She didn't understand what he

was saying, but she put a blue mark on the triangular label on his wrist to show that he was to have immediate attention as soon as he was off the train because there were too many for the operating table tonight.

She had learned to move her body with the swaying train, so that even when it rattled across points she didn't spill anything in the linoleum covered corridor. Tonight the gas had given out and the white enamelled tunnel of the ward coach was lit by paraffin lanterns swinging from the roof, bringing pitiful faces too suddenly into the light. Hands touched her uniform as she passed, and she stopped to offer what comfort she could.

She stood in the corridor of the rocking train, holding on to the bunks on either side. Since that night in London when she'd given Dochie a bath she'd seen many fine bodies. But that was different because they had been damaged, and they brought out other instincts in her because they were helpless like children. But Dochie had wakened her body and brought joy into the gloomy house in Eaton Square. Freddie wasn't like that. He was stiff and formal, the military man and precious little else.

'That boy up there with the bandage round his eyes needs more morphia,' the sister said to her.

He was only eighteen, and had been in a hospital behind the lines. The train had picked him up on the way to the front, and he was being transferred home. She'd become skilled at giving injections. It was amazing how quickly you learned, when you had to. As she was on her way back she saw the boy beginning to unwind the bandage.

'No!' she shouted as she ran.

But he had the bandage off, his hands up to his face.

'Where are my eyes? Oh, I've no eyes left!' He rolled from his bunk and clawed his way along the corridor, screaming, bumping into the bunks.

'It's all right, son,' a wounded man said, reaching for his shoulder.

'My eyes, my eyes! Where are my eyes?' His face was raised to the lantern swinging from the roof, his fingers in the raw sockets.

Alanna Richardson caught him. She held him tight, with his face to her breasts till the doctor could get the syringe into his arm.

'I would like to be among the men,' Lieutenant Lauder told the nurse.

'But you can't, sir,' she said earnestly. 'The rule is that there's a separate compartment for officers.'

'I could walk through to visit them,' he suggested.

'You'd better stay where you are, sir, otherwise the doctor will get angry. We're very busy tonight.'

The hospital train Lieutenant Lauder was on rattled through the darkness, one of dozens from different sectors of the lines making for channel ports before dawn. He'd argued strenuously with the Colonel that his wound was superficial. A few days' rest and he would be back at duty. But Kilberry had insisted on sending him home, and the Lieutenant suspected that he wanted him out of the way because he still wasn't getting on with the men.

He was sitting smoking in the top bunk. He felt ashamed of his wound, a scratch compared to the ones the other 8th Argylls had got. Some of the men on the train wouldn't make the morning. His parents were out of the country and he hadn't asked the Adjutant to send a message to Mildred because he didn't want to worry her.

Maybe he should ask for a transfer to another regiment – the Gordons, say. But that would only be to admit defeat. Once the Argylls got into the line and were fighting in earnest it would be all right; it was the long wait at Bedford that had caused all the frustrations and tensions.

'Is there anything you would like, sir?' the same nurse, an attractive girl, asked.

'No, thank you.'

'You're allowed a drink if it'll help you to sleep.'

'I don't want one, thanks.'

She moved on to the next.

12

Sam had already been waiting an hour for Maggie at Wade's Bridge, raking a match on the parapet for his third cigarette and throwing the used flame into the river. It had been the same the other night. She'd appeared eventually, with the excuse that the boss had come through as usual and kept her. Because the light had gone all they had been able to do was to turn and walk back up the avenue again. Well, he wasn't waiting any longer, so he began walking along the road, away from the big house.

Was she angry with him because she thought he wanted to join up? He'd felt like taking the next train when he was up in the village for the papers in the morning. Maggie kept sending him into the store for messages, and Munro kept telling him to remind her about the bill. When he came out of the store children were crowded round the gig. He'd lifted one little girl out of the way in case she went under the big wheel. She said something in Gaelic as she held out her hand. The other children were watching expectantly. He put out his hand because he thought it was a game, but when he opened his fist he had three grubby white feathers.

The children ran away laughing as the women watched from the door of the store. They shouted after him as he took the whip from the socket, using it too heavily, but he had to get away. What was the point in telling Maggie when she had enough worries already, the way the boss was drinking? Anyway, he had to fight his own battles.

He was striding along the road now, filled with a new sense of purpose. His love for her was worth a lot more than a handful of white feathers. Let them shout what they liked, he wasn't going away to leave Maggie behind. He loved her. That wasn't something to be ashamed of. He would swear on the Bible tonight that he wouldn't join up, but she would have to agree to get engaged before the end of the year. He'd enough money by now put aside for a ring. They could save together for the wedding, which needn't be for a while, till the war was over, even though it looked like a long wait.

He crossed the dyke and went down the meadow towards the river. Invernevis was a beautiful place, but he didn't want to make his home here. Maggie was better away from the big house because the boss was just taking advantage of her. Anyway, he wanted a family. He could get a job with a cottage on a farm and use his spare time to study so that he could become a manager, then get his own farm. He wanted to do well for her sake.

He stopped to talk to the old workhorse from the Home Farm lying in the daisies, then crossed the stepping stones resolutely. He would take a short cut up the lawn to tell Maggie about his plans. A late lark was trembling in song overhead as he stopped to pick her some marigolds. She would be so pleased he wasn't going to enlist. Before he went to bed he would write to his mother, telling her he was staying where he was.

Later he would ask himself why he'd taken that way, which he'd never done before. The lamp was on in the library, its yellow rectangle shining on the gravel. On an impulse he joined his hands through the hole in the wishing stone, watching the pale new moon as he made his request for their future together. An owl called as he turned the corner of the house, and he saw Maggie through the other window of the library.

She was standing, the knuckles of one hand resting on the edge of the library desk. What was she watching with that strange look? He moved behind the monkey puzzle tree and saw the boss lying sprawled in the arm-chair, his waistcoat open. He watched Maggie take the empty glass from his dangling hand and put it on a bookshelf behind him. He watched her pick up the fishing book that had fallen at his shoes, smoothing out the tissue paper over the illustration before closing it and putting it back in its space on the shelf.

He saw her expression change as she bent over him. She put her hands behind his back, trying to lift him up. Should he go in and help? But he stayed behind the tree, uncertain. The boss put his arms round Maggie's neck and pulled her down on top of him, and he didn't see any resistance.

In his agitation he backed into the tree, disturbing roosting birds. He threw the marigolds away as he ran up the lawn. What a fool he'd been. He should have known how things were by the look she gave the boss every time he appeared in the kitchen. It must have been going on long before he came on the scene. He was breathless by the time he reached the stables, but he ran up the steps, flinging open the door, hauling his suitcase from under the bed. He tipped the contents of the drawers into it, including his Bible, then lifted down his good suit from the nail and crushed it into the case.

When he was at the bottom of the steps he hesitated because he could see the silhouette of a horse's head at the half-door. At that hour of the night he usually had a lump of sugar in his waistcoat for this one, but it would only make things worse if he went to the animal he'd come to know so well and which responded to the lightest touch of the reins.

He took the mossy path at the back of the house and saw there was now a light in the kitchen. He stopped, his case heavy in his fist, knowing that this was a moment of decision which would affect the rest of his life, but he'd seen them, and confronting her would only make it worse. He didn't want any lies. It had obviously been going on for a long time, and he should have seen the signs. As he went round the blind bend the fragrance of the scents recalled the night he'd arrived, meeting Maggie there and seeing her face for the first time in the spurt of the match. He set down his case on Wade's Bridge. Which way? There wasn't a train till the morning, but he wasn't going near the village. He lit a cigarette and sat on the parapet, looking down into the darkening water. No, it was best to go, so he picked up his case and began walking south.

MacDougall heard the Lights Out pipes from the billets, but the woman's legs were round his back, refusing to release him. He was too late anyway, so he took a swig from the bottle of wine.

She was moaning and he gave her a few more thrusts to keep her quiet. He'd picked her up in the *estaminet*, but he was tired already of French women. He had to find out which train Alanna was nursing on, so that he could ask for leave to visit her.

The woman under him moaned again. This time he put the bottle of wine to her mouth and it ran down her tits. He would never have believed that you could feel lonely with a woman, and this one was only a packet of Gold Flake. He'd thought France was going to be much better than this. He didn't like the countryside. It was the mountains and the loch that he missed. Who wanted to fish in a canal, catching ugly bastards of eels? And their wine was piss compared to whisky, whose taste he'd forgotten.

Maybe it would be different once they got up for a decent length of time to the front line, so that he could get stuck into the Boches. He had a few throats to cut on account of the shells they'd sent over, mangling six of the company.

'Aye, and you too,' he said to the moaning woman as he buckled on his kilt.

She lay on the bank, naked, pleading for more, but he was already climbing the wall. As he went up between the tall poplars in the hushed evening he sniffed the letters Alanna had sent him before the war broke out and which he carried about with him as a talisman. Christ, that scent was almost worth deserting for. It seemed stronger than ever and every time he sniffed, his cock stirred.

'Where have you been, MacDougall?' the Sergeant demanded.

'I went for a wee walk, sir.'

But he wasn't challenged. He was proving too valuable to the battalion, the way he kept up their spirits as they alternated between being in reserve and being in the line. When they were on a railway move from Dieppe to Corbie the train had stopped at Amiens. A French infantry battalion had turned out to pay its compliments to Scotland, its band playing the British and French national anthems. Kilberry had called up the 8th Argylls choir to return the compliment. MacDougall had led the singing of 'Scots Wha Hae' while the French stood to attention at salute.

He'd wasted a packet of Gold Flake on that one. As he pulled off his shirt in the billet he looked at Hector, his head resting on his arm on his pipe box. Aye, there was something to be said for the sleep of innocence, he was thinking as he put Alanna's letters under his makeshift pillow.

The Master had been a terrible weight, getting him upstairs. She'd practically to drag him because of his game leg, but she didn't want the maids to know because they would only talk. After taking his cigarettes away in case he set fire to the house in the night she went down to the kitchen to make herself a pot of tea and some bread and butter. It was too late to go to meet Sam, but she would have to make it up to him. She was tired but she sat on, fondling the cat on her lap, but even its therapeutic purr didn't help tonight. As it got darker she began to worry that something had happened to Sam. When it came eleven she took a torch and the dog and went up to the stables.

The door at the top of the staircase was off the latch, and as soon as she was inside the torch showed that his suitcase had gone from under the bed. The drawers of the chest hung open, and one of them was on the floor. He'd left the little lamp with the shell-shaped shade. She picked it up and held it to her breasts, but it was cold.

Those bitches in the village had been going on at him, but it was the Master who'd made him go away to enlist. She heard the restless horses below and in her loss she hugged the lamp tighter, as if her body heat could make it light up, like that night he'd brought her up, so proud of what he'd done to the room. Seeing the way he'd made the room so neat made her cry. Oh, maybe she should have given him more encouragement when he'd kissed her, but there were so many ifs and buts in life.

Then she noticed the letters at the back of the drawer. She knew she shouldn't be doing it, but she sat down on the bed to read them.

My Dear Sam,
    George went into Aberdeen yesterday and joined up, which means that all my sons are now in the Gordons, except yourself of course. I don't know whether to

140

feel proud or to cry. The wound that James got
at Neuve Chapelle has almost healed and he'll
have to go back next month. Your sisters and myself
can just about manage the farm, but we really need
a pair of man's hands. Are you going to stay on
down there? I know you made your own life before
because you thought there was no room on the farm
because of your brothers, but things are
different now.

So that was what had been on his mind all the time. His mother
was wanting him home, to work on the farm. He'd sat at her
kitchen table reading the letters, but he'd never once said. It
showed you how you couldn't trust people.

She stripped the bed and folded the blankets neatly. She took
the case off the pillow and bundled the sheet because there
wouldn't be anyone else coming into this place. Then she shut
the door quietly behind her, as if someone had died in there.

As she went back down to the house with the blankets in her
arms she was trying to work out how he'd gone. He could have
gone on the late train, but it was unlikely. The thought that he'd
walked away in the darkness upset her even more. He could
catch a chill from sleeping out, then what use would he be to
the army?

Oh, this awful war. She felt that she wanted to throw back
her head and scream. But what was the use in fighting with
the Master about Sam when he was turning into a drunkard?
She never thought she'd have used that word for him, even to
herself, but he was at it every day. He wasn't making any attempt
to hide the unpaid bills that were piling up on his desk. It was as
if he wanted her to see them, but she couldn't cut back any more,
and besides, everything was getting so dear, double what it was
before the war.

When she woke next morning she somehow hoped that
Sam would be down in the servants' hall waiting for his
breakfast, but only the maids were there, and she didn't say
anything about it to them. She found work for her hands in

the kitchen while she waited for the Master to come down to breakfast.

When he eventually came looking for coffee and toast he kept his head bent, as if he was ashamed about last night.

'Sam's gone, sir.'

'Gone?'

'He left last night.'

'Where's he gone to?'

'I don't know, sir.'

'But I thought he was happy here.'

'So did I, sir. Anyway, he's away, and that's that. I've sent for Roddy, sir, to tell him he's needed again.'

'Thank you, Maggie. But I have to go up to the village, so I'll drive myself this morning.'

She left him to his breakfast.

It was a pity about Raeburn, Invernevis thought, because he was so good with horses, but maybe he'd found the place too quiet.

Invernevis was conscious of people standing staring as he drove himself along main street. He braked the gig outside the Arms and rang the bell. It was answered by Carmichael's slovenly wife, who shuffled away to get her husband from the cellar.

'I would like a case of brandy,' Invernevis said.

Carmichael stood with one hand on the lintel, as if supporting the weight of the building with his massive frame.

'Is your coachman not well?' he enquired.

'He's gone away,' was the curt reply.

'Gone away?' Carmichael nodded slowly as if he understood the implication. Unlike the locals he had no reason to be servile to this man: his lease came direct from the trustees.

'As a matter of fact I don't have any brandy. You got the last case a fortnight ago. It's difficult to get brandy now because it comes from France. The generals must be drinking it out there.'

Invernevis had no wish to discuss the conduct of the war with this crude man who was only interested in making money.

'What do you have?'

He rubbed his chin. 'There's a case of gin. I got it in for the Brigadier who came for the fishing, the one with the good-looking wife.'

'Brigadier and Mrs Richardson.'

'That's the name,' Carmichael said. 'Big MacDougall was doing the ghillieing for her.' He looked at Invernevis. 'What's the news of the Argylls?'

'They're somewhere in France.'

'I lost a lot of customers when they went away. If this war lasts much longer I may have to give up the lease, things are becoming so dear.'

'I'm sorry to hear that,' Invernevis said. 'But I can't do anything about it.'

'Oh, I know that,' Carmichael said. 'It's the trustees who decide things.'

'I'll take the case of gin,' Invernevis said.

'It's a good job I didn't send it back,' Carmichael said. He returned with the wooden box of twelve bottles on his shoulder and slid it on to the back of the gig.

'Have you something to cover it with?'

Carmichael came back with a sack to throw over the box.

'I'll be sending in the account at the end of the month. That's three cases so far. I'll be grateful for prompt payment because the quarterly rent on this place is due.'

But Invernevis was already up on the seat, shaking the whip over the horses' backs.

The old man had been sitting for an hour on the stone by the roadside, watching the bend. A lark rose behind the hedge and began singing high in the air as the postman came round the bend, but this time he was waving something. The old man hurried towards him with his small dainty steps, as if he would fall over at any moment.

'Is this what you've been waiting for?' the postman asked, putting the big brown envelope into his hands.

The old man held it close to his face.

'It's a Bedford postmark,' the postman said.

The old man hurried into the porch and up the stairs. After sitting for weeks by the fire, the old woman had taken to her bed. Her hat was over the bedpost as she lay there, getting weaker because she wouldn't eat, not even the white potatoes the boy had planted and which the old man dug up. He lifted her head and put pillows behind it, then laid the photograph on the blanket in front of her.

'It's the boy, *Pheigi bheag.*'

In the light coming through the small window she looked at the kilted soldier with his brogue up on the rustic bench. The background was all grey, with not a tree or a house in sight, which meant that he was between two worlds.

'He's looking well,' the old man said, sitting on the bed to study the photograph with her.

But she was getting up. She put on her dress and laced up her boots, lifting her hat from the bedpost before she went downstairs.

'Where are you going, *Pheigi bheag?*' he called after her.

But she was gone. She lifted the hook on the shed door. When the hens saw her coming in they hopped along their spars into the shadows. This time something drastic was needed, and when she came into the kitchen she had the cockerel by the legs, its wings still lifting though its neck had been drawn. Its feathers floated and settled round the old man in the kitchen, its head with the comb half over the baleful eye watching him from between her boots.

'There's too much eating in it for us, *Pheigi bheag,*' he protested. 'I could have got a wee bit of meat from the butcher's instead of you going to this bother.'

She glared at him before she went through to the scullery to remove the guts. When she came back her hands were bloody.

'Get me a bit of string,' she ordered.

He cut a length from the ball in the drawer and she held out the claws so he could bind them. Then she laid the twitching fowl on the table.

'Make a parcel of it for the boy.'

By the time it reached him in France – if it ever reached

him – it would be rotten. But he was only too grateful that she was up and about again, so he took brown paper and the string from the drawer. He printed out the address with the calligraphy that had made his teacher put his copy books on show.

Private Duncan MacDougall (Of Invernevis)
With the 8th Argyll and Sutherland Highlanders
With the 51st Highland Regiment
IN FRANCE

But it could be Belgium, so he added that country too. Then he put the parcel on her lap so she could test that the string was taut.

'Put wax on the knots,' she instructed.

He lit the candle, but when he tried to hold the dripping red stick over the knots, most of it went on to the paper. He put it back on her lap so she could test it again.

'Now take it up to the post office.'

He set out with the parcel under his arm, with his short dainty steps, taking many rests before he reached the post office.

'What is it?' the postmistress asked suspiciously.

'It's a cockerel she's sending to the boy. She got a picture of him this morning.'

'It won't keep,' she warned.

'Send it, it'll put her mind at rest,' the old man pleaded.

The postmistress had seen plenty evidence of *Peigi bheag na biorraide*'s powers. She could curse as well as cure. She put the parcel on the scales.

'And how is the boy getting on?' she asked as she licked the stamp.

'Oh, fine. He's looking well.'

The postmistress put her face close to the grille. 'There's still some about here that should have gone. They say they've got crofts to work in the national interest, but they spend most of their time in the Arms.'

The old man was exhausted by the time he got back down. He could have done with a dram but there was none in the house.

The photograph was now propped on the mantelpiece, against the brass shoe from Dunoon. The old woman had the fire on, and something in the pot.

'Did you send the cockerel?' she demanded.

'It'll be away on tonight's train, and he could be eating it by the weekend,' the old man said.

She nodded curtly. That would build up his strength so that the fire-eater, the one who had got into the *pit* of *Mairi Peigidh bheag na biorraide* wouldn't entice him into the other world.

'What's in the pot?' he asked.

'The giblets. You'll eat them because there's a lot of goodness in them,' she told him.

13

Sam set down his case on the bridge, using the rest of the match from his cigarette to look at the watch he pulled from his waistcoat pocket. One-thirty; he'd been walking for nearly three hours and had no idea where he was. The dark water murmured through the stone underneath him as he leaned on the parapet, smoking. If he turned back he could get to Invernevis with an hour or so in bed before he fed the horses, and Maggie would be none the wiser that he'd left.

But he had his pride. Had he not seen them together with his own eyes? They could be in bed together. The image made him throw the unfinished cigarette over his shoulder and pick up the case again, though he didn't know where he was going. If he went home for a few days he could think things out. But then his mother would try to persuade him to stay on the farm. Was that what he wanted? He didn't know, but he strode on. As he went round the bend he saw a fire ahead, as if the verge was alight. It was a tinkers' camp, tarpaulins thrown over hooped wattles. He moved on cautiously, but a barking dog was coming and he tried to ward it off with his suitcase till someone called it back. There was more shouting and when he turned he saw a hand that seemed to rise out of the fire signalling him back.

The tinkers had spent the winter at Vinegar Hill, Glasgow. They were moving towards their summer stance and they had all the time in the world. They ignored Kitchener's pointing finger on the recruiting posters in the windows of the villages they passed through with their carts, not because they weren't patriotic, but because they couldn't read the phrase *Your Country Needs You*. They moved north through the summer heat, with their naked children and unruly dogs, and in the evenings they rested, taking what sustenance they needed from the river and the wood.

As they made a space for Sam he thought he recognized the faces round the fire. In summer they camped up at the standing stones beside the Home Farm at Invernevis. He was sure that the young woman sitting opposite him had come to the back door of the big house, because she was pretty and she wouldn't look at him as she stood barefooted on the step, waiting for Maggie to fill the can of tea in exchange for six clothes pegs. Now her dress was slipped from her shoulder and she was watching him defiantly as she fed a baby. An old woman was sitting beside him, with an earring like a golden spark, and he was sure that he'd met her on the road at Invernevis.

They went round the doors, selling the tin ware they'd made, offering to repair kettles in return for cans of tea. They wore the assorted clothes of the dead and spoke their own language of cant which they weren't willing to share with outsiders. In the evenings they sat in the corner of the Arms and though nobody put up whiskies for them, nobody bothered them.

Stew was ladled from the big black pot on the fire and passed to Sam. It was hot and spiced with plants from the hedgerows, and as he ate it with one of their horn spoons he noticed the barn owl on the branch above the young woman's head, its saucer-shaped face watching him. He realized that it was tame and was moving with them, sleeping by day in one of the carts, vigilant by night. The old woman held a piece of meat over her shoulder and it flapped down silently for it, its wings fanning the fire. The baby had fallen asleep, holding the globe of the breast, the nipple in its mouth.

They passed Sam a tin of bitter tea, and he shared out his cigarettes, breaking several in two to make them go round. When the old woman had smoked hers she took up his hand and began to study the lines on it. She was watching him, and though he wasn't superstitious he was trying to read the message in her face. But she put his hand back on his knee and patted it. He could have fallen asleep there, in the pine scent from the fire, but that would be intruding on their hospitality and besides, he had to get on the move again. He shook their hands before he left and when he turned and looked back the owl's head had swung round and was following him.

It was now four o' clock and birds were singing. He stopped, thinking of Maggie getting up, going down to start the stove. In an hour or so she would know that he'd gone. As he passed a farmyard a man was walking a horse up a ramp into a lorry, and he leaned on the wall to watch.

'Where are you making for?' the farmer asked.

'The nearest railway station.'

'Stirling, if that's any help?'

'That would be grand,' Sam said, lifting his case in.

'Where are you from?' he asked, when they were on the road.

'Buchan.'

'You're a long way away.'

'I was working at a place called Invernevis.'

'I've heard of it,' the man said. 'What are you going to do at Stirling?'

'Get the train to Buchan,' he answered spontaneously, because he didn't want to get into complicated explanations.

'There shouldn't be any shortage of jobs with the numbers that are away at the war,' the driver told him. 'We need the farm workers to feed the troops.'

Sam could see Stirling Castle on its high rock in the distance, like out of one of the storybooks of his childhood. It gave him a sudden desire to see his mother again.

'I'll take you to the station,' the driver said.

He studied the timetable and worked out that there wasn't a train to Aberdeen for two hours. He also saw that in the other direction with one change he could get back to Invernevis by mid-day. No; he would go home and help on the farm till his brothers came back from the war.

He was sitting on a bench, smoking his last cigarette, hoping the bookstall would open soon, when a young woman in a large floppy hat trundled a trolley with an urn on to the platform.

'A cup of tea, please.'

'Are you a soldier?' she asked in a cultured voice.

'No, I'm not.'

'I'm sorry, but I only serve soldiers.'

He sat again. A train clattered in. When it pulled out a few minutes later there was a soldier and a woman standing on the opposite platform. His tin helmet was a hump on his back, and his boots were down at the heel. They were standing stock still, locked in each others arms in a prolonged kiss. The woman was up on her toes, almost out of her shoes. Her eyes were closed, and her face had such a look of intensity that Sam could almost feel the kiss himself across the track. They came across the latticed bridge hand-in-hand, stopping to cuddle again. When they descended to Sam's platform the woman in the floppy hat had a steaming mug of tea made.

'Will you take sugar?' she said in a voice that was used to giving orders.

He nodded, and she spooned it in, stirring it for him. He stood drinking, erect, confident, his bonnet with the gleaming boar's head crest of the Argyll and Sutherland Highlanders pushed back, the pleats of his kilt hanging like dark blades. The woman took a packet of Gold Flake from her clasp bag. She opened the silver paper and pushed a cigarette between his lips, but he put it behind his ear, preferring another kiss. It was as if they had all the time in the world as they went out of the station hand-in-hand, his kit bag slung over his shoulder. The woman in the floppy hat washed his mug reverently at the tap before she put it back on the trolley and waited for the next train, her eyes shining as if she herself had been kissed.

Sam sat staring at the polished rails. Then he picked up his case and went out of the station. The soldier and the woman were driving away in a cab, kissing in the small back window.

'Which way is it up to the castle?' he asked the next cab driver in the row.

'I can take you there for threepence.'

'I'll walk.'

He went up the steep street without setting down his case.

'I want to join the Argylls,' he told the sentry at the door.

He was shown into a large chilly apartment. In five minutes a sergeant appeared and sat at the table.

'Name?'

The pen was scratching.

'Address?'

He hesitated. What was he to say? He'd left Invernevis.

'Address?'

'Invernevis House.'

The Sergeant wrote it. 'Any disabilities?' he asked.

'No, sir.'

'The doctor better have a look at you. You'll have to go to his surgery. It's just down the road.'

But as he went back down the cobbles Sam was beginning to have second thoughts. He hadn't signed anything, so he could tear up the paper in his hand and go back to Invernevis, to Maggie. But the Sergeant would remember his name and would write to Invernevis, and anyway, his pride wouldn't let him.

He had to wait for half an hour on the doorstep because the doctor was still at his breakfast. Then he was standing naked, the first time in manhood he'd taken his clothes off in front of anyone. He wanted to cover his doings with his hands as the doctor scrutinized him over small gold glasses.

'Walk,' the doctor ordered, as if talking to a horse. 'Stop. Bend over.' Then he was scrawling his signature and handing over a paper to take back up to the castle. The examination hadn't even taken five minutes.

This time it was an officer who was sitting behind the table.

'I see you're from Invernevis,' he said. He had the same cultured voice as the boss. 'Major Macdonald is a very respected name in this regiment. What were you working at?'

'I was his coachman, sir.'

'Good,' he said as he wrote. 'There's plenty of scope for working with horses.'

'I want to go to the 8th Argylls, sir,' Sam said anxiously.

'I don't see any difficulty,' the officer murmured. 'Now I'm going to administer the oath to you.'

He saw the Bible produced from the drawer of the table, and remembered the day that Maggie had asked him to take her oath. He laid his hand on it and repeated after the officer's casual voice.

'I swear by . . . '

'I don't think there's any use sending you all the way back to Invernevis to wait,' the officer said when he'd sat down again. The implication was that Sam had been sent to enlist. 'I'll give you a form for the stores.'

An hour later he was buckling on a kilt, a queer thing to walk in, the way it swayed against the back of your legs.

The leader of the orchestra had his head bent as Mildred whispered to him in the lull between numbers. As she came back it began to play 'Roamin' in the Gloamin''.

'To remind us of happy days at Glenbranter,' she told Lieutenant Lauder as she resumed her seat beside him in the lounge of the Savoy. But he wasn't listening to his father's tune. He was smoking with his left hand because his right was in a sling made from a silk headscarf of Mildred's.

'I should be back out there,' he complained.

The pounding of the orchestra's drums became gunfire. The 8th Argylls were probably in the front line by now. These were his men out there, across the dark channel, somewhere in France. This life in London with its frivolity no longer appealed to him. He saw no sign of sacrifice in his surroundings, with waiters bringing trays of brandy balloons, boxes of cigars, and even a platter of grouse in aspic for one of the uniformed revellers. He was thankful his parents were on another coast-to-coast tour of America, otherwise his father would have insisted on a grand party.

'You can't go back till that arm's completely healed,' Mildred warned him. 'The doctor says that if you get an infection in the wound it could be very serious.'

He put another cigarette into his mouth and leaned forward for her to light it. Some of the officers at the surrounding tables were telling the world that they were returning to the front that night, their canes lying among the glasses and the overflowing ashtrays. At the other end of the room officers and their escorts were dancing, cheek to cheek, a last ruminative smooch before they went back to the fray.

A young Captain came up to Lauder's table.

'How are you, Johnnie?' he said boisterously.

The Lieutenant introduced him as one of his year from Jesus College. The blond man sat on the arm of Lauder's chair, his back turned on Mildred.

'Got a bit of a wound, I see?'

'It's nothing,' Lauder said. He'd never liked this fellow.

'Tommy Nairn got a rough time,' the Captain said.

'I didn't hear,' Lauder muttered, wishing he'd go away.

'He got it at Loos, and Greenlaw's a wreck.'

Lauder saw the effect the conversation was having on Mildred, and would have moved to another table if it hadn't meant making a scene.

'And what about you?' Lauder asked him.

'I go back tomorrow. I've had a super war so far. I was at Ypres.'

His rooms had been near Lauder's in Jesus. On summer afternoons he would lie in bed in a woman's silk dressing-gown with ribbons at the bust, listening to a gramophone, with a barrow boy he'd taken off the street and given a bath to. Lauder suddenly understood the nature of this man's destructive impulse. This was a war for men only, at least at the front. The violence of it appealed to him. It was a form of masochism, like flagellation. He'd heard the swish of a cane, the cries on an early summer afternoon, and later saw the thin lines of blood on his cricket flannels. The throb of the gun was orgiastic, like the throb of Elgar from that fluted gramophone horn as he penetrated the barrow boy, having promised him a guinea.

The young officer who was standing on tiptoe, searching the crowded lounge came across. He was obviously the Captain's lover, the way they looked at each other. The Captain talked of casualties as if he was keeping a cricket score at his public school by counting how many of his team had been knocked out, some never to come back for a second innings.

'Any chance of a Captaincy?' he asked Lauder.

Lauder smiled wryly. 'I'm quite happy as I am.'

'I find it gives you that bit extra edge. I'll be looking for my Majority before this show's over.'

They were taking their leave, bringing their glasses together in a toast before setting them down and putting their canes into their armpits. They would take a cab to the station and cross the dark channel to the throb of guns in the unnatural act of war in which they felt at ease among the hot barrels and the blood.

'I can't stand them,' Lauder complained to Mildred.

But he would like to catch the boat train himself. He still had to prove himself to the men. Wounded before even getting into the fight wasn't a very good start. The longer he was away, the more difficult it would be with his company, especially with that troublemaker MacDougall.

'I've got a job, Johnnie.'

He didn't hear Mildred the first time.

'I'm working for the VAD.'

'I hope it's not dangerous,' he said, irritated.

'No, no. I'm helping at a hospital telephone switchboard.'

He nodded, abstracted. Then he called across the waiter and whispered to him. The waiter returned with a pair of scissors on a silver tray.

'No – don't!' Mildred said.

He had already cut through the silk sling.

Maggie was sitting at the kitchen table, with the door open behind her, the dog on the step. She seemed to have lost interest in life, and even her baking was suffering, as if she'd forgotten the vital ingredient to make things rise.

The dog was growling at a man in long leather boots standing on the steps.

'I've come to see the horses,' he said abruptly.

'There's nothing wrong with the horses,' Maggie told him. This wasn't Mr Madden the vet; he must be a horse dealer.

'War requisition,' the man said.

'What does that mean?'

'It means that I want to see your boss.'

Invernevis was at his desk in the library, trying to make sense of his financial affairs, a glass within reach.

'It's about the horses, sir. I don't know what he's after, but I don't like the look of him.'

'I'll come through and see what he wants, Maggie.'

'They need all the horses they can get for the war effort,' the man explained. 'I've been going round the district, buying up beasts.'

'I don't have any horses available,' Invernevis told him.

'I want to see what you have,' the man persisted.

They walked in silence up to the stables.

'You've got two there,' the man said, pointing to the heads at the open half-doors.

'Yes, but I need both of them for the gig.'

'Why can't you run something smaller, like a dog-cart?'

'Because things have to be brought down from the village. It's out of the question.'

The man was walking along, opening doors, as if horses had been hidden away from him.

'What about this one?'

The animal was lying on its side on the bed of hay, its eye watery.

'That's Captain. He's very old. I keep him for sentimental reasons.' It was one of the horses that had taken him to the train on the day he'd left for the South Africa war, and it had been his sister's favourite.

'I'll take him,' the man said.

'But he's no use for anything,' Invernevis said incredulously.

'You'll be surprised at what we're shipping out, and how well they do once they get there,' the man said. 'This one doesn't look any more useless than the one I gave the man at the Home Farm forty pounds for.'

'I'm surprised that MacPherson would let one of his plough horses go. He takes a lot of pride in them.'

'It wasn't one of his plough horses,' the man said. 'It was the old one in the field across the river.'

'But it's hardly got the strength to get up the meadow,' Invernevis said.

'I'll give you the same money for this one,' the man said.

The old horse was watching him as Invernevis made his decision. The money would certainly help to pay some of his most pressing debts.

'Very well.'

The man took a book from his pocket, scribbled a note and tore it out for Invernevis.

'You'll get the cheque within the week. I'll arrange to have the horse collected today.'

The man departed on the motor cycle and Invernevis went back through to the library.

'Was everything all right about the horses, sir?' Maggie asked anxiously as she served him his lunch, along with the habitual glass of wine.

'Yes, fine.' He was ashamed to tell her what he'd just done.

As she was rolling out dough in the afternoon she heard the sound of an engine and went out to investigate. She was waving the lorry back down the avenue, but the driver kept coming on.

'You've taken a wrong turning!' Maggie called up to him.

'Is this Invernevis House?'

'Yes. What's your business here?'

'I have to collect a horse,' the driver said.

She went through to the library for Invernevis, who was sleeping in his arm-chair, the new *Field* spread at his brogues.

'There's some mistake, sir. There's a man with a lorry here to collect a horse.'

'He's here for Captain, Maggie.'

'For Captain? Where's he going?'

'He's needed for the war, Maggie.'

She was aghast. 'For meat, sir?' She'd read in a magazine that the French ate horse meat.

'No, no, Maggie, to do work, like pulling guns.'

She was close to tears. She often went up to the stable with sugar for Captain, now that Sam had gone.

'Is everything to be sent to the war, sir?'

As Hector Macdonald halted behind Kilberry's chair in the mess tent his pipes changed from a strathspey to a lament. The Colonel's head began to sink nearer and nearer to the table as if the chanter being fingered slowly behind him was charming him. When the Colonel's forehead was resting on the map he'd intended to study over his post-prandial drams, Hector held the note as he reached over to take a swig from the whisky bottle without interrupting the tune.

The turf behind the Colonel's folding chair had been trampled to bare earth by Hector's brogues marking time night after night as he played to an audience of one, because there was no possibility of the other officers conversing. It was also disturbing the camp, and the piper got the complaints.

Hector gave him a few more minutes, then folded his pipes and made his way among the guy-ropes to Lawrie's tent. The Pipe Major was in his bed.

'This is the last night,' Hector vowed. 'It's going for my playing with the band. Did you not hear me out of tune this morning?'

'My playing's buggered too,' the Pipe Major complained. 'Look at these.' He held out his fingers. 'I can hardly straighten them now. I know the Colonel loves the pipes, but he doesn't realize what he's doing to the player.'

When Kilberry lifted his head he thought he was in his own house in Argyll until he saw the stars through the pinned-back flaps of the tent. As he straightened up he felt his age in his bones, and emptied the remains of the whisky bottle into his glass before carrying it outside into the warm night where the only respite from mosquitos was constant cigarette smoke.

There were no camp fires lit in case of a night attack, because daring enemy aviators were flying by the moon that stood full above the poplar trees. The men were sleeping in their tents, but in the morning an order could come through for a move up to the front line. By tomorrow evening some of them could be dead.

It was a thought to chill him on a humid night in France. He'd come out with the battalion because he believed that his experience in India with the Tochi Field Force would help, but what was a hurled spear compared with guns that could send shells for twenty miles? Jura used to complain that they hadn't been trained properly, but how could you train Territorials for a fight like this, when even the regular army men weren't prepared for what the Germans were throwing across, like the gas that filled the lungs with a green froth?

There were several mosquitos floating in his whisky, but it was too precious to waste. It wasn't worth getting more sent out. It wasn't that he was drinking more; he was getting tired. He was going to have to go home. He owed it to these men sleeping in their tents because the only way they would stand a chance was if a younger man was brought in from another battalion, or even another regiment, someone who understood what French and his staff were trying to do in the instructions that came over the miles of telephone wires run out over the mud at the front.

At the annual camp the 8th Argylls had been a big family, but not out here. There was no room for individuality, for that kind of loyalty. There was no clan system in France or Flanders. The battalion was only a small part of the 51st Highland Division which was only a part – not even an arm – of the huge army.

The Colonel moved restlessly with his glass among the tents, with the night's piping recital still ringing in his ears. There was something he had to do before he went home to his castle on the coast of Argyll, where he would have to help with the harvest because most of his estate workers had come out with him. In Lauder's absence there had been a lot of snide remarks about 'the laird of Glenbranter' over dinner in the mess. But Lauder had to get his chance: it was the battalion that was going to have to change to accommodate men like him, if it was to have a chance of survival, though he himself didn't particularly like Lauder. But he was going to recommend him for a Captaincy.

14

After Invernevis's late breakfast the post was waiting for him in the library. He used to look forward to news from Jura and other friends from his army days, and to the fishing books he'd sent for. Now he dreaded the bills in their buff-coloured envelopes, and the tightly rolled copy of the *Times*, sad reading with friends and acquaintances in the casualty lists that seemed to get longer each morning.

As he settled at his desk he noticed that the top envelope on the pile had the crest of the Argylls. He'd already written to Stirling Castle to tell them that he couldn't raise another man in the village, now that the 8th Battalion was in the thick of the war and suffering casualties.

> Thank you for sending us your coachman Raeburn.
> He's a big strapping fellow, just the kind we
> need for the 8th. I do hope you've got more
> like him to send!

He was angry at Raeburn putting him in this position by not telling him that he was going to enlist. He wouldn't reply to the letter, but instead of putting it into the wastepaper basket he was looking at the next envelope. It was marked Strictly Private and he knew by its bulk that his financial crisis had arrived. Maybe he should leave it till he'd had a restorative drink. But he was inserting the ivory paper knife under the flap, sawing slowly as if he'd changed his mind about opening it, then extracting the contents with fumbling fingers. Cheques with his own signature spilled over the blotter as he spread out the letter.

> We much regret having to return the enclosed
> cheques, but you have had repeated warnings
> about exceeding the agreed limit of your overdraft.
> Provided that you lodge sufficient funds to meet

them, these cheques will be honoured upon
representation.

He shuffled through the cheques as if he'd been dealt a
ruinous hand of cards. Two were to spirits merchants; four
were for household supplies for Maggie. The last one was to
the Home Farm for four months of accounts. MacPherson would
tell everyone in the place that the Laird hadn't even got £15.

He swung his chair away from the mess of his financial affairs
to the view of the river. This bloody war was going to ruin
him. He'd always managed on his dividends, but they would
be worth next to nothing soon. He'd taken men from Invernevis
out against the Boers and some of them had been killed, but
after he'd arranged relief for the widows life had returned to
normal. They'd said that this war would be over by Christmas,
but it was well into another year. Even if it stopped tomorrow
things would never be the same again. It was more than the
value of money that had changed. They no longer touched their
caps when he went up to the village, and though he didn't want
servility, respect was another matter.

He turned the chair back to the room in which he spent most of
his time. But even the familiar objects around him – the fishing
books on the shelves with his plate inside, the pieces of crested
silver on the desk, to hold his matches, to write with – had lost
their comfort and reassurance.

He blamed his father. He'd been cynical because he'd had to
wait too long to come into the place, and when he'd eventually
inherited he had been too old and too ill to enjoy it, lying upstairs
behind muslin, having to be handled with gloves because of
what he'd brought back from the brothels of India. He'd wanted
Alexander to succeed him, which was why he'd saddled the heir
with trustees, as if he didn't want the place to go on. But it had
been too long a struggle over five hundred years to give up now.
They had carried the Invernevis chieftain home on a litter from
Flodden, accompanied by wailing women. After the Forty-five
the house itself had been demolished, nail by nail, and it must
have looked as if the place was lost for good. But they'd got the

land back and rebuilt the house, and now he owed it to his son in Switzerland to make sure that there was a place to come home to, otherwise what had all the struggle and sacrifice been for?

He uncapped his pen and calculated his most pressing liabilities. Maggie was due six months' wages. She hadn't complained, but he mustn't take advantage of her loyalty. Miss Fraser the governess needed money to pay for the children's lodgings and lessons in Switzerland. When he added up his figures, he reckoned he needed £200 immediately. Where was he going to get that sum? He sat thinking in a haze of cigarette smoke till Maggie brought through the morning coffee.

'I'll be upstairs, dusting the paintings if you want me, sir.'

'Thank you, Maggie.' Then he put down the cup suddenly and followed her up because she'd given him an idea.

'Is there any news of the children?' his mother asked plaintively, waking from a stifling dream of India, where it wasn't pigs dear Sandy had been sticking.

'They'll have to stay where they are,' he told her abruptly. 'It's too dangerous trying to get them home just now.'

'I want to see them again before I die. Sometimes I think I hear them playing out on the landing, then I find I've been dreaming and I'm so disappointed. My life's just one long useless dream now.'

'I need another loan, to tide me over till I can sort things out,' he told her.

But this time it wasn't going to be a matter of being sent to her desk for her bank book.

'Come and sit here,' she urged, patting the bed with her good hand, a gesture she'd used when he'd come into her room as a child and she wanted to give him a gentle lecture because there had been a complaint about his behaviour from Aunt Carlotta.

He used to be so fastidious about taking the nicotine off his fingers with a pumice stone, but they were badly stained, trembling as he fumbled with the silver cigarette case she'd given him on his coming of age but which was now dented. She could smell drink off him. If she'd had the use of both her arms she would have put them round him because she understood what he was going through. She'd been the same, after dear Sandy's death.

'I'll pay you back,' he pledged as he got his cigarette lit.

'It's not the money, Niall. What need do I have of it, as long as there's enough to get me to the chapel, and a little legacy for Maggie since she's been so good to me?' Her hand found his arm. She'd never liked this house and would have preferred to die in the furnace of India instead of among such ponderous gloom, the deep pools of mirrors, so much dark wood. But Sandy had always stressed how important it was for the family to go on.

'You're too much alone, Niall. You need to get out and about more and make the effort to meet people. There's no reason why you shouldn't remarry if you met a nice girl.'

This was too high a rate of interest to pay on borrowing money from her. He made to go back downstairs.

'You know where the bank book is.'

'Do you have any cash?' he asked.

She was surprised by the question, but made him retrieve the beaded bag from the floor by the bed. It was tipped out on to the quilt by the good hand, the contents separated. She would need to keep these shillings for Maggie, for helping with the commode, but she counted aside six sovereigns. 'I was keeping them for dear Queen Victoria's face, but what does that matter now?'

'I'll replace them,' he promised, putting them into his pocket. Then he went to her desk for her bank book, but there was only £60 left in it, £50 for Maggie's legacy, so he put it back into the pigeon-hole.

He went down to the kitchen to tell Maggie that he was going to Edinburgh on business the next day. She was worried about him drinking when he was away, but what could she do about it? Before dinner he went upstairs. The door of his bedroom was open and she was bent over his bed, folding the arms across the shirts she'd ironed for him going away. The evening sun was coming through the window. She looked beautiful. This was only a servant, but the war was changing everything. He had drink in him, and he was tempted.

She straightened up when she saw him in the doorway. 'Will I pack for you, sir?'

'No, I'll manage myself, Maggie. I'll only be away for the one night. Would you help me with something out here, please?'

She followed him along the line of family portraits on the landing, mostly men, some with vigilant hands near swords. He went to the end of the corridor and lifted the small painting of the Virgin and Child from the wall.

She wouldn't allow the maids to touch the paintings and dusted them herself, but the paint on this one was badly cracked. It made the woman look too old to be the mother of the baby she had in her arms. Was he going to accuse her of damaging it?

'I need some strong paper and string, Maggie. I'm taking it to Edinburgh tomorrow.'

What a queer world, she was thinking as she went down the stairs. She couldn't get a sack of flour because the bills weren't paid, yet he was taking a painting to Edinburgh to be restored. She padded the canvas with old copies of the *Times* while he put the string round it. Then it was covered in brown paper and secured with more string. 'You'll have to be very careful with it, sir, in case it gets a knock. And tell them to pack it well when they send it back.'

He hesitated, then said:

'It won't be coming back. I'm going to sell it.'

'Oh no, sir,' she said, shocked. 'It's your mother's favourite.' She didn't tell him that one evening the old lady had got on her nerves so much, going on about never seeing the painting again that Maggie had lifted it off the wall and propped it on a chair beside her bed. When she went in half an hour later the old lady had tears on her face.

'I have to sell it, Maggie,' he said sadly. 'I need the money to keep the house going.'

To pay your drink bill, she wanted to say. As she stood on the landing, watching him carrying the painting downstairs, into the library, she felt sorry that he'd been reduced to this.

'Here comes the Hindu horseman,' MacDougall said, nudging the man standing to attention beside him.

Kilberry had gone back to his castle on the west coast of Argyll. The new commanding officer of the 8th Argylls was riding one of the magnificent horses he'd brought with him from the Bengal Cavalry, along with the two Indian orderlies in flowing white tunics and incongruous tacketed boots who were walking on either side. While one held the reins the other helped Major Douglas Baird to dismount. As he walked along the ranks for his first inspection he stopped in front of MacDougall and rubbed the back of his hand against his face.

'Did you shave this morning?'

'I did that, sir,' MacDougall said earnestly. 'But it just seems to start growing again as soon as I put my razor away.'

'He has the same trouble with his cock,' someone muttered.

As the Major moved on, his cane rapped a buckle. 'That's not cleaning,' he warned the wearer. He took a rifle off a man and slipped the bolt. 'The standard of care of arms of this battalion is very poor,' he told the Sergeant Major.

'Weapons,' MacDougall said contemptuously to Hector when they'd been dismissed. 'We haven't even got a machine gun between us. They'll be asking you to batter the Germans over the head with your pipes yet, Eachainn.'

Hector was subdued. He'd had a letter from Maggie, saying that Sam had gone. He was sorry because he'd seen that there had been something deep between them. She didn't mention anything about the boss, but someone else in the company had had a letter from his malicious wife, saying that the boss had been up in the village with a good drink in him. Hector could have done with some leave to make sure his sister was all right, but there wasn't much chance of that.

'There's that bastard,' MacDougall said.

They watched Lauder striding across the parade ground with his cane.

'Christ knows why they made him a Captain. It shows you what we've got looking after us, and it's going to be worse now, with Kilberry gone,' the big man said vehemently. 'Lauder gets on well with Baird because they're two of a kind, with their fancy ways. Well, I'm not taking anything from either of them. One word to me and he'll get that cane of his up his arse.'

'You'll have to be careful,' Hector warned him.

'Oh, I'll be careful,' MacDougall assured him. 'It's not the Germans that are the biggest menace out here, Eachainn. It's these bloody jump-ups of officers like Lauder. We're being led by boys with as much in their heads as they've got between their legs.'

The post had arrived, and a man came round with his arms full of parcels. 'There's one for you, but I left it over there,' he told MacDougall.

The cockerel's claws had come through the brown paper.

'It's from the old folks,' MacDougall said.

'What a stink,' Hector complained.

'It's the thought that counts,' MacDougall said, offended. 'I'll go and get a spade.'

The two men buried it reverently, under a tree.

Maggie opened the fragrant tin of beeswax, getting ready to spring-clean the library while he was away in Edinburgh. She would do the desk first herself, before she got Jessie in to help her shift the furniture. They'd lift the carpet and take it out to the lawn to beat it. As she moved the papers she kept the cheques together, noting that one was from the Home Farm. But he would get a lot of money for the painting in Edinburgh because the old lady was always saying how valuable it was. It should be the end of his worries, poor soul.

She was handling the paperweight, fascinated by the way the morning sunlight was striking it, as if the anemone was going to burst into bloom through the domed glass. The Master said it was a real flower, but how had it got in there and why didn't it die? She held it up to the light and the colour dazzled her. As she set it down carefully the boar's head crest of the Argylls caught her eye on the letter.

She stood behind his desk, the letter in her hand in the motes of dust she'd disturbed. If he'd come through the door at that moment she would have struck him. He'd pretended he didn't know where Sam had gone, yet he'd sent him to Stirling Castle to join up. What a dirty trick, after all the years of faithful service she'd given him and his family. She had to practically drag him up the stairs to bed, but she was finished. She would get all her things together and go on the evening train before he got back. She would get a job in London as a cook, even without his references.

A bell rang from the kitchen. The old lady would be wanting to talk about India. Someone else could listen to her from now on. Maggie went through to the kitchen to make herself a pot of tea. She took a chair out and sat at the back door in the sun. The more she thought about going away, the more determined she became. She would write to Sam and they could meet when he came home on leave. She could make a home for Hector somewhere else. When she looked at the clock she saw she'd been sitting for an hour in her anger. She would take the old lady's tea tray up, then pack her things.

She had tired herself, pulling at the bell and had fallen asleep. She looked like a child. Maggie sat down on the bed beside her, taking up her dead hand because she knew that wouldn't disturb her. This old woman had been like a mother to her since her own had died. This was the only home she had now, and she knew she couldn't leave it.

The old lady opened her eyes.

'What time is it?' she enquired.

'It's nearly five, ma'am. I'm sorry I'm a wee bit late with your tea.'

'That's all right. I was having a beautiful dream about India. Do you know where I was with dear Sandy?'

'No, ma'am.'

'Up in the hills.'

'What were you doing?'

'Now that would be telling,' she said, with the coy look of a girl. 'What will I be having for supper?'

'What would you like, ma'am?'

166

He carried the painting down the stairs of his club. It was legally the property of the trustees, but there was nothing else he could do, and they wouldn't check the inventory till he was dead. He was doing this for the sake of his son.

There was a sizeable drinks bill to be settled, and he wrote his cheque with a flourish because he knew that there would be plenty of funds lodged to meet it. The porter offered to carry the painting, but he took it with him into the back seat of the cab in case it got a knock.

The painting was taken from him at the dealers on Princes Street, and he had to wait for ten minutes in a room with arts magazines arranged on a table. When he was shown through, the frock-coated dealer had the painting on an easel, in the light. He took a pair of pince-nez from his floral waistcoat pocket and clipped them to his nose.

Invernevis noticed the view of the castle and looked down on the people in Princes Street. Those sitting in the open-topped omnibus seemed solemn, as if they were thinking of relatives in France and Belgium.

The dealer was taking his time, head slightly back, hands under his swallow tails.

'Il Parmigiano.'

'I beg your pardon?' Invernevis said.

'Francesco Mazzola. Born in Palma, beginning of the six-teenth century. As you can see, influenced by Raphael and Michelangelo.' He was crossing to a bookcase as he spoke, pulling out a volume as if he knew immediately where it was on the shelf. He turned over pages.

He began to read, like a schoolmaster:

'But while he was painting a picture for S. Salvadore del Lauro came the ruin and sack of Rome, which not only banished all art for the time, but cost the lives of many artists, and Francesco was very near losing his; for at the beginning of the tumult he was so intent on his work that when the soldiers began entering the houses — and some Germans were already in his — he, for all the noise they made, did not move from his place. But they, coming suddenly upon him, and seeing his painting, were so astonished by it that, like good fellows, they let him alone.'

He closed the book and restored it to its place. 'I doubt if the Germans would do that today.'

But Invernevis hadn't come to discuss the war.

'How much is it worth?' he asked.

The dealer put his pince-nez back into his top pocket, leaving the black cord looped.

'That's a difficult question. It's wartime and the market's flat. Even in Edinburgh people aren't buying pictures in case they're bombed by the zeppelins, and who can blame them? In fact I have a considerable number of canvases in storage for clients. But this is a nice picture, in reasonable condition. I can give you five hundred guineas for it.'

Invernevis waited while the cheque was written out and took it immediately to his own bank, withdrawing £100 in cash. He took the cab back to the post office, watching the elegant women parading on Princes Street. Maybe he should stay another night.

He sent £50 to the governess in Switzerland, £5 for her to buy a present for herself for her patience. He stopped the cab at a tobacconist's to buy a box of good quality cigars for the train, and went to licensed premises to have his hip flask filled from a barrel of choice brandy. Then he went into Jenners and asked the way to the hosiery counter.

'Can I help you, sir?' the elderly assistant enquired.

'I would like two pairs of silk stockings.'

She pulled out a drawer and laid it on the counter. 'What size is your wife's foot, sir?'

'I don't know, but it's small,' he said, because the real explanation was too complicated and embarrassing.

'What colour would suit her, sir?'

'She has dark hair.'

On the train home he relaxed in the carriage with a Havana and hip flask as he watched the moors go by. The silk stockings were in his portmanteau in the rack above his reclining head. It was wonderful what money could do.

15

It seemed to be the same funeral going past hour after hour, day after day from the hospital, the same mourners bent into the breeze from the sea or into the driving rain, following the cart covered with a Union Jack. When it reached the cemetery bugles blew the last post before it came back for the next load.

'Run!'

It was the turn of the man in front of Sam, but the sand was slippery after the rain and his bayonet grazed off the sand-filled sack swinging on the frame.

'What a fucking effort!' the instructor yelled. 'If that was a Hun he would have cut the balls off you.'

The sack was now swinging for Sam against the greyness of the sea. He shrugged his shoulders to make the pack sit better on his back, then levelled his bayonet. Ploughing taught you to aim straight and true, even when the soil under you was slimy, when the horses wanted to go sideways with the lie of the land. He ran and his bayonet ripped the heart from the sack.

'That's more like it!' the instructor shouted grudgingly.

Spilling sand, the sack was swung again.

'Next!'

It was cold by the sea, but a lot of men still had to make their run. Etaples was the British Army's No. 1 training camp, providing the thousands of troops that the insatiable front line demanded. The training ground, the Bull Ring, stretched for more than a mile on either side of the Boulogne Road and its staked-out areas in the sand dunes were equipped with every kind of obstacle a soldier would encounter at the front, from barbed wire to water, walls to trenches. But the instructors, called Canaries because of their yellow armbands, liked to concentrate on bayonet practice.

It was noon, time to eat the one slice of bread that had been issued that morning. Sam went for a half pint of tea from the charity canteen that had been trundled down on to the sands. Lady Angela Forbes herself was serving today.

'It's too chilly for you here! You should be tucked up in bed in London, your ladyship!' one of the instructors shouted at her.

Sam stood by himself, taking the tea and bread, thinking of the dinner that Maggie would be putting into the servants' hall. But if he hadn't left Invernevis he would have been called up anyway – because of the new law about single men they'd passed. It was time to resume training, to march along the beach for target practice. They lay down on the sand on their bellies while the instructors stood over them. Sam shot carefully, putting all the bullets into the inner circle in the hope of getting sent up to the front as soon as possible.

The man beside him was whipping up the sea with his shots.

'What's the matter?' the instructor asked, boots on either side of him. 'Are you trying to hit the White Cliffs of Dover? Because they're a long way away, son, and you won't be seeing them for a fucking long time. In fact if you keep on shooting like this you'll never see them again.'

'I can't see the target, sir.'

'Can't see it? But your bloody eyes were tested before you were sent out here.'

The man was shivering from the wetness and from fear.

'We'll have to give you some help,' the instructor said, standing on the shooter's back to stop him shaking while the water oozed up out of the sand as he sank into it.

He was hitting the target now.

Sam watched the covered cart drawn by a horse coming from the hospital. It was going in the direction of the tall chimney whose stench you couldn't get off your skin. One of the men who'd gone into town, though it was out of bounds, said that that was where they burned the gangrenous limbs before the remains were buried a few days later overlooking the Bull Ring, where they'd been put through their training in the sand.

'Gas practice!'

Sam lined up outside the canvas chamber. The masks didn't fit properly. One of the men who'd taken a long time to get through was kneeling, retching in the sand, but a boot sent him back through again. Sam filled his lungs before he pulled the mask down over his mouth. He struggled through the gloom but the stuff was getting into his eyes and his feet were dragging in the sand. It was like trying to plough sodden clay, but he could see the brightness of the exit, and he made a last effort, lunging out, then recovering his balance because a Canary was standing there with a stopwatch. He made the line in the sand before the instructor's thumb pressed down.

But there was still a four-mile quick march back to camp, past fences where men were tied by the wrist for minor offences, the way he'd fixed crows by the wings to the fences in Buchan to deter others. The Canaries stood on either side of the road, lashing out where they saw a loose puttee or a rifle not at the correct angle.

The infantry-base depots stretched behind barbed wire for a mile on either side of a road up a hill behind the little fishing port of Etaples on the river Canche. The village was out of bounds to Bull Ring troops, but some of the hardened cases slipped out from camp to the two brothels that were reserved for officers and instructors. Men with money to spend ran after La Comtesse, the resident whore, as she stood up in her carriage, whipping her team through the streets.

Though Sam was still shy about undressing in front of other men he joined them in the bath-house that Lady Forbes had organized, but as soon as he put back on his clothes the lice began again. He went into the Expeditionary Force canteen and bought a mug of tea. An officer was passing among the tables, and he was about to get to his feet to salute when the man sitting beside him put a restraining hand on his arm.

'That's not the kind you salute.'

'But he's a Colonel,' Sam said.

'And I'm fucking General Douglas Haig,' the man said. 'That's a dead man's gear.'

'I don't follow you,' Sam said, watching the officer sitting down at a corner table.

'It's simple. He was up at the front and he didn't like what he had seen so he started to run, and on the way he bumped into an officer in the Guards. Living or dead, it doesn't make much difference there. So he came back here a Colonel, when he left a private. It takes some doing, you'll admit.'

Men were beginning to leave other tables to go and sit with the Colonel, who had produced a cloth from his tunic and was rolling it out.

'It's crown-and-anchor,' the man said contemptuously. 'He'll take every penny off them and then he'll go back to the billet he shares with the hundreds of others in the woods and dunes. It's not like that game over there, where at least you win and lose. But these men, they can't go forward and they can't go back. They come out at night to forage.'

'He's going to get caught now,' Sam said.

A military policeman was moving about, tapping the tables with his stick. He stopped to study the board game. Then he saluted the Colonel and moved on.

'He gets a cut,' the man explained. 'That's the rule you play by here.'

The first day he'd arrived in the camp Sam had decided that he wasn't going to risk anything. He was fit and could do everything they put in front of him. He wanted to get to the front as soon as possible because Hector was there. He gave the man a cigarette for his insight and went up to the canteen for several sheets of paper. He had a letter to write to Maggie, but how was he going to explain why he'd left without saying cheerio? He sat chewing the end of the pencil in his frustration.

The game was over in the corner. The Colonel was rolling up the crown-and-anchor board and putting his winnings into the pocket of his smart tunic. In case he met anyone on the way back to his home in the chalk escarpment he had a bag filled with sand down his thigh.

Invernevis's library was a friendly, intimate room again, now that he'd solved his financial problems by selling the painting. He started reading the new book about salmon flies but he couldn't settle in the yellow circle of the lamp, so he turned it down and took the bottle of whisky and an extra glass through with him.

Maggie was sitting at the table, thinking what a mistake it had been not to go when she'd seen the letter from Stirling Castle about Sam. He'd come back from Edinburgh, so pleased with himself because of what he'd got for the painting, but that had only made her more angry with him. If he could afford all that whisky he could get a nurse in to look after the old lady.

Where would Sam be now? If only he'd send even a postcard, just to say that he was all right, but he'd probably be in France by now. He could even be dead. She was startled to see Invernevis standing in the doorway, with the bottle of Mackinlay's and an extra glass.

'Not for me, sir.'

But he was pouring her a generous dram.

'It'll make you sleep,' he said as he sat down.

She had to rise to get him a saucer for an ashtray. He was so settled it looked as if he was going to stay the night. She was tired and she was angry about what he'd done to Sam. If she stayed silent he might go away, then she could go up to bed.

'It's a pity about Raeburn,' he began.

She may as well have it out with him.

'But you sent him to join up, sir.'

He suddenly realized the reason for her mood.

'Oh no, Maggie, I didn't send him. The first I knew of it was when I got a letter from Stirling Castle the other day. I thought he would have at least told you that he was going.'

She was confused, but knew that he was telling the truth. It made it even worse, Sam going off like that by himself. He couldn't have felt much for her to do a thing like that.

'His job will still be here when he comes back,' Invernevis said.

'He won't come back, sir. Very few of them will come back.'

She'd stopped looking at the newspapers that came into the house because of the long lists. She dreaded the sound of the postman's bicycle at the back door because she expected to be handed a telegram about Hector. All she got from him were issue postcards with *I am well* ticked off, as if he couldn't be bothered writing.

But he wasn't going to go. He started talking about the old days.

'Do you remember my sister?'

'How could anyone forget her?' Maggie said. 'She was so affectionate.'

'Yes, there's been a lot of sorrow in this house. But I could never manage here without you, Maggie.'

'You would soon find someone else, sir,' she said coyly.

'Nobody like you, Maggie. You've been so good to my mother and myself. She thinks the world of you.'

She flushed with pleasure and reached to take a sip from the glass of whisky. She didn't like the taste but once it went down it relaxed her as she stood in the warm glow of the lamp, listening to him reminisce. There were sad memories, and memories to laugh at as she reached again for her glass, and he refilled his from the bottle. She touched his shoulder; she looked down with affection on his bald patch. She felt the heat in her face as he struck another match for another cigarette.

The cat went on his knees, purring sonorously. It was after one when he tried to stand up. She had a struggle getting him up the stairs by the moonlight streaming through the stained glass window because she felt so light-headed, as if her feet were floating above the steps. As she helped him along the dark corridor his shoulder left the gilt frames of paintings rocking on their chains. He sprawled on the bed and she removed his silver cigarette case and matches. She unthreaded the watch chain from his waistcoat, then unlaced his brogues and pulled them off.

The whisky was making her feel even lighter, as if she was floating above the bed. She began to fumble with his buttons.

Kilberry was standing at the window of his castle, watching the sun setting over the bens of Jura, a glass of whisky in his hand. It wasn't the silence without the guns that he found strange; it was the silence without the pipes. That fellow Macdonald, Niall Invernevis's piper, was one of the best he'd ever heard.

He would have to see about getting his lament for Jock of Jura published.

He looked across to the darkening island. It was so sad to think of Jura lying over there, so sad to think of the fighting that was going on in France, of all the dead, including men he'd commanded; men in their prime. When the guns eventually fell silent – and that could be years – there would be a terrible shortage of men. He turned to his desk. Jura's photograph stood on it, and it seemed as if he was riding the black charger out of the silver frame.

Hector MacDonald was hungry. He'd had nothing to eat since the previous day because the action had being going on since dawn, stopping any rations being brought up.

A pigeon had alighted on an uprooted tree in the remains of the wood he was lying in. He was watching its silhouette against the red glow in the sky. All he needed to do was to reach out, wring its neck, pluck it and put a few twigs under it to cook it. There was plenty of smoke about already.

His hand was close to it when he noticed the cylinder tied to its leg. It had flown through the shells and the smoke with a message. It might be an order for another attack, or an order stopping an attack. If he killed the pigeon he could be killing men.

He clapped his hands.

16

On a September evening two soldiers came off the train at Invernevis station. They went down the hill into the countryside with their kitbags on their shoulders, remarking to each other how quiet it was. The small man had the additional burden of a black box.

The old man was sitting in the porch when he saw them coming round the bend. He went into the old woman who was dozing beside the fire and put his hand gently on her arm.

'*Pheigi bheag*, when you open your eyes it's not a ghost you'll be seeing,' he said.

When she saw him standing against the brightness of the window she let out a cackle, the first since he'd gone away. The charm of the cockerel had worked; he'd been rescued from between the two worlds. MacDougall hugged the old man and kissed the top of his whitened head as though he were a boy. Then he stooped over the old woman, sliding a hand under her skinny knees, the other gently easing her back forward. He lifted her and danced her round the room, her arms round his neck as she cackled and cackled.

The kit-bag was opened, the gifts handed out. The old man got French tobacco in gold foil. He carved the black block against his thumb with his curved knife, and soon it was smouldering aromatically in the bowl of his pipe, the nape of his neck against the back of the chair as he watched the boy kneeling beside the old woman to show her the ornament he'd brought back, wrapped in a shirt. A man in a blue coat and breeches was holding up the small porcelain hand of a woman in a white gown, his other hand round her waist. She had a flower between her breasts. MacDougall turned the key in the bottom and they began to waltz to the tinkling French music. The old woman's eyes were wide. He'd brought magic back from the other world.

He'd also brought back dark chocolates with soft centres for her gums, and every time a flavour burst against her palate she grinned at him, touching the dark pleats of his kilt as he knelt beside her with the box.

There was one more gift, a bottle of French brandy. At first she was suspicious of its fire, but when its warmth hit her insides she began cackling, swinging the glass for a refill. The old man took his tot daintily, lifting his little finger like a lady taking tea.

The old man asked him about the war, and he used his hands as he tried to find Gaelic to tell them about the flares and cascades of the star shells, more brilliant than the *Fir-Chlis*, the Northern Lights, as they burst every night over no-man's-land. The old woman reached out to touch his kilt because the spell of her cockerel had brought him back safely from that other world beyond the mountains where men breathed fire.

Word had spread that MacDougall was home, and people began to arrive to shake his hand. There was soon standing room only in the kitchen, but they were still coming in without knocking, paying homage to the cackling hostess in her rocking chair before hearing in Gaelic about *an Cogadh Mòr*. It was as well that the Somme wouldn't translate, because MacDougall didn't want to speak about it. They wanted news of husbands, brothers, sons, but if somebody had been wounded MacDougall made it easier for them by telling them that it was 'only a scratch', even if they were at death's door.

There were women arriving too, most of them former lovers of MacDougall's. One of them had hot scones wrapped in a cloth; another had brought a cheese. The table was becoming crowded with gifts, bread and home-killed mutton. A man came in with his fingers through the gills of a dozen mackerel taken that afternoon in the turning tide at the mouth of the loch. *Peigi bheag* was in her element. She had her hat on as she went round, cackling, showing people the musical box she'd put on the mantelpiece, but always coming back to touch MacDougall's kilt as if she couldn't quite believe he was home. She went through to the scullery, gutting the glittering fish with a sure blade. She scrubbed the new potatoes that someone had dug up in the dusk and brought in a wicker basket as a gift. Both pots were carried through to the fire.

Carmichael sent down two bottles of special reserve whisky from the Arms because MacDougall would fill his pub and his till for the length of his leave. Someone was now playing a fiddle, and they were shouting for MacDougall to sing.

He stood with his back to the fire, his hands clasped, brogues planted wide. But he didn't sing a Gaelic song. Instead he sang the song a woman with almond eyes and a perfumed mound had taught him night after night in a bed with scrolled ends in Armentières. *Peigi bheag* was watching him. If it had been an English song she would have put him out of the house, but it was in a strange pleasing language, and as he shaped his mouth for the word *l'amour* and put out his arms every woman in the room, including *Peigi bheag*, went weak at the knees.

The bowl Maggie was mixing the cake in almost left the table when she saw her brother standing on the doorstep like a ghost.

'You should have written to say that you were coming! You've frightened the life out of me, and I haven't even got your bed aired.' She hugged him as she scolded him, settling him in her chair before she put the kettle on.

'I wanted to give you a surprise.'

'A heart attack, more like. Did anyone else come with you?'

'Aye, Dochie MacDougall.'

'Oh, him,' she said dismissively. 'So you're still keeping the same bad company.'

He was rolling a cigarette at the table. He'd become expert at doing it in the dark, in a trench in the teeming rain when at any moment a shell might destroy the thin membrane of the paper in his fingers. He stopped rolling.

'He's been a bloody good friend to me.'

When he swore she would rebuke him, but as she filled the tea-pot with her back to him, she heard something more in his voice, like the time it had changed overnight when he was fourteen, and his piping had changed at the same time, becoming deeper, richer, ringing in her ears long after he'd stopped playing.

178

Her brother was sobbing.

'What is it, Hector?' she asked, putting her arm round his shoulders.

It took him time to find the words.

'I never told you in the letter, but when I had the measles it was MacDougall who put the life back into me.'

'What does that mean?' she asked, frightened.

'He poured whisky into me when they'd put the sheet over my face.' He didn't add that he'd been given the last rites.

'Oh,' Maggie said, nodding. In that one word her attitude towards MacDougall changed, though she wasn't going to show her brother.

'And another thing, he saved a lot of the boys. That man should get a medal, only Lauder doesn't like him, so he won't recommend him for anything. It's a damned disgrace. None of the officers like Lauder. You hear a lot of things between tunes when you play in the mess.' But he couldn't tell her how he was petrified with fear when the shells came across, and how the big man stayed with him until the attack was over.

She put a generous spoon of tea into the pot from the caddy, then did something she'd never done before with him, but he was home safe, and he was upset. She always kept a small bottle of whisky in a cupboard for emergencies, and she poured him a dram.

'*Slàinte*,' he toasted her, then tasted it, his eyes closed. 'I've been dreaming about this for months.'

'Well, see that you don't do your dreaming in the Arms when you're home. I've got enough on my hands.'

He saw that she wanted to talk.

'Is the boss still at it?'

'Still at what?' she asked sharply.

'The drink.'

'And how do you know about that?'

'One of the boys got a letter from his wife. He said the boss was taking a big bucket.'

'My God it's great how gossip travels,' she said, then added wearily: 'he's very heavy on it, just as bad as his mother was.'

'Where's he getting the money?'

'You'll soon see when you go upstairs. He's been taking paintings to Edinburgh to sell. He'll get into trouble with the trustees because they're not his.' She didn't say that she'd seen the inventory on the library desk.

'You'd better not let Father Macdonald up the stairs if he comes,' her brother warned her.

'What do you mean? Nobody gets into this house.'

'Maybe the time's come for you to leave,' he suggested.

If he'd said that to her before the war she would have flown at him. But her face told him that she'd considered it.

'If you got a job in Glasgow I could go there after the war,' he said. 'I could take up a trade. I don't want to come back here, just to be a piper. I've had too much of that already. I've met some soldiers who work in the shipyards and they say there's good money in it.'

She was touched by his offer, but she shook her head. 'No, he needs looking after. He's got no one else.'

'What about the old lady? '

'She's never left India.'

'Have you thought of having a word with Dr MacNiven about the boss's drinking?' Hector suggested.

'I've thought of it, but he would know it was me, and that would only make things worse. You know how proud he can be. He thinks he's solving his problems by selling all these things, but he doesn't realize that he's only making them worse.'

'He'll run out of pictures to sell,' Hector said.

'Not before the drink kills him.'

'It's a pity he wouldn't get married again,' he said as she put the cup of tea in front of him. Since going out to the war he'd learnt to read faces. You could see the fear in men's faces as they prepared to go into battle, and you could see the end coming when you lifted them on to the stretcher. He'd also learnt to read the desire in the faces of the French women sitting in the *estaminets* with glasses of wine, thinking about their husbands at the front. Now he saw his sister coloured slightly in the soft evening light, and it wasn't the heat from the stove.

'How's he going to meet anyone when he doesn't go anywhere, except to Edinburgh to sell things, and doesn't invite anyone here? What woman would put up with drinking like that?'

But it was a different world now, Hector was thinking as he lit his smoke after his tea. MacDougall was going with the Brigadier's wife, or at least, would be going with her if her hospital train stopped long enough for him to catch up with it.

There was a silence now in which his smoke drifted out the door, but the main topic hadn't been covered. Hector knew that he had to bring it up. He opened his pipe box and handed her the letter.

'That's from Sam.'

She didn't read it; she kept it under her hand as she sat there, as if some vibrations were coming through her fingers that were allowing her to decipher its contents.

Since she wasn't going to ask, Hector said:

'He's getting on fine.'

But she wasn't going to give her feelings away, so they sat over cups of tea, chatting about local men who were out in France and Belgium. She was glad to be using her Gaelic again.

'There's a few widows up in the village now,' she said sadly. 'It must be very hard on them, trying to work the crofts and raise a family.'

There'll be a lot more widows yet, he could have said. The 8th Argylls had been in the battle of the Somme, which was probably still going on, but he and MacDougall had agreed on the train that they weren't going to speak to anyone about their experiences. There were a lot of crosses on the mounds of mud, and sometimes the shells dug them up again, so he found himself lifting men he'd already buried back on the stretcher.

'I see you brought home his pipes,' Maggie said.

They both looked at the long black box on the floor. Those pipes had gone arrogantly into battle with the rush of men on the Somme and come out, subdued, at evening from shattered High Wood with the men on stretchers.

'Aye, you know what like he is about them,' he said.

'And you haven't met a girl?'

It was said so suddenly that it took him by surprise.

'A girl?' He laughed. 'You don't see many of them out there.'

But it wasn't true. They'd had a week's rest in Armentières, where the whores lifted their skirts for a few francs. But MacDougall wouldn't join the queue in case he was put out of action with the clap. He was visiting a big farmhouse, and had taken Hector along with him one night, with a bottle of peach brandy.

'I'll take the mother, and you can have the daughter.'

The mother, the wife of a French officer, was a striking-looking woman in her thirties, and MacDougall soon disappeared upstairs with her. Hector sat with the girl at the big table. She was watching him. She couldn't have been more than fifteen, with pigtails down her back, and a neat white collar like a nun's. He hadn't the language, so he'd sat there, smiling and nodding. Then she'd got up suddenly, closed the book of wild flowers and took his hand, leading him through to a bedroom. It was his first time, but she tied her pigtails at the top of her head so that they wouldn't get in the way of her exertions as she mounted him.

He sat there in the secret knowledge of his initiation; that was another thing he'd had to thank MacDougall for.

'I'd better go through and see the boss,' he said, rising.

'He's fishing.'

'Oh, well. I'll see him later,' he said, settling again. 'There's a wee drop left,' he said, indicating the whisky bottle.

Invernevis loved fishing. Since he was a boy it had been his way of getting away from the house, from his father, from Aunt Carlotta. It was more than the silence; it was the way you learnt to read the water; the hint of a fin. Maggie's father had taught him how to do that. But when the fly fell short of the place he was watching on the river he saw what the drinking was doing to him. It was like having to relearn how to cast, sending out the wild line again and again because of the tremor in his hand.

If there was anything on the other side it wasn't taking. He cast again, and this time the lure landed where he wanted it, by the boulder, where fish usually lay.

His affairs were in better shape, though it was regrettable that he'd had to sell paintings. However, the most pressing debts were settled, and he'd sent enough money out to Switzerland to keep the children going for quite some time.

For the first time in a year he had a fish. There was the old excitement of stopping it going down into the next pool, or upriver, of taking back line from it, of not giving it the chance to go down to the bottom. He had the hook of the gaff poised as it came into the shallows.

He carried the fish up the lawn, round the corner of the house to the kitchen, laying it on the table.

'It's a nice one, sir,' Maggie said. 'You can have it tomorrow.'

He shook hands with Hector.

'I'm glad to see the pipes are safe,' he said.

Maggie went away to get on with work as he questioned Hector about the part the 8th Argylls had so far played in the war. Since he'd been the company commander, Hector knew that he had to tell him the truth. It wasn't what Invernevis had read in the papers, and he listened intently about the huge wastage on the Somme.

'I think you should be careful about what you say about the war when you're home,' Invernevis cautioned. 'Some of the women are nervous about their men, and there's no point in upsetting them.'

Hector assured him that he wouldn't say anything, and the conversation moved to the news that Baird was being replaced as commanding officer by Colonel Robin Campbell from the Camerons.

'You're very fortunate in the officers you have.'

But Hector didn't bring up Lauder's name.

'He didn't even offer me a dram,' Hector complained to Maggie when he went back through.

'Just as well, when you see what the drink can do to a person.'

'I think I'll take a walk up to the village.'

'To the Arms, you mean?' Maggie said. 'Don't you go getting into bad company and letting yourself down, after doing so well.' She was opening a drawer as she spoke, and drew out the purse. 'Here you are,' she said, giving him a sovereign.

As soon as he was gone she went upstairs and sat for some time on her bed with the letter on her lap. She knew that if she opened it she would be bringing him back into her life.

Dear Maggie,

I shouldn't have left without saying cheerio to you but it was the way things were at the time. I wasn't intending to join the Argylls; I was on my way home to Buchan and I saw an Argyll at Stirling Station and that's what made me decide to join up. Of course I knew that Hector was out here with them and I would have a friend.

Things aren't too bad out here. I'm not allowed to say where we are but Hector will very likely tell you. It seems a long time since I left Invernevis and I often think about the horses. I hope they're all right and that the boss can drive them all right. I still think of you all the time and when they give me some leave I'll come and see you.

Love,
Sam.

She sat holding the letter in both hands. So the Master hadn't sent him to join the Argylls after all, but it was a bit late for her to apologize to him. She put the letter in her bottom drawer.

Hector found the Arms deserted because the whole village seemed to be at MacDougall's. He bought a half bottle of whisky to take as a gift and ten cigarettes for himself. He strolled down the brae savouring the quiet evening countryside as he smoked, the way the officers did, holding the cigarette between two fingers, in and out of the corners of their mouths.

It was as if the noises of war had sharpened his hearing for more subtle sounds. He stretched out in the grass of the verge, for the sheer pleasure of hearing a mistle thrush singing without interruption, perched near the toe of his boots.

There was a sudden salvo of shots from the wood on the hill, where they poached pigeons. He started to tremble as the awful thing that had happened just before coming on leave came back.

A parade had been called in a field as the sun was setting over the Somme, its rays distorted by the flicker of the guns. Major Baird had appeared with his two Indian orderlies in attendance, like ghosts in the twilight.

The Sergeant Major read out the particulars. Not a man moved as Captain Henderson walked the ranks.

'You, step forward.'

He hesitated when he came to MacDougall, then passed on. He had chosen twelve men. Then he turned to Hector.

'You too.'

'Will I bring my pipes, sir?'

'No. Bring a chair, a blanket and two ropes as well as your weapon.'

'The men who have been selected will muster here at six in the morning,' Captain Henderson told them before Major Baird walked away, his two orderlies fading into the night.

'I'm not going through with it,' Hector told MacDougall.

'You'll have to. Here.' He passed him a bottle in the darkness. 'Take a good drink of that before you go out.'

He didn't sleep, and he drank the brandy as he went out under the lightening sky. The dozen men were boarding a lorry with their rifles. They couldn't see where they were going because of the canvas sides. The officer who was travelling with them allowed them to smoke. A bad sign, Hector was thinking.

When the lorry braked thirty minutes later they jumped out into a field.

There was no sound of guns.

Sand martins were flitting from a bank in the new day. Hector had seen them down at the river at Invernevis, as a boy while his father fished.

Then another lorry arrived and a man was led out, his hands manacled behind his back, his eyes bandaged, but Hector knew who it was by his bandy legs which some of the men had made fun of. Higgins had transferred from the 9th to the 8th battalion, and hadn't been there one morning.

'He won't get far with these legs,' MacDougall had said.

They'd caught the deserter at one of the channel ports, wearing riding breeches and no badges. Now the medical officer was pinning a small square of lint at his heart. The condemned man was tied to the chair, and the officer told the squad to line up.

'You too,' he said to Hector.

He'd been hoping desperately that since he was holding the blanket he wouldn't be called, but he had to pick up his gun and go into line. The officer loaded the weapons, putting live ammunition into twelve, a blank in the thirteenth.

'Aim!'

He was used to pipes, not a gun. He squinted along the sights at the white square on the man's chest, but his hands were trembling so much that the barrel swung from side to side.

The officer brought down his hand.

The lint was weeping red as the man slumped at the stake. Hector had tried to fire wide, but would never know where his bullet had gone, or even if his gun had been the one with the blank.

The medical officer went forward.

'He's not dead,' he announced.

There was a silence such as Hector had never heard before. By the look of the squad, they would turn their guns on the officer if they were asked to fire at the man again. The salvo had broken the sandbank, the shells from a dozen nests scattered.

The officer took his revolver from his pouch and went forward, administering the *coup de grâce* to the prisoner's skull.

'Bury him,' the officer ordered.

Hector and the man who was usually on the stretcher with him had to cut the bleeding corpse from the post and wrap it in the blanket before carrying it to the field where the shallow temporary grave had already been dug and recorded on the map.

The chaplain came to speak a prayer about forgiveness. The blindfold had come off. Higgins's eyes were open, and he seemed to be staring at them, as if he hadn't died.

'Hurry up,' the officer said.

When the officer's back was turned Hector let the clay soil trickle from the spade, covering his eyes. Now as he sat by the roadside at Invernevis he was swigging from the whisky bottle he'd bought to take to MacDougall's. He couldn't get these eyes out of his mind, and he knew that for the rest of his life every time he heard a shotgun or rifle something would slip down from his mind and he would see those eyes.

He no longer felt like going to MacDougall's house, so he went home.

It was time for *Peigi bheag's* party piece. MacDougall stood her on a chair, her hat touching the ceiling. It was a *Rann ri Ghabhail a dh'Aon Anail*, a 'Rhyme to be Said in one Breath'.

> 'Trì làraichean deug donna donna donna-ghorm
> Le'n trì searraich dheug dhonna dhonna dhonna-ghorm
> Trì mnathan deug geala geala geala-bhraghdach
> Le'n trì leanban deug geala geala geala – bhraghdach
> Dà ghille dheug bhreac-luirgneach
> Aona n-uiseag dheug fhad-sporach . . . '

(Thirteen blue-brown mares
With their thirteen blue-brown foals
Thirteen white-breasted women
With their thirteen white-breasted children
Twelve feckle-shanked boys
Eleven long-clawed larks . . .)

While the old woman was chanting some of the listeners stood

round her chair, holding their hands on her stomach to make sure
that she wasn't drawing breath.

'Isein circe 's chas briste
Beairt air a mhuin:
Astaraibh siod, astaraibh siod.'

(A hen's chick with a broken leg
A loom on its back:
Recite that, recite that.)

She hadn't drawn the smallest breath. They crowded round
her, laughing and clapping while she stood cheering. One of the
twins offered her whisky.
'Where's that boy?' she asked.
MacDougall was in the scullery, attending to a woman.

17

The 8th Argylls with the 152nd Brigade had reached their destination with an hour to spare before zero, having stopped for food and tea. It was a bitterly cold night, with fog rolling up from the valley of the Ancre obscuring the weak moon. Hector and Sam stumbled over feet as they entered the assembly trench to stand in water and mud up to their shins. They had khaki aprons over their kilts for camouflage. Hector was frightened that the nervous tickle in his throat was going to betray them, so he took the last of his rum tot, letting the hot liquid go down slowly.

Sam still hadn't touched his. He nudged Hector to look at MacDougall. The big man was standing with his dixie out while an officer filled it. It was brimming as MacDougall lifted it to his mouth with both hands like a chalice. He'd been in another fight. The 8th Argylls hated the 6th battalion from Renfrewshire and had shouted insults at them in Gaelic as they pumped water from the trenches in the chalk escarpment of the White City at Beaumont Hamel. The 6th Argylls were well supplied with gifts from local firms and clubs, cigarettes, whisky, even a football. Coats the Paisley thread manufacturers had presented each officer of the 6th Argylls with a breast-plate, and every man with a heart-shaped mirror of polished steel to wear in his tunic pocket for protection.

'Fucking Jessies!' MacDougall had jeered at them. 'They'll be sending you out roses next.'

A fight had broken out in the trenches, involving shovels as well as fists. But MacDougall wasn't put on a charge. He was needed for the big battle, and an officer was refilling his dixie with rum. Another officer had his wrist up, checking his watch against the lightening sky. Hector put an arm round Sam's shoulder and hugged him. Then he opened his pipe-box on the parapet of the trench.

Sam saw the officer with the watch put a whistle into his mouth and realized that he hadn't drunk his rum. He didn't like alcohol but he gulped it for the courage he knew it would give him because this was his first battle. As Hector was hoisting his pipes on to his shoulder to tune them the earth seemed to lift him up as if some giant prehistoric creature had been wakened by this war. Thirteen tons of explosives made the dawn rain down with stones and earth, entombing more than three hundred Germans in their dug-outs.

The intense barrage began, and the pipes led the advance through the dawn fog, veering away after a hundred yards. But the 8th Argylls weren't following the officer with the pistol in his gloved hand. They were following MacDougall. The big man was drunk. Head thrown back, he was roaring as he ran uphill, weaving between knife-rests splintered by the spattering bullets, throwing the pineapple-shaped grenades from the bucket he was carrying as if he were sowing a crop on his croft. Behind him men were up to their waists in water, using their rifle butts as paddles to cross the shell-holes. But the Argylls were pinned down in the mud by machine-gun fire, and the 6th Gordons, Jura's old battalion, were brought up to help.

MacDougall ran on, leaving the machine gun pointed at the sky, a nest of burst limbs and the scattered buckets of helmets. Hector came behind with the stretcher. For the first time he was terrified of this task because that man lying there, face-down in the mud, his kilt in tatters, could be Sam. He realized not only how much Sam meant to his sister Maggie, but to himself. It wasn't Sam; it was another Invernevis man he helped to roll on to the stretcher, but he was finished, so they tipped him off and went for the next casualty.

At the time of the Wars of Religion tunnels had been dug in the chalk to shelter the villagers. The Germans were known to have enlarged them, creating a small underground town beneath Beaumont Hamel, which had once produced powder puffs. MacDougall was going down the steep flight of stairs with his bucket. There was a door in the chalk face with a red skull and crossbones painted on it, but the big man blew it open. Sam and the others followed him down into the earth. It was incredible. Electric light was burning in the tunnel they were running along, an underground street with shops on either side. MacDougall smashed the window with his boot, hauled out the tailor's dummy with the military uniform and kicked it along in front of him.

Another door gave way for him. Officers were sitting in leather armchairs in a panelled room. One had a tall stemmed glass by his dangling fingers, his blue tongue protruding. As MacDougall tore the iron cross from his neck and dropped it into his bucket as a souvenir the corpse fell sideways. Then he crossed to the table and put the decanter to his head before splintering a cupboard and handing out boxes of cigars. When they couldn't get them to light the Argylls hacked off the ends with their bayonets.

They were in the street again, another window giving way for MacDougall's boot. He tipped the tray of signet rings with the German eagle into his bucket and broke glass again.

'Take them for the missus, sir!' he shouted, throwing a pair of silk stockings over the officer's shoulder.

Sam felt ashamed, taking a pair for Maggie, but the feel of them made him think of her in them.

The next door led deeper down into the earth. It was a huge cavern cut out of the chalk, with men lying on the rows of beds. Two naked men were lying, joined at the front and back.

'Dirty bastards!' MacDougall said, and used his bayonet to part them.

An officer came in, a handkerchief over his mouth.

'You get used to it, sir!' MacDougall said cheerfully, in his element. 'The gas we sent across did for the bastards.'

Sam stayed in the corridor, watching. It wasn't only the stench that was sickening him. The piano was being opened up.

'All that's missing is women!' MacDougall said.

The officer was ordering them up into the battle again, but the piano was being pounded. The real Beaumont Hamel was underground, and it had fallen to the 8th Argylls. Whatever was happening above was no longer any concern of theirs.

As Hector arrived the Invernevis company was shouting for a song from MacDougall. Hector was expecting a victory rant, but the big man began to sing with the soft voice of a young woman.

'Fhuaras naidheachd an-dè –
'S fhad bhios tàire 'na déidh –
Nach do thill thu on eug,
Fhir a b'fhìrinniche 'beul,
Dhan robh 'n inntinne gheur gun bhòsd.'

(News came yesterday –
We shall long rue the day –
That you had not escaped from Death,
You of the most truthful mouth,
With the keen mind without vainglory.)

Hector realized that MacDougall's song was for the sweethearts and wives of the men in the wire beds who had drowned in their own vomit when the gas came under the doors they thought were so secure.

''Bu tu 'n gallan gun mheang
Nach bu mhalairneach greann,
Nach bu ghalanach fann,
Duine sgafanta seang:
Bha thu tamull 'sa' Fhraing air bhòrd.'

(You were a scion without blemish,
Without frown or scowl,
No plaintive weakling
But a handsome lean man:
You lodged for some time in France.)

In the silence after MacDougall finished the hand of a dead man slipped from a bunk and swung. Then suddenly the big man banged the piano with his fist, making the hammers jump as he launched into another song, this time an *iorram*, a rowing song, pulling the imaginary oars to his chest as the war galley sped over the waves. The other men joined in the boastful chorus as they passed around bottles of wine, cigars glowing between their knuckles.

'Sometimes the big fellow goes too far,' Hector said to Sam. 'It's a good job Captain Lauder's not here.'

But MacDougall had drawn a cork with his teeth and was offering his friend the first swig.

Invernevis had made love to Maggie, the most wonderful experience of his life, and now he was falling asleep without a care in the world, her arms round him, her soft hair on his skin.

'It's past nine, sir.'

He was turning to her warmth again when she pulled the curtains and the sun burst into his eyes. She poured the fragrant tea from the tray, the silver spoon tinkling on the Spode saucer as she set it beside him. He lay, naked under the quilt, unable to look at her.

'I've brought up some Gentleman's Relish on toast, sir.'

But he couldn't face it.

'Thank you, Maggie,' he said as she closed the door. The tea was getting cold as he lay trying trying to remember how he'd got to bed. She must have helped him up the stairs again and removed his clothes. Was it a dream, or had he really been in bed with her? She could have got up early and gone, treating it as if nothing had happened.

He had to go down sometime and face her. She'd left the jug of hot water for shaving. He stropped the open razor on the belt hanging from the marble wash-stand and pulled out the mirror on its latticed arm. But the blade slipped, cutting his neck. He missed having Hector to help him in the morning to lay out his clothes.

'I put the mail in, sir,' Maggie told him as she passed through the hall.

The bank was returning more cheques, and he was going to have to make another trip to Edinburgh.

He went through to the kitchen.

'I'm afraid it's the Millet this time, Maggie.'

'Oh no, sir,' she said in despair.

'The prices keep going up because of this war,' he complained.

'It's too big for you to take to Edinburgh by yourself, sir.'

'I can manage.'

She helped him to lift the painting off the wall. It was her favourite, because of the way the golden glow of the sunset seemed to light up the peasant woman's skin as she carried the bowl along a country road that was very like Invernevis. Sometimes she stood staring at it as if it were a window, always bright, whatever the weather.

'You'll have to get it put into a proper box, sir,' she advised him.

'All right, ask the joiner to do it as soon as possible.'

He sat in the library, hearing the sawing and hammering as the crate was made for the picture. At the station it was put into the guard's van. He had it taken straight off the train by a barrow to a taxi, and went directly to the dealer's. It took two porters to carry the crate up the stairs and open it. The painting was lifted on to an easel in the same room with the view of the castle. The dealer, who'd already paid Invernevis £1200 for four paintings, stood back with his pince-nez at arm's length.

'One of my ancestors brought it back from the continent last century,' Invernevis informed him. 'From Barbizon. He had a pistol in the coach with him because he knew what a bargain he'd got, and he was frightened of being robbed.'

The dealer was tapping his pince-nez against his chin.

'Wonderful, isn't it?'

'Wonderful,' Invernevis concurred.

'Look at that detail,' the dealer said, tapping his pince-nez on the fingers gripping the bowl. 'You can feel them. And the glaze of the inside of the bowl is so . . . 'His hand was searching the air for a word.

'I'm very sorry at having to part with it, but these are difficult times as you know,' Invernevis said.

'A wonderful copy,' the dealer said. 'You would swear it was the real thing.'

'That isn't a copy,' Invernevis told him scornfully. 'It's got Millet's signature in the corner.'

But the dealer had gone to his bookcase. He was turning over the tissues covering the illustrations as he brought the volume to his client.

'This is the original, in the Louvre.'

'But how do you know that's not the original?' Invernevis challenged him.

The dealer looked horrified. 'Seeing it's such a good copy I could go to £40.'

'I'm not interested,' he said angrily.

'You won't get any more for it elsewhere,' the dealer warned.

But he had to salvage something from this humiliation.

'If you get your man to put it back in the crate, I'll have it collected later,' he told the dealer.

He went back to his club for a lunch that consisted of large whiskies. What could he do now? He could go along to the lawyers and explain his predicament, but they would sell land to save the situation, the last thing he wanted. There was nothing for it but to go to a moneylender, but where was he to find one? He walked the length of Princes Street, but there was no sign. Then he tried Queen Street, and saw an engraved window:

WILLIAM MORRIS, LOANS

The man behind the desk was wearing a bowler hat. It was a shabby room, and Invernevis came to the point immediately. The man listened till he'd finished.

'How much do you require?'

'Five hundred.'

That didn't seem to shock him. 'What collateral do you have?' he asked.

'I beg your pardon?'

'Collateral — security.'

'I have an estate,' he informed the man.

'Do you have the title deeds?'

'Of course not. They're at my lawyers.'

The man had had clients like this before. Usually they were for small loans, women who'd spent money, lawyers who'd embezzled and wanted to make good before the police were brought in. Since the war he'd had more of this class in. At first they'd intimidated him, but he had something they needed.

'The rate will be twenty per cent, repayable over twenty months,' he stated.

'That's outrageous.' Invernevis complained. 'That's nearly three times the bank rate.'

'Then go and get it from the bank.'

'When can you give it to me?' Invernevis asked.

'There's paperwork,' the man said, opening an appointments book. 'Come back at nine in the morning.'

'I'm going home tonight. I need it now.'

'It'll take half an hour,' the man said as he rang the little brass bell for his clerk with the pen and ruled paper.

He took the cheque to his bank and drew a substantial sum in cash, then walked along Princes Street to Jenners. Every time he'd sold a painting he'd bought silk stockings for Maggie, but she must have a dozen pairs by now, so he walked round the counters, looking for something else.

'May I help you, sir?' an assistant came forward.

'I'm looking for a present for a lady.'

'Do you have anything in mind, sir?'

'Perhaps something to wear,' he said vaguely.

'Day or evening wear, sir?

'Perhaps evening wear.'

She took him up in an elevator to a floor of dummies wearing fine gowns, trailing stoles on their outstretched arms.

'I don't think this is quite what I want.'

'Perhaps night attire, sir?'

He knew by the slight change in her tone that she surmised he was looking for a present for a mistress. She led him through to the lingerie department. He stood studying a model in a silk nightdress, with ribbons at the bust, trying to see Maggie in it.

'Where are your perfumes?' he asked.

They returned to the ground floor. The assistant left him with an elegant woman who seemed to be in no hurry to make a sale. She kept bringing out golden bottles from small boxes, dabbing the scent on to the back of his hand for his appreciation, then cleansing his skin for the next one. He sniffed, eyes closed, trying to match them to Maggie.

The assistant had an atomizer now. She pressed the little black bulb and sprayed his hand.

'I like this one,' he said.

She showed him the cut crystal bottle in the shape of a swan.

'It's our last of this line, sir. French, of course. But we shan't get any more of it because of the war. It's called Reverie.' She pronounced it in the French mode. 'After the perfume is finished – and of course it will last a long time – the bottle is a beautiful little ornament.'

It was only after she'd wrapped it that she told him the price. He was taken aback but paid with a five pound note. He went back to his club for dinner, the speciality dish with the best bottle of claret, then asked the waiter to take a large brandy to the fire for him.

He hardly recognized the man slumped in the opposite chair, staring into the flames. Campbell of Jura had become so old-looking since his heir's death.

'How is Jock's wife?' Invernevis asked.

'She had a little girl months after he was killed. That saved her sanity. I also lost my son Ronald. He was with the Royal Fusiliers.'

'I'm so sorry,' Invernevis said.

'I'm here to see my lawyers. I'm turning the island over to my son Charles, now that Jock's gone. I doubt if he'll be able to hold on to it, but he's got more energy – and hope – than I have.'

Invernevis knew that the Campbells had had the island of Jura for a long time, and seemed as permanent as the paps themselves.

'What's this world coming to?' old Jura asked, turning bewildered eyes on Invernevis.

'Two large brandies,' Invernevis told the steward who had answered the bell by his chair.

* * *

Maggie liked to make the plum puddings well in advance, so that they could mature in the larder, but this year she was even earlier than usual. She had a pile of silver threepenny pieces beside the bowl of mixture and she wrapped them in little bits of paper before dropping them in. This pudding was going to be sent to Hector, and if she didn't stop there would be more pieces of silver than currants. She put one more in for luck, and this time she hoped he would share it with MacDougall, if it ever reached him.

When the four puddings were in the oven she sat down to a pot of tea, wondering how the Master was getting on in Edinburgh. He would have got a big price for the Millet painting. This time he would surely pay all the bills, and she would get what she needed for the house, though things were getting short because of the war. Now that he was away, she missed him coming through with his glass of whisky to talk, but hoped he wouldn't bring back any more silk stockings. When was she ever going to wear the ones she had upstairs?

Mildred was watching his face as they sat on the carpet in front of the fire in the Glenbranter drawing-room. He was staring into the flames with a strained look as if he were witnessing a battle in which his men were following.

'Don't look so sad, Johnnie.'

'I'm all right.'

She couldn't work out if it was fear, or a desire to get back among his men. She studied the engagement ring he'd given her in the summer when he'd been invalided home with pleurisy, as if she could foretell their future in the flicker of the fire in the circle of diamonds.

'It's a pity that things have been set back by the war,' he said. 'The old man's stopped work on our house. Not even he can sing for a bag of cement.'

'The house doesn't matter. It's us that matters.'

He only needed to turn to her and lay her on the carpet in

front of the fire and she would let him take her. But the coals had shifted, and the flames were now flaring in his spectacles. It frightened her and she took up the poker to subdue the fire.

'That's twice I've been out of action,' he said.

'You say it as if it's your fault. You should thank God it hasn't been more serious.'

She heard a clock strike deep in the eerie house which, she was now convinced, she would never live in.

18

It was the strangest Christmas that Alanna Richardson had ever spent. Festooned with holly cut from the wayside, the train was running as usual, and they had taken on board a group of Indians, the remnants of a cavalry unit from a shell attack. She was standing unravelling a turban with a bullet hole in· it as the train clattered through the darkness to the coast. The wearer was sitting so still in the bunk in the swaying carriage, smiling serenely, his hands folded, that Alanna was sure he was a prince used to sitting up on an elephant. The yellow combs from the turban were in her mouth, and as she unwound the last length of blood-stained cloth long fine dark hair like a woman's tumbled down over his shoulders.

It was incredible: the piece of shrapnel seemed to have passed through the side of his head, leaving a hole, but without affecting him. When she'd dressed it he turned and salaamed her, his right palm on his forehead. She couldn't get back down the train for other Indians, down on their knees, talking to themselves in their strange language.

'Do they hold Christmas?' she asked another nurse as she avoided a paper lantern swinging from the roof.

'They're jolly well going to have to, after all the work we've put in.'

As the nurses went round giving out gifts, one of them was stopped by an Indian.

'Sing?' he said eagerly, holding up a finger.

She had a hand over her mouth, holding back her laughter as he gave a version of 'Bonnie Dundee'.

'Where on earth did you learn that?'

'From a Jock,' he said, beaming.

Some of the Indians had removed their tattered uniforms and were sitting naked.

'Don't tell me this is another custom,' the nurse said.

'I think they've got lice,' Alanna said, and helped to gather up their infested clothing. She was tired, but the men were opening their presents, and soon the speeding train was filled with the aromas of cigars and cigarettes. But they were wounded and they had to settle down to sleep. Alanna went along the swaying train to her compartment, her hands out on either side like a sleepwalker. She washed her face in cold water in the canvas basin. At times like these she missed her London home, lying in a hot bath, her maid waiting with the big white warmed towel. But there was something so satisfying in this work.

As she lay down for a few minutes on the couch that converted to her bed she was thinking of Dochie MacDougall. Where was he, out there in the darkness as 1916 was coming to an end? Huddled in a trench somewhere on the western front, or perhaps lying under a wooden cross? But he wasn't the type to get killed; he was larger than life. She was due leave in the new year, and she was going to visit Freddie at Divisional Headquarters, though he said that it was no place for women. He'd know where the 8th Argylls were, and she would make him take her on a morale-boosting visit. The war was having a strange effect. Women were now free. Things would be easier for herself and Dochie. But she must seize the moment. She would find him, and as she lay on her couch in the swaying train she was burning for him.

The big man had a rope knotted round his waist and was leaning backwards, his gumboots sinking into the mud. Church bells from one of the few unshelled spires in the Somme began ringing out Christmas morning, and at each peal he strained. Hector had seen him as anchorman on the tug of war at the Invernevis sports, laughing as he walked backwards, pulling the half dozen men in the opposing team with him, but this was different: the other end of the rope was attached to the horse in the shell hole. Sam couldn't bear the pitiful sounds in the audible mud. The bells swung again and MacDougall strained until the veins stood out blue on his forehead, but only the animal's head was showing now.

As the peals stopped someone cut the rope with a bayonet.

'You shouldn't have done that, you bastard!' MacDougall roared, lunging at the man. 'I could have saved it.'

'You did your best, didn't he, boys?' Hector said, restraining his friend. 'Come on or we won't get our Christmas dinner.'

The 51st Highland Division were at Courcelette in the churned Somme, having taken over a sector of the line captured by the Canadians. The gumboots had caused weals on their thighs under their kilts, so six thousand pairs of trousers had been issued. But that only made it more awkward, with the constant dysentery. The ground was so sodden that trenches caved in as soon as they were dug, so the front and support line troops lived in the shell-holes.

The horse's nostrils were bubbling under the mud as the men left it. MacDougall was depressed because for once his strength had failed him.

'If I don't get out of this place, I'll go mad,' he told Hector and Sam.

The battalion no longer used Gaelic in conversation, and MacDougall had not sung since before the macabre ceilidh underground at Beaumont Hamel.

The horse that had sunk under the mud had been helping to bring up gun ammunition, but it was the conditions, not the Germans they were fighting. It seemed to have been raining for weeks. The buses which were to take them to Wolfe Huts after their night operation had stuck in the mud, and they were walking. The firmer ground Sam was treading on turned into the chest of a dead man. The whole Somme battlefield was a huge swamp-like cemetery in which corpses kept coming to the surface and sinking again in a ghastly mockery of resurrection.

'Form up in a column!' a voice ordered.

'Christ, he's not back!' MacDougall said.

They turned to see Captain Lauder sitting up on a white horse, reining his way among the shell holes as if waltzing his animal.

'A column?' MacDougall said. 'You can hardly walk in these fucking boots, never mind in a straight line.'

'Form up, I said!'

The Captain's cane touched the big man's shoulder as he rode past.

The men tried to form in behind the flanks of the white horse. Hector was remembering when they'd marched together at the camp at Dunoon through the hedgerows. What would he give for the scent of a flower, instead of the stench of death? Men were swaying in the column as if they were sleepwalking, and all the time the mud was sucking, sucking, as if it was a living creature with so many mouths. Small slopes had become mountains. They slithered back, and some of them were crying with the pain of their feet when they began the climb again.

'Sing one of my father's songs!' Lauder shouted.

'Fuck your father!'

He pulled up and turned in the saddle, his palm resting on the horse's back.

'Who said that?'

He was looking down at the rows of sullen unshaven faces. His eyes met the big man's who'd been nothing but trouble since Dunoon, but he knew he wasn't going to get an admission.

'March on!'

'That bastard's going to get it yet,' MacDougall vowed.

Hector was frightened by the look of the big man. He was wearing a sheepskin waistcoat tied with a length of rope and he looked like an animal, his face thin, eyes bright, the face of a wolf.

'March on!'

Sleet was now falling. It settled as a mantle round the men's shoulders. The soldier in front of MacDougall was swaying as if he was beginning to sleep on his feet. The big man caught him before he fell over. Stragglers supported each other, coated in mud from head to foot, their feet swollen into the gumboots. Some lay down to sleep by the road and would never get up again.

Sam's feet were aching, but the years of walking behind a plough in the rain helped. He was carrying Hector's pipe-box for him. When they reached the billets they took their Christmas dinner in a shell hole, using empty ammunition boxes with a board laid across them for a table. Maggie's Christmas pudding was in the centre, bashed after its long journey. They were cooking their own meal, a tin of meat and vegetables warmed on a small tin of solidified alcohol, the same fare they'd been eating for weeks because the men were too weak to carry portable hot-food containers over a mile of slime and shell-craters. They spooned their food noisily, as if this was the first time they'd tasted it. Then Hector shared out the pudding with MacDougall and Sam.

When MacDougall spat out the hard bit of fruit on his palm it turned into a silver threepenny.

'You can't spend them out here,' he complained.

'It's for luck,' Hector explained.

'Some fucking luck out here,' the big man said, but put the coin into his pocket.

Sam got the next one, and put it carefully into his cigarette tin. They ate the whole pudding, and then someone came round with a can of tea. MacDougall was thinking of the old folks. The old woman always killed a hen for Christmas. He would have to write to the old man, but he hadn't got anything to say, so he just made up things, saying it was nice countryside.

The little metal Christmas boxes from the king and queen were distributed, the second Hector had had. MacDougall tipped the cigarettes into his pocket and threw the box into the mud.

'You're wanted at the mess,' Pipe Major Lawrie came to tell Hector.

'What the hell for?'

'To play for their Christmas dinner.'

'I thought this was supposed to be a rest day.'

'I'd get moving if I were you. You'll probably get a dram.'

He used his spoon to try to scrape the mud from the pleats of his kilt and gave his boots a wipe with his sleeve. A motor cycle had been sent to convey him. He crouched in the sidecar, clutching his pipe box as the driver swerved and jolted among the shell holes. What would Maggie say if she could see him now? He'd sent her a wee bottle of perfume for her Christmas, all he could get.

He couldn't believe his eyes. The mess hut had been decorated, and there was actually holly on the king's picture in a landscape where you couldn't even find a blade of grass. Wood was blazing in the stove. On the long table glasses sparkled among the silver, and the orderlies had spotless white jackets and napkins over their arms. He piped in the officers in their mess jackets and trews, as if there were no war going on. The commanding officer, Colonel Robin Campbell, said grace, giving thanks for the victory behind them and the fare to come.

A tureen of tomato soup was brought in.

Hector could feel the heat and taste of it in his mouth as he stood with his pipes in the crook of his arm. Two large turkeys from a farm behind the line were borne in on salvers and carved. Hector watched the thick white slices fall from the knife. He was angry at what they were getting, considering the muck the men in the trenches were having to live on. He watched the roast potatoes being piled on the plates, the cranberry sauce being spooned out. It was as good as the boss got back home. If he had to stand and watch them eating he would go mad. He closed his eyes, but he could smell the food, and kept shifting from boot to boot.

He heard the sound of an engine, then the door opened. It was like a vision. A woman was standing in a blue cape over a white garment down to her ankles, with a red cross on her breasts. It was Alanna Richardson.

'The ambulance train's in Albert for a couple of hours and I just had to see you all,' she told them.

They left their hot feast and crowded round for the privilege of lifting her wet cloak from her shoulders and kissing her. Colonel Campbell led her on his arm to his own chair. They said grace again for her, blessing her coming, 'like an angel,' the Colonel said. A waiter brought a warmed plate for her. The breast of the turkey was carved in delicate slices, the cranberry sauce tapped on to the crested lip of her plate with a silver spoon. Wine was poured for her. But she hardly got the chance to enjoy her dinner because she was talking so much, answering their questions, explaining about the ambulance train, reminiscing about that camp in the summer before the war. Even Hector forgot his hunger and felt the warmth and light that this beautiful woman had brought into the hut in the cold miles of mud. Every man in that room would have given up his rank and his decorations to lie with her for an hour, not for the sex, but for the consolation of her arms around him.

There was Scotch woodcock on toast, followed by cheese, and jars of caviare from Fortnum & Mason. A tangerine from a piled bowl was touched by an elbow and rolled off the table. Hector helped it on his way with his brogue so that he could get it later, but one of the officers stooped to retrieve it. Then a champagne cork made the corrugated iron roof of the hut ring, and Alanna Richardson's glass was full of froth as they toasted her. This was followed by whisky. Kilberry would never have left a piper without a dram, Hector was thinking bitterly.

'Can you play 'Silent Night'?' the Colonel asked him.

He did his best, and Alanna Richardson turned her chair round to sit gazing at him, her face resting on her hand. There was silence after he stopped.

'What would you like?' the Colonel asked, as if she could have anything in the world at that moment.

'I would like 'The Bens of Jura'.'

As Hector played it they could see the tears in her eyes for the dying Highland troops she had comforted, for Jock Campbell for whom each lurch of the train had been an agony because of the bayonet wound in his side, but who never showed it to the end.

They asked Hector to play 'Old Lang Syne' and they stood with their arms crossed, hands linked, above the littered walnut shells, the candied fruit of their feast.

'I must thank the piper,' Alanna told the Colonel. 'We met at the camp at Dunoon,' she reminded Hector as she shook his hand. 'You were with Dochie MacDougall.'

'He's my best friend, ma'am.'

'He told me. Tell him I'm here,' she whispered. 'I'll try to delay the train.'

On the way back Hector told the motorcyclist to go faster.

'I'll land in a shell hole and we'll both drown!' the driver yelled as his lamp snaked over the mud.

'Dochie! Dochie!' he shouted as he stumbled across men's legs in the waterlogged trench.

'I hope you've brought back a drink,' the big man said morosely from under the dripping sack that was over his head in the hole he was squatting in.

'I've seen Mrs Richardson,' Hector said.

'Fucking liar.' He had his friend by the lapels of his greatcoat. 'Don't you make a joke about that.'

'I'm telling you. She came into the mess. Her train's at Albert. Hey, wait!'

But MacDougall had gone.

Even in daylight men got lost in this wilderness of mud. Runners with life-and-death dispatches went round and round until they fell exhausted, drowning in shell-holes. In the dawn platoons failed to return, though they hadn't been taken prisoner. But instinctively MacDougall turned south-east. He splashed through the mud, swerving to avoid shell holes he couldn't see. He was fired at but he kept on running because he knew the bullets couldn't touch him. At Invernevis he would lap every man in the race several times, making the crowd laugh. He had a stitch in his side, but he kept on running, stumbling over the dark landscape. He could see the shapes of the transport moving with their unlit lamps on the road to Albert. Now he was running backwards along the shell-pocked road, his arms out to the lorries. One of them braked.

'If you're a deserter, mate, I'd advise you to get the hell out of here,' the driver told him. 'The place is thick with military police.'

Then he felt the bayonet in his ribs as the big man reached through the window.

'You're going to the railway station,' MacDougall advised him as he climbed in.

The driver kept his eyes on the road without saying anything because he could smell the desperation of the man beside him. They were moving through bomb-shattered streets now.

'This is as far as I can get,' he told his passenger.

MacDougall ran past the broken spire of the basilica with its hanging golden Virgin. He leapt blocks of masonry that the shelling had scattered and upset a hand-cart being pulled by an old woman who shouted curses after him. He was jumping over the rails, among wagons with war supplies. He ran the length of the train, rubbing the rain-streaked windows with his sleeve, but there were rows and rows of empty seats.

Then he saw a row of lights on a siding and leapt across the rails. But the lights were beginning to move, and he was running between the rails now. A figure was leaning out of a window, waving and shouting, but he couldn't hear for the hiss of steam. As the train clattered away with its wounded via Amiens to Boulogne he lunged at it, catching metal, gritting his teeth, digging in his boots by the heels as if trying to drag it back, but it gave a shudder and he was dropped. As he saw its tail lamp disappear he lay on the sharp cinders, but the pain was all inside him.

He didn't care what happened on the way back. A woman came and took his arm under the shelled basilica, but he pushed her away roughly. He was thinking of the train speeding through the dark countryside, out of this mud, this filth. As he was trudging along the road in the driving rain a car braked behind him. Captain Lauder had escorted Alanna Richardson to the station in the Colonel's vehicle. He wound down the window.

'This is desertion,' he said.

MacDougall turned and looked at him with wild eyes before veering away into the night like an animal.

The blind girl sat beside Mildred Thomson at the hospital switchboard. Somehow she knew where to put the plugs in and was always cheerful to the caller, even when they were going to receive bad news about a loved one. Because she lived alone in a hostel Mildred had invited the girl home for Christmas dinner. The plum pudding had been set on fire and consumed, and now they were sitting round the candles. The blind girl had her hands pressed down on the dark wood.

'What are you doing, Alice?' Mildred asked, intrigued.

'Usually I can feel the vibrations from the guns.'

'What guns?' Mr Thomson asked.

'The guns across in France.'

They watched her as she pressed her hands on the dark wood, as if about to summon a spirit. But the guns of the western front weren't speaking through her tonight.

'It's gone quiet because it's Christmas,' she explained. 'Perhaps they'll stop firing for good. Peace and goodwill among men from now on.'

'I doubt that,' Mildred said. She was thinking of Johnnie out there and wishing that they'd got married.

Harry Lauder was rehearsing his song as he shaved in his London hotel room, his elbows swinging as the blade scraped on his throat. The revue *Three Cheers* was a sell-out at the Shaftesbury Theatre because of his new song 'The Laddies who Fought and Won'. It sent the audience into raptures, especially at the end of the song when a company of Scots Guards in full uniform marched on to the stage. The secret of its success was that he was thinking of his son John and the rest of the 51st Highland Division as he sang, willing their safety. He had always liked reading about himself but now he dreaded buying a newspaper because of the long lists of casualties, some of whom had been at Cambridge with his boy.

It was New Year's Day and his wife was up in Scotland, celebrating with her own folks. He cleaned the razor blade and folded it back into the handle, then went next door to dress. He would take it easy today before the evening's performance. He heard the doorbell as he slipped the links through his cuff sleeves. There was a knock. The maid was standing there with the telegram on a silver tray and without touching it he knew what it was. She was watching him sympathetically as if she already knew the content. He took it off the tray and she closed the door.

He propped it on the dressing-table, against the mirror. He

knew that pale official envelope represented the death of his dream.

Captain John Lauder killed in action.

Then he noticed the Dunoon postmark. His place was with Nance, and the revue would have to be cancelled though it was a full house again tonight. Throughout the day a succession of visitors called to offer their condolences, and before midnight the taxi came to take him to the midnight mail train north.

It took them some time to find him in the morning mist. Captain Lauder was lying face-down in the mud, a red stain on his back. Hector pulled down his kilt before taking his ankles and swinging him on to the stretcher. Then he noticed the spectacles lying in the mud, and on an impulse he folded them and put them into his pocket.

'Let's get to hell out of here in case the sniper gets us too,' the other bearer said.

But it wasn't the thought of a sniper that was frightening Hector as he stumbled back with his load, the strap of the stretcher round his neck like a halter. That part of the line had been quiet for days, as if the snipers were taking the festive season off.

The doctor confirmed that Lauder was dead, and told them to get him ready for burial because the rats were bad. Hector went to the elephant shelter for his pipes. MacDougall was cleaning his rifle.

'So he got it at last,' he said with grim satisfaction.

Hector was looking at the gun, wondering if it had been fired recently. There was a strange look of satisfaction in the big man's eyes, the same look he'd seen that day under the ground among the dead at Beaumont Hamel.

'What was he doing out at that hour of the morning?' MacDougall said contemptuously. 'He was probably a spy.'

'He wasn't as bad as all that,' Hector said. 'It was just that he hadn't the experience in handling men.'

'Oh, he knew how to handle men all right,' MacDougall said vehemently. 'As if they were dirt. He thought having a big house meant that you had to treat people like that. Invernevis doesn't.'

'That's true,' Hector conceded.

'And Captain Campbell of Jura didn't. No, I'm glad the bastard's gone.'

For the first time in his life Hector was frightened of the big man with his thin face and burning eyes.

'Don't go making a tune for that one, unless I can fucking well dance to it,' MacDougall said, rolling a cigarette.

That afternoon Hector went with Captain Lauder's body to the gentle slope at Ovillers where there were already graves. As he adjusted his pipes he could see the golden Virgin hanging from the steeple at Albert over the hill, the infant in her arms. They said that when she fell the war would be over. Some of the men actually prayed for it to happen. He had his eyes on the statue in the fading light as he played 'The Flowers of the Forest' at the grave.

He'd helped to carry and bury so many men now that he felt immune himself, but he wanted out of this landscape that held you by the ankles, pulling you under. He followed the officers back to the billets. They were wrapped in their greatcoats, each with his own thoughts and regrets about Lauder, because they'd never really accepted him in the mess, even when it was only a shelter in a trench in France. He hadn't been the kind of man Hector could have made a tune for, but he'd always felt there was some good in Lauder, though he daren't say that to MacDougall.

'What time is it?' Mildred Thomson asked when the maid opened the curtains.

'It's gone ten, miss.'

She had stayed up till after midnight to see in the New Year, though it hadn't been the same without Johnnie. She had had this dream: they were at Glenbranter, becalmed in a boat on Loch Eck, making love.

'Thank you, Effie.'

There was a knock on the door, and her father came in in his dressing-gown. She knew he was the bearer of bad news even before he sat on the edge of her bed, holding her hand.

'Where did it happen?' she asked. Her tears were those of pride, because he'd died fighting, the way he'd wanted.

'On the Somme,' her father said. 'It was a sniper.'

Oh no, it couldn't have been. It had to be in a battle.

'But how?' she insisted.

'His father didn't have any details, except that it was in the early morning.'

There had to be some mistake. The blind girl said that there had been no fighting.

'I'm so sorry.'

'I'm going to work at the hospital,' she said.

'No, no, you must rest, after this.'

'I'm on duty today. I must go. The soldiers will be getting New Year calls.'

Her parents were worried about her composure as she came downstairs. She steadied herself as she went into the car, a lesson in abiding love. But she made the driver go via the War Office, and she banged on the door without getting an answer. As the car went through the silent streets of the capital she was even more convinced that there was something wrong about the story of Johnnie's death, and when she got to the switchboard she put through a call.

19

The postmistress leaned over the scales to watch the soldier coming up from the station. She couldn't see his face for the kitbag on his shoulder, and it was only when he turned to go down the brae instead of coming along main street that she recognized him. Now why was he back, when so many others weren't? Her mouth was grim as she turned towards the counter again to dispense the day's stamps.

Maggie had the back door open as she baked. She liked the spring because the place was so cheerful and busy. The shadow of a blackbird kept crossing the floor with nesting material in its beak as she kneaded the mixture.

'Hullo!' Before she could say anything Sam had lifted her off the floor and carried her round the table, the ball of dough still in her grip.

'You should have written to say you were coming,' she told him, close to tears. 'My, but you suit the kilt.' She stepped back to admire the hang of the dark tartan that the Master also wore. Sam had fine strong legs to carry it. 'Have you eaten anything?' she began to fuss.

'I could take something.'

She went out to the larder, bringing in the leg of lamb that had been supplied by the Home Farm, now that the bills were being paid again. She carved off thick slices, then put on the potatoes that the Master was to have for his lunch. When she had a plate set in front of him she sat watching him eating. Despite the uniform it was still the same man who'd come off the train – goodness, it was nearly three summers now – and had his supper at the same place. The trenches hadn't made him forget how to use a knife and fork, though he was very hungry, the quick way he cleared his plate. But as she carved more meat she saw his face looking older and sadder. While he was eating, the apple tart for the Master's lunch was warming in the oven, and she served him a big wedge with cream before she sat opposite him, holding his Argylls bonnet to her heart.

'How's Hector?'

'He's fine. He sends his love.'

'I wish he'd send a letter.'

'It's not easy, out there.'

She noticed that his hand was shaking a little as he drank his tea. This time he didn't need to ask permission to smoke. It smelt pungent, like a pot on fire. 'It's French,' he said.

She wondered if he'd got them from a woman. But why would he have come all this way when he should have gone home to his mother? She'd never really given him up and had known instinctively that he would come back, though she'd never dared to dwell on it. The past was the past and here he was, ready for more tea.

'Have long have you got?' she dared to ask.

'A week. But one day's gone already, getting here.'

Obviously he expected to stay, but this put her in an awkward position. It wouldn't be any holiday for him, going back up to the place above the stables and, anyway, the room must be very damp. But if she let him stay in the house it would have to be Hector's room, up on the top floor with her, and the Master might not be pleased.

'How's the boss?' he asked, as if reading her thoughts.

Since he'd come all this way he was entitled to her confidences. 'I expect Hector told you he was drinking heavily.'

'Is he still on it?'

'It's an awful job,' she said, shaking her head. 'If he hadn't got the money from selling paintings he would have had to stop it, but it's been cases of whisky coming off the train.'

He could see how painful the subject was to her. Maybe he'd made a mistake that night, when he'd seen them through the window. The boss was probably drunk and she'd been trying to get him to bed. What a great pity he hadn't stayed longer to see. He would still have had to go to the war, with the conscription, but he would have had a little more time with her.

'Has there been a lot of fighting?' she wanted to know.

'It was quite bad, in the winter, but we've had a rest recently.'
She could see by the look in his eyes that he didn't want to speak about it. 'You'd better go through and see him.'

But first Sam gave her the present he'd brought back for her, a little porcelain lamb wrapped in tissue paper.

'It's lovely,' she said as she stood it on the palm of her hand.

Invernevis shook hands. He was impressed by his former coachman's bearing in uniform, and he was also eager to hear the war news he couldn't get from the papers. He made Sam sit down, and gave him a cigarette while he heard about Beaumont Hamel. Sam described the huge mine, the subterranean house of the dead. Invernevis listened, engrossed and enthralled.

'What's the mood of the 8th Argylls?'

'Good, sir, now that we've got that awful winter behind us. Courcelette was hellish.'

'That's where Captain Lauder was killed,' Invernevis said. 'How did it happen?'

'They say it was a sniper,' Sam said.

Though Invernevis sensed that there was more to it, he left it at that. He had to admit that he'd never really liked Lauder, who hadn't belonged with the battalion.

'I hope you'll come back to work here when it's over,' he said. 'Now you must stay and have a good holiday.' As he spoke he was opening a drawer. He put an envelope in front of Sam. 'These are the wages I owed you when you went away. I didn't know where to post them on to.'

'That's very good of you, sir.'

He got a great welcome in the servants' hall at supper, and the maids insisted on treating him like an officer. One of them even curtseyed before she put the cutlery in front of him. He wished he was out of his uniform, but he didn't have any other clothes. Hector's bedroom was two doors from Maggie's. He lay looking at the moon on the skylight. War had made him sleepless, nervous as he'd never been before. He couldn't forget that July night of bombardment on the Somme when the shells had filled Mametz Valley with sickening, blinding gas. He smoked till he'd finished the packet of French cigarettes, then started on the Woodbines he'd bought in Glasgow. He shouldn't have come to Invernevis. He'd never forgotten Maggie in the trenches, but coming back and seeing her unchanged had made his love for her even stronger. He couldn't bear the prospect of going away, even though he still had five days left. He wanted to go along the passage and get into bed with her, his arms round her for the comfort.

During the day he went up to the village so as not to get in her way. When he went into the store Munro leaned over the counter to shake his hand, refusing to take his money for the cigarettes, and the women patted him on the back and asked about their men. He tried to make the news as good as possible. The children who'd shouted names after the gig and given him the white feathers now clustered round him and offered him sweets as they asked him about their fathers.

In the evening after dinner he and Maggie went for a walk, usually by the same way, down to the loch where they sat on the rocks. He spoke about his past life in Buchan because he couldn't bear to talk about the mud of the trenches which he would have to return to.

'Three more nights,' he told her, as they walked home, arm in arm. They left the avenue to kiss among the trees, and he picked flowers for her.

Then it was two nights.

The cook had jumped from the ambulance train to pick Alanna Richardson a bunch of primroses from the bank beside the track. She arranged them in a dressings jar in her cubicle and sat with their perfume close to her face, staring out of the window as the countryside shunted past. Tonight there would be more wounded. It seemed to her that she had been on this train for many years, going round and round the same looped track. How many dying men had she held in her arms?

The only thought that kept her going was that she would see Dochie soon. He was the reason she'd gone to the officers' mess at Albert at Christmas time. She had tried to delay the hospital train until he reached her, but it was needed many miles away.

Each time she had leave due there was another big battle, with men calling out for help in the crowded train. But she would go and see Freddie at Divisional Headquarters and make him take her to the 8th Argylls. After all, if the Duke of Argyll could visit them, so could she.

The train jolted to a halt. At night that meant that a body was being removed, so as not to distress the others, but this bright morning the engine was drinking from a river and she sat staring at the bobbing ducks.

After their successful role in the battle of Arras the 51st Highland Division had retired to rest at the red-roofed hamlet of Monts-en-Ternois behind the lines. The orchards were in blossom, the woods in new leaf in perfect weather, and hens wandered the dusty lanes with their chicks. Tents were pitched in the undulating pastures, under the trees, and in the cool of the evening women appeared at the edge of the wood with flagons of wine in their arms like figures from a classical frieze as they called *'Ici! Ici!'* to *'le grand Ecossais'*. Spring had made MacDougall his old self after Courcelette. His soul as well as his feet had healed from the weals of winter, and when he emerged from the woods in the gloaming he glowed with good health:

'Aye, Hector, you'll have to come with me tomorrow night. There's a wee one that rides like a rabbit.'

A football match was arranged against the 5th Seaforths, and MacDougall was the centre forward. The officers of the 8th Argylls sat under the trees with their canes across their knees, cheering him on as he dribbled, knocking down big men till he came to the goal where the velocity of the ball in the keeper's stomach sent him back between the posts.

At an open concert a dozen soldiers arranged on an arc of benches played violins. Hector sat watching the writer Neil Munro, who was a guest of honour. The death of his son had been even more foolhardy than any of the actions of the characters in his Highland novels. The Lieutenant had gone behind the line to capture a German flag, and several of the NCOs had risked their own lives bringing back the body. Hector had played at his burial. Munro looked close to tears as he sat with the officers listening to the concert.

It was MacDougall's turn to perform. He sang a Gaelic love song, and his voice rang through the trees to the French women waiting in the foliage for the concert to finish. They only needed a few minutes with him and then they would sleep peacefully in their lonely beds.

Hector was missing Sam, who'd become like a brother to him. Though he didn't say much, he knew he was keen on Maggie. But he was hoping he wouldn't buy his sister a ring till it was all over, because you never knew the minute.

Most of the men slept out in the balmy weather. Hector and MacDougall had spread their blankets under the trees and they smoked late to keep away the mosquitos as the horses settled beside them.

'I wouldn't mind staying in this place for a while, the women are so good,' MacDougall said. 'Much warmer than the ones at home. It must be all the sun they get. The one I was with tonight's hoping her man won't come back from the war. She says I can move in to run the farm, and she'll teach me the lingo.'

'What about the old folks?' Hector asked.

'Aye, there's that. This war will be over by the summer, you'll see. I'll have a lot to do on the croft, and you'll be going back to the big house to waken the laird in the morning with your pipes.'

'I don't think so,' Hector said. It would be difficult, after what he'd seen. 'I think I'll try and get a job in Glasgow.'

'What about Maggie?'

'I suppose she'll marry Sam.'

'If she's any sense she will,' MacDougall said before he turned over to sleep, and during the night fruit ripened on the laden branches above them.

It was Sam's last night of leave.

Instead of going along the road above the river they climbed the hill to the standing stones by the Home Farm. It was a place

Maggie didn't like, because they used to say that people had been sacrificed there on the big flat stone. They went through the blackened circles of the tinkers' fires. She could see how tense Sam was as he struck a match on one of the pillars, holding the wavering flame to his mouth. He looked old, angry.

'I don't want to go back. It's terrible out there.'

'I don't want you to go either,' Maggie said gently, taking his hand. 'But you have to, or you'll get into trouble.'

He knew about the firing squads for deserters, though thank God he'd never been picked to serve on one. But sometimes as he squatted in the trenches, having to do his business in front of other men because there was no latrine, not even able to wipe himself, he thought that those who went that way were the lucky ones.

'We could go to Glasgow till it's all over. It would be all right then.'

'It'll be over soon, you'll see,' Maggie assured him. 'You'll come back with a medal.'

'Then we'll get married?'

'Yes, we'll get married.'

But that wasn't enough for him. He was pacing about.

'I need to take back a bit of you, to see me through.'

She put her hands up behind her head and removed the little Celtic silverwork cross that had been her mother's and which never left her neck. She made him sit down on the stone while she put it round his neck, tucking it inside his shirt.

'That will see you through,' she said.

But it wasn't enough. Another match spurted, and he was sucking on the cigarette as he sat looking down at the big white house across the river in the peace of the evening haze from its chimneys. He hadn't realized before how attached he was to the place, and would give anything to be going along that road to it for the first time, with Maggie waiting for him with that supper whose taste he'd never forgotten.

'I'm going to desert,' he said as he roamed among the stones.

'No, Sam. Don't do anything foolish,' she pleaded.

'I need something else to take back with me,' he said desperately.

'What do you mean?' she asked uneasily.

But he was pacing again. He slapped one of the pillars. The thought of leaving her was unbearable.

'Something else,' he repeated.

When he turned she was unbuttoning her blouse.

Tomorrow they moved on, back to war. MacDougall had gone into the wood for his last amorous encounter and Hector went up to the church. The old curé was hobbling among the perfumed flowers of his garden with a watering can in the evening of birdsong. Tomorrow would be another hot day.

'*Bonsoir*,' he nodded to Hector.

He pushed open the door of the little whitewashed church. A life-size statue of Christ was hanging in a corner, and the more devout soldiers had lit candles round his feet for wives and sweethearts. Hector lit a candle for Maggie and fixed it on the iron spike before dropping a franc into the box. Then he sat in the front pew. He hadn't come to pray, but to sit in peace. The birds had stopped singing outside, and the stained-glass windows were getting dark. He was looking at the haze of the candles. Tomorrow they would march away from this place which reminded him of home and where he'd been so happy.

The next day they moved by tactical trains to relieve the 4th Division in the sector of the Rouex chemical works just north of Arras, which had had nine assaults launched on it, but which had now been taken by the British.

It was clear that the Germans intended to re-take the sector because of their intense artillery bombardment directed by lookouts in the crows-nests of trees stripped of their spring foliage by the slipstream of shells. There were also many low-flying planes, but the Baron von Richthofen, whom Ludendorff said was worth as much as two divisions of German infantry because of his April tally of twenty-one kills, had flown home reluctantly on leave of absence from the front on the orders of the High Command.

In peaceful times barges drifted down the river Scarpe, wandering through swampy land to Rouex, where the chemical works lay conveniently beside the Arras-Douai railway. But the Germans had come swarming along the railway embankment to occupy the British trenches in the area, from which they launched a series of flank attacks, occupying the chemical works and the railway buildings, then tried to push southwards.

Captain MacTaggart gave the signal by firing his revolver and the company of the 8th Argylls left their trenches to rout the enemy at their backs. As the Captain was running his right hand and revolver were blown away by a piece of shell, but he kept going. He kept running even when a second shell took away an eye.

But the third shell stopped him. As Hector reached him with the stretcher the Captain's guts were showing, but he was still waving on the advance with the bloody stump of his right hand.

Realizing that the enemy had penetrated deeply into the British lines, Colonel Campbell, the Commanding Officer, led the counter-attack against the Germans north of the railway line. Captain Pollard threw rifle grenades into their shell-holes. As the Germans emerged, stumbling into the dawn, MacDougall rolled them over one by one as if they were rabbits. As he calmly fitted a new clip of rounds into his Lee Enfield one German was getting away. MacDougall raised his rifle, shot the man in the foot, turned him over head over heels, then shot away the strap of his helmet before putting the next bullet into his head.

But there was now heavy rifle fire on the other side of the railway, and Colonel Campbell led a party up the embankment. He could see a group of Germans west of the chemical works being engaged by the 6th Seaforths from their front and from their left flank with rifle fire. The Colonel sent his Adjutant to tell the Seaforths to deliver a frontal attack while he enfiladed the Germans from the embankment. The tactic was successful, though a bullet went through Captain Pollard's heart and one narrowly missed the Colonel as it ricocheted off the railway line he was lying across. His party then joined the Seaforths and advanced through the chemical works, digging themselves in east of it.

MacDougall was leaning on the remains of a wall, having a smoke in the lull in the fighting.

'By Christ, Colonel Campbell showed them!' MacDougall said.

'So did you,' Hector said. 'You must have shot twenty of them across there.'

'Aye, and I've got a lot more of the bastards to get, to make up for Captain MacTaggart,' he vowed. 'He was a fine man, like Jura.'

A shell came screaming and what was left of the walls was breaking up around them. When the dust began to clear Hector felt something against his boots. He looked down and saw MacDougall's head, the glowing cigarette still between the teeth of his grinning mouth. 'No! No!' Hector picked up the head, hugging it to his chest as he searched frantically for the body to fit it back on to. 'Help me! For Jesus' sake help me!'

'Leave it!' the officer shouted.

But Hector was still staggering around with the head among the rubble.

'There are wounded men out there that need stretchers!' an officer shouted, and when Hector didn't stop howling he took the back of his hand hard across his mouth.

Peigi bheag na biorraide, who had been dozing in her chair, suddenly woke up.

'*Dèan àite dha aig an teine*,' ('Make room for him at the fire,') she told the old man opposite her.

'You've been dreaming, that's all, *a Pheigi bheag*,' he told her.

Then he felt the warm breeze on the back of his neck, though the door and the window to the west were closed. He shifted his chair and she began to cackle.

He looked at his wife sadly then shook his head. Their daughter Mildred was kneeling on the carpet of their London drawing-room, pasting another cutting into her scrapbook. It had been sent that morning from the agency and had appeared in an

American paper. She pasted it in lovingly, smoothing out the creases. That made ninety-eight cuttings to date.

'It's so strange, how different they are.'

Her parents looked at each other. They'd had this conversation before.

'This one says: Harry's Brave Son Shot on New Year's Eve. Other papers give every date from Christmas to the New Year.' She turned a page. 'Listen to this: Harry Lauder's son was dancing a jig on the top of his trench when he was hit by a sniper. They make him sound like a fool.'

'You're only torturing yourself, darling,' her mother pleaded. 'You should get out more with your friends.'

'Why don't we all go out to dinner tomorrow night at the Savoy?' her father suggested eagerly.

But she wasn't listening. She was engrossed in her scrapbook again, like a child. She needed to know how he died, because all those stories couldn't be true. But why were they all so different? She was his fiancée and had a right to know. She'd written to the War Office, but had got the brief reply that he had been 'killed in action by a sniper in the early morning'. She'd written to the commanding officer of the 8th Argylls in France, and he'd replied with an expression of: ' . . . the deepest sympathy of all the officers. Captain Lauder was killed by a sniper in the early morning.' There was no mention of what he'd been doing. Why couldn't she get a story she could trust?

She thought of enlisting as a nurse so that she could get out to France to see the place where he'd been killed. If she could stand on the spot, she would understand how he had died. 'I'm tired,' she said. I think I'll go to bed early.'

They kissed her good night, and she took the scrapbook with her. In the letter she'd asked Colonel Campbell for a memento of Johnnie, and he'd sent a piece of his kilt. It was pinned to the wall above her bed. Before she put the light out she knelt on the bed and kissed the dark tartan. She knew now that she would never marry or have a lover. Because she hadn't given herself to him at Glenbranter, when there had been so many opportunities she regretted so much now, she would keep herself for him.

20

Maggie had gone through to Stirling to see Sam off. The platform was crowded with soldiers going back, their arms round their wives and children. Sam was holding her hand so tightly that it was hurting, but she didn't say anything because there was far more pain in her heart. Women were crying around her, and a child was clinging to an Argylls kilt. She was looking at Sam's boots because she couldn't bear to look at his face. He'd tried to polish them, but they were so misshapen, down at the heel, with mud ingrained in their seams.

The train that came in from the north was crowded with troops, standing room only. The guard came along the platform, unlocking the doors, but no-one got off. Sam tried to stay by the door, but other men were pushing to say goodbye to their women. Maggie reached up for his hand, but the guard came along, twisting a big T-shaped key in the doors.

A whistle sounded and the train began to move. Some of the women began running with it. Maggie tried to keep up with Sam's carriage in the crowd, but it was going away from her, and there were waving arms at all the windows.

She was on the moor above the house, picking sphagnum moss at the edge of the bog because she'd read that it was needed for the soldiers' wounds. A curlew was crying as she went back down to the house with the basket over her arm. It was a lovely evening, but she was depressed because she was frightened that he was going to desert. That was why they must have locked the doors; men were desperate enough to jump from the train. Would she hear a knock at the back door one night, to see him standing there? But she knew that he would be back in France by now.

She was making up a parcel for Sam with cigarettes and a cake she'd baked for him when Invernevis appeared in the kitchen with a bottle of Mackinlay's and two glasses. At least it was better than him drinking alone through in the library. He'd been so drunk the night she came back from Stirling.

Tonight he had something special for her. He laid the little black box on the table.

'I want you to have that, Maggie.'

She hesitated, then opened it. A pearl-and-diamond pendant glittered in satin.

'I can't, sir.'

'Do take it, Maggie. It belonged to my wife.'

He tipped it from the box and pinned it to her black dress at the neck with the little gold safety pin on the chain.

'It looks very nice on you, Maggie.'

'Oh, but it's too much, sir,' she said as she went to the mirror. The pearls were arranged in a little crown.

'I want you to have it because of all you've done for me.'

He poured two glasses of whisky and sat down.

She was tired and wanted to go to bed, but he kept talking, and every now and then she took a sip of whisky and touched the pendant at her throat.

The level went down and down in the bottle and he became more and more garrulous. At midnight the cat was at the door, wanting out into the moonlight, and the bottle was empty. He was dozing, his elbow keeping slipping from the table. She tried to get him up out of the chair, but he was such a weight. She got his arm round her neck and had to practically drag him through the passage to the front hall. She dreaded the stairs because of his game leg, and he kept lunging at the banister. She was frightened he was going to go head-first through the stained-glass window on the landing.

She got him across his bed, and found matches in his pocket to light the lamp. She was used to undressing him by now.

When Harry Lauder crossed the Channel to visit the troops he had with him a portable piano and thousands of packets of cigarettes. The cigarettes were all gone within a few hours of landing, in the base hospital at Boulogne, a former casino where men crawled to hear him sing. But he carried the portable piano to the front. On an early summer evening at Arras five thousand Scottish troops assembled in an amphitheatre of ruins in the twilight. Aeroplanes circulated overhead to make sure that he wasn't interrupted by the Red Baron, now back from his leave of absence, eager to order another miniature silver cup from Berlin as his trophies of war accumulated as a Richthofen family heirloom.

An officer played the portable piano as Harry swaggered on the makeshift platform, singing 'The Laddies Who Fought and Won', the hit song of the revue he'd been in when he'd received word of his son's death. He was close to tears as he sang it to the 51st Highland Division, and the men joined in the chorus, momentarily interrupted by a shell passing overhead. They kept calling out for requests.

'I'm frae Aberfeldy, Harry — for God's sake sing us 'The Wee House 'mang the Heather'!'

The men swayed around Hector as they sang, but he sat silent. He was thinking of MacDougall. He'd been so upset over his death that he couldn't play at his funeral, which was all over in a few minutes anyway, a mound of mud, a wooden cross for someone who'd had so much life. Maybe in time he could make a tune for him. But he smiled to think at the number of wee MacDougalls that must have been left behind in France. The Frenchies returning from the war would find that they had strapping sons.

After a dozen songs it was dark, but Harry was still singing requests, and they kept on cheering him after he'd left the platform. Sam and Hector had a last smoke before turning in. Hector was pleased with the news that Sam was going to marry his sister, though it would change things for him.

'I've been thinking,' he said to Sam. 'One of us should ask for a transfer.'

'Why?'

'Because the Highland Division's been in the thick of it. If MacDougall could get it, any of us can. We don't know where we're off to next. If we were in different regiments it would give Maggie a chance.'

Sam could see the sense in the idea.

'You can't leave the Argylls,' he said. 'They'll never let a piper go — especially not one like you. I'll make the move.'

Then someone was calling for Piper Macdonald.

'If I've to pipe in the mess at this hour I'm not going, especially if it's a dinner for Harry Lauder,' Hector said resolutely.

'You won't need your pipes,' the officer said.

He was told to wait in a small room off the mess. Then the door opened and Harry Lauder came in, shaking his hand. He gave Hector a packet of cigarettes from his sporran.

'Did you enjoy the concert?' the comedian asked.

'Aye, it was fine,' Hector said, ill at ease. What the hell was this all about?

'Sit down,' Lauder said, and drew up a chair beside him. 'I'm told that you were one of the men on the stretcher that lifted my boy at Courcelette.'

Hector nodded.

'Describe to me how he died.'

'What do you mean? I wasn't there,' Hector said defensively.

Lauder put a steadying hand on his knee. 'Now I know it's upsetting, son, losing an officer, but try and tell me.'

Here was a man who half an hour before was singing so confidently to all those men, yet his hands were trembling now, and his eyes looked pathetic.

'When I got there he was dead.'

'Where had he been shot?'

'In the back.'

'How did you know that?'

Hector didn't like Lauder's tone, but he had asked, hadn't he? 'You get to know when a person gets it in the back,' he explained, 'the way the blood goes.'

The comedian's face changed momentarily.

'Was there a lot of shooting at that time in the morning?'

He was tired of this questioning. What did it matter now? Lauder was gone and so was MacDougall. So many were dead who had been at Courcelette. Why open up an old wound? He wanted to forget the eerie silence that morning when he reached

Lauder's body. He wasn't the only one who'd been shot by his own men, if that was what had happened.

'Oh aye, a lot of shooting,' Hector said. 'There was a sniper working, you see.'

'How do you know that?' Lauder asked eagerly.

'Because I heard him, and a bullet hit a tree when we were carrying the Captain away.'

He'd made up the story to make the comedian go away, but he wasn't moving.

'My boy was a popular officer.'

The way Lauder put it, Hector wasn't sure if it was a question or a statement. Perhaps it was intended to be neither, a kind of no-man's-land statement.

'He's missed,' Hector said. 'I kept something for you.' He went to his pipe case and brought across the spectacles with the gold frames, one of the lenses cracked.

Harry Lauder clutched them to his chest. Then he stood up and tipped a handful of money from his sporran. The man with a worldwide reputation for meanness handed Hector a sovereign.

'Get yourself something when you're in town again, laddie.'

Hector took the money because he'd earned it.

Alanna Richardson had at last reached London. She hadn't even taken her cloak off. She was sitting in the hall, waiting. She'd telephoned her husband, who was across from Divisional Headquarters in France for consultations with the War Office, and the secretary said he was on his way home. She felt guilty as she sat waiting. The ambulance train would be running again tonight, away from some new battle towards the coast, but men would die before they reached it.

When she heard the throb of the engine outside she went to meet him.

'You should have telegraphed that you were coming. Your room won't be ready,' he said, irritated.

'I didn't know I was getting away till last night, and there was no time to let you know,' she told him as she followed him into the drawing-room. It seemed so big and unfriendly after her snug cubicle on the train.

'Will you take sherry?' he asked, as if living in France might have changed her tastes.

She took a glass of sherry while he had his whisky.

'How's the work going?'

'It's tiring, but worthwhile,' she said, sitting beside him on the sofa. She knew that if she rushed it it would seem suspicious.

'You all do a lot of good work,' he said wearily. 'I know that Haig's most appreciative.'

'Will it be over soon?' she asked with the ease of one entitled to secret information. Dying soldiers had whispered unrepeatable things to her.

'I doubt it,' he said into his glass.

'Well, I've got a week and I'm going to enjoy myself,' she said gaily. 'Will you take me to the Savoy tonight?'

'If I can get a table.'

'How is your work going?' she then asked.

'It's only administration.'

'How are the brave lads?'

'Which brave lads?'

'Your Division, the 51st?'

He was pleased with the enquiry. 'They acquitted themselves very well at Arras.'

'And the 8th Argylls? I keep thinking about Jock Campbell.'

'They're having a good war. Campbell who's in command is a particularly good man.'

'You mean Kilberry?' she said, taking her time.

'He went home a long time ago. There are rather a lot of Campbells in the Argylls,' he said with a smile.

She got up and went to his silver cigarette box. She fumbled for a match, striking it on the fluted dish. She was trembling, as if with the expectation of love.

'You know, sometimes I lie awake thinking of that last camp at Dunoon. It was all so happy, with Jura and the sports. Do you remember that big man who tossed the caber when the others couldn't?'

'That was the ghillie you had at Invernevis,' he said.

She was going to have to be careful.

'Ah, yes, Macdonald. The one who taught me to cast.'

'MacDougall,' he corrected her.

'Was that his name? I wonder what happened to him.'

She was standing behind the sofa, smoking quickly.

'He was killed.'

'What?' She didn't recognize her own voice.

'I saw a report on him. He was being recommended for a Military Medal because of his bravery at Arras. That's where he got it. It's a great loss because he was a natural leader.'

She hadn't noticed that the cigarette had dropped from her fingers and was burning the Chinese carpet he was so proud of. She picked it up and snuffed it slowly, feeling the fire.

'I think I'll go for a bath, after my journey,' she said weakly.

'Will I still book the Savoy?' he called after her.

But she was already climbing the staircase, holding on to the banister with both hands. She looked into her bedroom, with the tight bolster at the four poster where he'd taken her one afternoon with orgasms that made her glow and glide long after he'd gone.

She went next door, sitting on the edge of the big bath in which she'd soaped him that afternoon when his yelling had sunk into delighted submission as she enveloped his balls in bubbles. She turned the handle to shut off the hole. Then she turned on the hot tap. The water gushed from the brass faucet. She went to the cupboard, bringing back the bottles in her arms, removing the stoppers, pouring in the contents. Bubbles began to rise and break in the fragrant steam. She went back for bath cubes, tore the gold foil from them and tossed them in.

She left her clothes lying in a heap as she stepped into the bath. She closed her eyes as she sank down. She couldn't bear to go on living, knowing that she would never see Dochie again. The frothing water was washing over the side of the bath now. There were men out there who would be laughing as they relaxed out of the line, but who were going to need her when they were lifted on to the hospital train after the next battle.

* * *

The 8th Argylls were gathered in the hollow on Sunday morning, singing a Gaelic hymn from the small book that had been handed out by the chaplin.

> *'O Dhè, ar cobhair anns gach linn,*
> *Ar dòigh san tim ri teachd,*
> *'S gach teinn bith fhèin duinn ad fhear-dion,*
> *'S ar dachaidh shìor, gu beachd.'*

Sam was standing beside Hector. He didn't know the Gaelic words, but he sang the English version.

> 'O God, our help in ages past,
> Our hope for years to come,
> Be thou our guard while troubles last,
> And our eternal home.'

He felt close to tears with the massed voices because it was his last day with the 8th Argylls. He'd gone to see the Colonel in his tent.

'Why do you want a transfer? Are you in some sort of trouble?'

'No trouble, sir. I've been very happy in the 8th Argylls.'

'Then why this request?' Colonel Campbell asked impatiently. He had paperwork to get on with, even on the sabbath.

'I signed up with the Argylls because I was working with Major Macdonald of Invernevis, sir, and because I knew a man in the battalion. But I'm from Buchan, and my brothers are in the Gordons.'

The commanding officer nodded to show that he understood. He had the report from Private Raeburn's Captain in front of him, saying that he was: 'a most satisfactory soldier, cool-headed and dependable, a particularly good shot.'

'You may not end up in your brothers' battalions,' he warned.

231

'I know that, sir. But my mother's keen for me to be a Gordon, too.'

'Very well, I'll see what I can do.'

It was done within a week, and Sam was transferred to the 10th Gordons of the 15th Highland Division. A lorry took him to the billets at the village of Wail on the river Canche. It was a beautiful peaceful place behind the lines, the red roofs of the barns tumbling down naturally. The tent Sam was sharing had been pitched at the edge of a field, under chestnut trees, beside the *chapelle funéraire* containing the tombs of the Hautecloques, the local landowning family. The château was across the road and in the dawn when he went to the nearby burn for a pail of water he saw a maid push open a small high window. She was dark-haired and clear-complexioned like Maggie. He stood among the trees with his full pail, watching her as she plumped out the pillow before laying it on the sill to await the sun.

The heat trapped between the hedges and the scents of the wild roses trailing in the grass made him soporific as he wandered through the village after the morning's training exercises, an easy hour with arms in a field, when even the Sergeant Major seemed subdued. At the weir he watched the mill wheel turning. They had been warned about swimming there because of a deep hole, but further down, where the river was in no hurry to reach Hesdin, the banks were lined with kilts as soldiers swam. *Pêche Interdite*, the sign boards warned, but soldiers were sitting on the banks with cigarettes in their mouths and slack lines in their hands as Sam wandered upriver, past the statue of the little bearded man in his brick shrine, coins scattered around him in the fountain. Sam made a wish for Maggie and left his offering in francs.

In the late afternoon when it was cooler he went to the Division horses in the field, helping to groom them as they stood in the shade, or talking to the smith by his glowing basket as he shod them for harder roads to come. In the evening when he went back to his billet for his supper, he saw that the white pillow had gone from the sill and that the little window was shut. He thought of Maggie, sitting at the kitchen table with her pot of tea. Was the boss still drinking? He began to feel jealous and uneasy, taking no part in the singing to a mouth-organ round the fire. He was lonely among all these men, though some of them were from Buchan and had ploughed fields near his bothy.

On the day of the regimental horse show he was up and about even before the casement in the château had been opened and the pillow plumped out. He brushed the horses as the sun began coming up through the trees, and then, one on each side, he walked them through the early lanes to the field three miles away where the show was being held. Their shoes thudded in the dust, their tails swishing across him as the flies began. When he stopped to look at flowers they cropped the wayside, or slewed their hindquarters to leave their dung steaming in the ditch.

They behaved with the same discipline and decorum in the ring, when he led them round, whispering to them as they went, and in the evening he walked them home by fragrant hedges with the two blue rosettes pinned to his cap. He didn't want to be a coachman again; he wanted to be a farmer, ploughing with his own team. Maggie and he would go up to Buchan and get the rent of a small place. It was dark when they reached Wail, and there was a lamp in the high window of the château. But when he came back from settling the horses in their field it was out, and he stood there, by the mausoleum, thinking about Maggie sleeping.

On his next free day, a Sunday, he went to visit Hector near Arras, getting a lift on a lorry. Church bells came in with the gentle breeze through the open window as he smoked and chatted to the driver.

'I think the place is called Ternas. Something like that.'

They found the sign, but there was no sight of tents.

'It must be the wrong place,' Sam said.

The driver was leaning out his window, asking a local woman about 'les soldats écossais'. She marched on the spot and swung her arms as she pointed up the road.

'You've missed them,' the driver told Sam.

Sam walked through the fields, past blackened places where fires had been, the discoloured cores of apples, heaps of horse dung round which flies were swarming. Maybe the Highland Division had been sent home; it had been a mistake, asking for a transfer at that time. He started walking back to his billet and it wasn't till after five miles that he got a lift.

He told the men he shared the tent with that the Highland Division had gone.

'We're going too,' one of them said.

'Where to?' Sam asked.

'I can guess,' the man said. 'I've been there before and it's a fucking awful place. Three times is going to be unlucky.'

'Where is it?' Sam asked again.

'You'll know soon enough,' the man said, to whom even the naming of the place had the superstition of death.

He was up even earlier that day, while it was still night. He stood waiting for the casement to open, and then he blew the maid a kiss. She threw something down to him and it landed in the dust at his boots. It was a St Christopher medal on a chain, and he put it round his neck with the Celtic cross Maggie had given him.

As his Brigade marched away from Wail he had a last look back at the tumbling water of the weir, wishing he could stay in that place where he'd been so happy. They began moving up country in the heatwave, through villages where women came out to stare at them, as if they were seeing other men going off before them. They billeted for the night and moved on through Ste Croix; Pernes; St Hilaire; Thiennes. The sun heated the water in their bottles, and the dust filmed their lips. Sam's feet were on fire in his boots.

The countryside was getting flatter as they marched towards the plain of Flanders, past fields of hops held up on poles. There seemed to be more and more wayside shrines containing statues of the Virgin and Child, small bunches of flowers at the plaster feet.

It took them eight days to reach Toronto and St Lawrence camps near Vlamertinge. The training area was marked with coloured flags and taped lines designating ravines, woods, strongpoints and other objectives of the battle to come.

But the 51st Highland Division had moved up a fortnight before, covering twenty-six kilometres in the warmest day it had experienced in France. The beer frothed in the water bottles that the locals had filled for the soldiers when they left the village where they'd been billeted, and ambulance cars followed to pick up the stragglers with blistered feet. Hector was thankful that the pipe band didn't have to play in the heatwave. He missed Sam's company, but he was safer were he was, back there with the 15th Scottish Division.

After a two-day rest the Highland Division reached St Omer for a period of intensive training. It was a landscape of canals and market gardens, of pavement cafés and friendly women. MacDougall would have been in his element. The mess of the 8th Argylls was in a château. They dined in a room with a huge chandelier, and there was plenty of food and drink. Hector was standing behind the Colonel's chair, having a rest between tunes when he overheard the conversation and realized with horror that he and Sam were bound for the same place.

Maggie was standing behind Invernevis's chair in the kitchen. She took a sip from her glass of whisky to give her courage to ask the question which had been preying on her mind ever since Sam had gone.

'What would happen if a soldier deserted, sir?'

He didn't answer immediately because he was lighting a cigarette.

'He would be court-martialled, Maggie.'

She took another sip.

'And what would happen after that, sir?'

'I presume he would be shot.'

The glass shattered on the stone floor.

21

Around him men were making water for the last time, kilts lifted, squatting like women. The soft purr of piss swirled round sodden boots, oozing into the mud, running in rivulets into shell-holes.

Sam Raeburn wanted to get up and run away, but the provost marshals were bobbing about on their horses behind the line, scouting for deserters, and he was weighed down with a rifle, a haversack, a water-bottle, a gas mask and bombs. Every fourth man had been given a trenching tool. Sam had a spade down his spine, like a splint. He needed a pee and had to lie on his side, and it ran back to soak his kilt.

The tea that had been poured into their dixies had been more than half rum. Some of the men around him were muttering about 'killing as many of these bastards as possible' as they fixed their bayonets. Sam was disorientated through lack of sleep because they'd spent most of the night moving up to their position. He was also terrified. As he watched the sky he could feel the chill metal of Maggie's Celtic cross against his throat. He'd lain so many mornings in his Buchan bothy, waiting for the sky to lighten through the small window so that he could make an early start with the day's ploughing. He'd lain watching the skylight brighten in his quarters above the Invernevis stables because he would see Maggie at breakfast. But he didn't want this sky to lighten. He had too much to live for, and he didn't want to die. Maggie was going to marry him and they would get a small farm in Buchan. As he looked across the dark rising terrain he felt his bowels opening down the backs of his legs.

The war correspondent trod on his cigarette as if it would attract enemy artillery in the darkness before he climbed the ladder to the high observation platform at the edge of the salient. This was going to be a momentous day, and he would have to call upon all his command of English for his many readers next morning across the channel. The King would be among them, and when this was all over, there was the possibility of an honour, since this war was being fought with words as well.

He had four pencils in his attaché case, a sharpener and several notebooks as well as one hundred cigarettes and a flask of brandy. He hadn't been allowed to describe the build-up, the weeks of intensive training, the white-faced tunnellers, the registered guns, the tanks crawling under cover of darkness to their stations like grotesque creatures, the cavalry cantering to their flanking positions, the massed movements of men and horses. But he was already beginning his dispatch in his head as he stood on the platform looking east, where this day was due to break violently, unnaturally. 'A storm threatened, but it did not arrive. Instead it was a moist night, and the darkness permitted our troops to take their places for one of the great battles of the world.'

Beyond him, in a line that stretched for three miles, one hundred thousand men of the Fifth Army were also watching the sky as they waited in the mud. The 10th Gordons were on the right, against the Ypres to Roulers railway. The officer standing beside Sam was following the sweep of the second hand of his wrist watch, its luminosity fading against the sky. The silence was eerie. There wasn't a blade of grass in the mud contaminated by corpses and gas from shells in three years of fighting for the salient, but a bird was moving in front of Sam's face. Buchan had been full of larks, singing over his bothy and over the landscape as he ploughed. The small bird seemed to be struggling in the mud as if it was injured, but as he reached out it rose singing on trembling wings into the lightening sky.

At 4.15 a.m. the train sitting in the special siding near Godewaersvelde was shaken by the beginning of the bombardment, almost throwing Sir Douglas Haig out of his bed. He lifted the blind on the dull dawn, then rapped the barometer with his knuckles. It was steady.

The immensity of what was happening at Ypres made him stand in silent prayer for a minute, asking guidance for the fulfilment of his wearing-down process. His batman brought him his shaving water and he used the blade carefully. If today went well, the Passchendaele-Staden ridge and the railway from Roulers to Thourout would be taken, which would facilitate a landing near Ostend, to get possession of the Belgian coast. Jellicoe, the First Sea Lord, had warned him that because of the grave shortage of shipping due to German submarines, it would be impossible for Great Britain to continue the war in 1918. If the ports of Ostend and Zeebrugge couldn't be taken, Dunkirk would have to be abandoned.

The train rocked again, but his blade didn't draw blood. He cleaned it carefully and folded it back into its ivory head. He clipped his moustache before his batman helped him into his uniform.

The 10th Gordons were attacking on a frontage of 350 yards with two companies, each with two platoons in line and two in support. Sam was in the front line, following the signalling arm of the platoon commander. They had practised taking the gentle heights of Frezenberg in the training area behind the lines, with white tapes representing their positions and officers pointing out manoeuvres with their canes. But there had been firm turf underfoot. As he tried to get up the slope he could see the heaps of bricks that had been a farm where a woman had made cheese and chickens had scratched in the courtyard, where children had played safely and said their prayers before bed. But the ruins were erupting, and the tank that had come to support them was stuck in the mud, whining. Sam couldn't duck and weave amid the machine-gun fire like the others because of the shovel jammed down his spine. The force sent him skidding back and flung his arm up into the sky.

It was only half past five, but Maggie was downstairs in her nightdress, sitting at the kitchen table. The back door was open but she wasn't listening to the dawn chorus. She was staring at her bare feet. What terrible trouble this war had caused. It had made people do things they would never have done before.

The lid of the kettle was lifting but she didn't rise to make tea.

'Sam!'

He was standing in the doorway, a cigarette between his teeth as he grinned at her. He had a tin helmet on the back of his head and his right arm was raised in greeting.

Before she reached him he had vanished.

Invernevis hadn't been up so early since he was a boy going fishing, but he knew what he had to do today. As he stropped the razor his door was knocked, but it wasn't Maggie. Jessie the maid slid the tea tray on to the table. The curtains were already opened, and she went down for the jug of hot water. The sun was flaring the mirror on its extendable arm, and the birds sang in the shrubberies as he shaved carefully. He cleaned the razor, then went next door. After undressing him Maggie had folded his clothes over the horse. He chose a fresh shirt from the chest, then a sober suit.

It was Jessie who served him breakfast. The house seemed strangely hushed.

'Is Maggie all right?'

'She's upstairs, sir.'

'Is Roddy in yet?'

'Yes, sir.'

'Tell him that I'll be going up to the village straight after breakfast.'

Though he had the key to the cellar he didn't go to see if he'd overlooked a bottle of Mackinlay's. He went through to the library and gathered up the papers he'd laid out on his desk before he'd got so drunk, putting them into a small leather case he'd used to keep fishing tackle in. Then he heard the gig coming round to the front.

Maggie had carried the basin of hot water up to her room. She was standing naked in front of the mirror, washing herself in a dream, as if the hand with the soap and the other with the sponge didn't belong to her. She washed all over her body and used lavender water before putting on clean underwear, and a pair of the silk stockings the Master had brought her from Edinburgh. She buttoned up her best black dress and sorted the little white lace collar before sitting on the bed to lace up her Sunday shoes.

'I'll not be long,' she told Jessie as she went out the back door.

It was a beautiful morning. The pungent scents from the

rhododendrons on the blind bend came to meet her, and the tunnel of the avenue was throbbing with birdsong.

Invernevis tugged the bell, but it took a long time for the shadow to appear behind the stained glass.

'Father Macdonald is at his breakfast,' the housekeeper rebuked the caller.

'I must see him.'

He wasn't asked through to join the priest for a cup of tea, but had to wait for twenty minutes in the chilly parlour beside the bowed plant.

'You're about early,' the priest said peremptorily. There was no handshake. 'Is it confession?' he asked sarcastically.

'I suppose it is, in a way,' his visitor said quietly. He put the case on his knee and took out the papers. 'I've a payment to make tomorrow which I can't meet.'

'What kind of payment?' the priest asked cautiously, still not accepting the papers that were being offered to him.

'An interest payment on money I borrowed.'

The priest took the papers.

'You borrowed five hundred pounds, at this rate of interest?' he said incredulously.

'I had bills to meet.'

'Why bring these to me?' the priest asked truculently.

'Because you're the chief trustee.'

'But the trustees won't pay this, even if we had the money. This is a personal debt, nothing to do with the estate.'

'I gave the house as security.'

'How could you give the house as security when the titles are with the lawyer?'

'The moneylender checked my name and address in *Who's Who*. He took my word.'

'A word you couldn't give, because the house isn't yours. No wonder your father didn't leave the place to you, when this is the kind of mess you get into.' He tossed the papers back across the desk. 'You'll have to get out of this one yourself.'

'But he'll take me to court. I signed a document,' Invernevis pleaded.

'That's your concern,' the priest shrugged.

'But it'll bring the family name into dishonour.'

'You should have thought of that before you borrowed the money. You should have gone to an institution for treatment for your drinking, before it got to this stage.' The priest sat back in his chair and put his fingertips together. 'The solution's in your own hands.'

'I can't borrow any more money,' Invernevis protested. He had expected the priest to capitulate by now.

'No, but you could marry.'

'That's a most insensitive thing to say, considering the circumstances in which I lost my wife.'

'Men remarry.'

The priest had left his chair and was at the window, his back to his visitor. He hadn't liked Invernevis's wife because of her flimsy dresses and advanced ideas.

'I don't happen to have met anyone,' Invernevis said defensively.

'Because you sit drinking down in that house. There are many intelligent, wealthy women looking for a husband, especially one from an old family.'

'I thought your church preached love.'

'You're in no position to afford love,' the priest said harshly. 'You're going to have to be practical for the first time in your life. Your children need a mother. They need to be brought home from the continent to a secure home.'

'With the whole of Europe at war?'

'It won't last much longer. There'll be a big push in Belgium. This war will leave a lot of widows.'

'I don't like the implication,' Invernevis said angrily.

'The implication of not settling this moneylender's debt is much worse.' He consulted the papers again. 'You're due to make a payment of £100 tomorrow.'

'Which I haven't got.'

'The trustees will pay this one and one only. Then you'd better start searching.'

Maggie had reached the village. People stopped to speak to

her, telling her how nice it was to see her, but she passed on after a few polite words. They thought she looked very pale, and wondered if she'd had bad news about Hector.

She turned up the lane and rang the bell.

'Well, *you're* a stranger,' Mrs MacNiven said, showing her into the waiting-room.

'I can't remember when I last saw you up here,' the doctor said warmly, holding her hand in both of his. 'You must be the healthiest person in the place.'

They always spoke Gaelic, but this morning she used English.

'I used to be,' she said sadly, following him through to the surgery. She took off her clothes behind the screen, including the silk stockings and lay naked while he examined her with his considerate hands. He told her to get dressed again.

'After thirty it can be tricky,' he said. 'Don't worry.' He patted her hand. 'I'm sure he'll do the right thing by you. He's a gentleman, after all.'

She was still in a dream.

'What did you say?' she asked.

'I said that the Laird's a gentleman. He'll see you right.'

The war correspondent had filled a notebook. 'I have never seen a sky like the sky of this dawn, not even on the Somme. As day was breaking the sky over Flanders was filled with the red flashes from our forward batteries and heavy guns heaving thousands of shells in the direction of the enemy. Hundreds of thousands of men were fighting for their lives in the swirling smoke of battle and the writhing morning mist in the landscape of death and destruction that was Ypres.'

But he'd left the platform and was on the move behind the lines, with his notebook.

'From where I watched it seemed that nothing could survive in the din of that ferocious battle for the already pulverized salient, but I was glad to get confirmation of our success from the long streams of lightly injured men coming from the dressing-stations.'

Sir Douglas Haig was visiting General Gough to hear about

the good progress that had been made. There were troops established beyond the Steenbeck river, and the French had had their successes.

'I believe we've taken over five thousand prisoners and more than sixty guns,' Gough told the Commander-in-Chief.

Haig had sent two emissaries to the casualty clearing stations. They reported many slight cases, mostly shell fire. The wounded were very cheery. Up to 6 p.m. over six thousand had been treated.

But the heavens opened even more and Haig had to take shelter.

Sam was lying out in the mud at Frezenberg in the downpour. There weren't enough stretchers and the battle was still raging. It wasn't till the late afternoon that he was lifted on to a stretcher which was slid on to the bogie of the light railway. But it kept stopping because of the congestion caused by so many casualties, and it was early evening before he reached Vlamertinge where he'd trained for the offensive. He lay on the stretcher beside hundreds of others on the grass in the rain outside the tent. Men were crying to be finished off. A nurse came around, kneeling, putting cigarettes into mouths and lighting them under her spreading cape. Padres and priests were also going among the stretchers, and the trains and motors kept coming.

Sam felt himself being lifted. He was lying on a hard surface now. He looked up and heard the rain drumming on the canvas.

'Is that you Hector?' he asked.

But it was a man in a mask.

'The arm will have to come off.'

He tried to struggle. How could you run a farm with one arm? How could you plough?

But the mud of the salient was already in his blood.

The war correspondent was now sitting in a tent, pounding out his report for next morning's newspaper. He was in a hurry because it had to go through the censor before being telegraphed to London. He had a hip flask to assist him because the carnage he'd seen that day was the worst, though he'd covered all the big battles since 1914. But you had to remember that there were wives and parents among his readers.

He heard the sound of the pipes and went to stand at the entrance, hoping for inspiration. The remains of a platoon of the Gordon Highlanders were coming out of the salient. Their faces were filthy, their kilts torn, and men were supporting each other. The piper leading them was lacking a boot, but his fingering of 'Highland Laddie' was impeccable as he led them through the rain in the darkening day.

The war correspondent couldn't find words.

The six men from the 8th Argylls were crouched in a German fox-hole. They'd taken the Steenbeck which had been a stream that morning, but which was turning into a torrent, welling round their boots in the teeming rain. The box of heirloom Invernevis pipes were roped to Hector's back. He put his head out. The four stretchers were covered with blankets because they couldn't carry them to the First Aid post through slime up to their kneecaps.

It had been hellish fighting. He was so worried about Sam, but there was no way of getting any news about him because they would have to spent the night here, holding the ground they'd taken. To take his mind off the cries of the wounded outside he thought of the mess in the Flanders farmhouse where he played to the officers. The girl who served him his supper in the kitchen hadn't a word of English, but she let him play with her tits when he gave her a tune on the chanter.

He heard the gurgling sound, and he put his head out again. The stretcher was level with his face, and was sinking into the mud. He tried to put his hand under it, but it was no use. The face on the stretcher was turned towards him. The man's mouth was open, and Hector didn't know if he was dead. Then he was sinking into the mud. His ear had disappeared. Jesus Christ: with the gas in the ground he was coming up again, with his mouth full of mud. If this went on all night he'd go crazy.

The train was packed with casualties from Ypres, the worst cases she'd ever seen, ghastly wounds. Alanna Richardson had helped to lift them through the sliding doors in the downpour and she was exhausted, but there was a long night ahead.

The Red Baron had been grounded by a bullet through his flying helmet and was in hospital, ordering his fifty-seventh silver trophy from his Berlin jeweller. The other pilots of the German Flying Corps were jealous of his prowess and intended to prove themselves in his absence. The aviator was racing the train. It was a long one, nearly half a kilometre. He followed it in the moonlight as it snaked along the track. He flew into the smoke from the engine and could see the glare of the fire-box as more coal was tossed in. The metal was shining in the moonlight and he thought it was an armoured train.

Alanna Richardson was on duty in the lying-down coach, standing in the swaying corridor holding on to the man's hand. He was a Gordon, far gone. She was thinking of MacDougall, his hands locked under the huge tree against his shoulder at the sports in another world, when the aviator pulled the bomb lever.

22

Maggie could hear the Armistice celebrations throughout the city as she put the baby to bed in her room at the top of the house in the fashionable London square. The child was crying because of the bangs of the rockets and the singing of the crowds as they ran through the streets with linked arms.

She sat rocking her daughter in her arms, her back to the window, facing the door as if she expected it to burst open, a bonnet of the Gordon Highlanders landing at her feet. But she hadn't heard from Sam since the previous July, after the big battle at Ypres. Hector had fought in it, and though he'd gone to look for Sam afterwards, he couldn't get any news of him because there were so many dead and wounded. But she didn't believe that Sam was dead. He would have deserted, as he said he was going to do on his last leave at Invernevis, when she'd given herself to him. Her worry was that he was hiding somewhere, cold and hungry, not knowing that the war was over.

Sometimes when she was baking at the table in the basement, with the city clattering past above in the autumn smog, she was back in the peace of the kitchen at Invernevis, the door open on the summer behind her. The Master had pleaded with her to stay at Invernevis, but she couldn't because of the embarrassment of having the baby in the house. It would only make the locals talk, and that wouldn't have been fair to the Master when he had so many other worries.

The baby was sleeping now, and as she laid her in the wooden cradle her new Mistress had given her, the flash of a rocket dazzled the child's face, but she didn't waken. Maggie still hadn't had her christened, and was thinking of calling her after the Master's mother, who had been so upset at her leaving.

The whole of the district of Invernevis seemed to be up at the bonfire on the hill above the village for the Armistice celebrations. Invernevis could see the blaze from the library window where he was standing with a glass of whisky. He had stayed away from the village because he knew that his presence would only inhibit their enjoyment, but he had ordered a case of whisky and a barrel of beer from the Arms to be sent down to the hall.

He was thinking about Maggie, as if at any moment he expected to hear her light knock, the door opening to tell him that his dinner was ready. He missed her conversation and cooking. He had to bring his children home from Switzerland, now that the war was over, and Maggie would have been so good with them. Her child would be no trouble, and he could get her extra help in the kitchen. A letter from her was lying on his desk at his back. She said she had settled in well, but he sensed that she was homesick.

Up at the bonfire Hector had tuned up his pipes and was now marching round the blaze, playing 'Auld Lang Syne'. It wasn't only the smoke that was making his eyes water; he was thinking of the good friends he had left out in France and Belgium under makeshift crosses, especially MacDougall and Sam. He still found it difficult to believe that the big man was dead, as if he expected to meet him with an arm round a woman on the other side of the radiant fire. Maggie was convinced that Sam had deserted, but her brother was sure that he was dead, though he would never say that to her.

Alanna Richardson had been invited with her husband to the celebration dinner at the War Office, but she was sitting in the bedroom of her London home, a shaded lamp by her elbow, listening to the bursting rockets and the chants in the street. She looked at herself calmly in the mirror despite the hideous injuries caused to her face by the bomb that had been dropped on the hospital train, which had been mistaken for a munitions train. She had been three hours on the operating table, and there was still steel in her body. Behind her she could see her dim canopied bed where she had lain naked with MacDougall while the scented foam from the bath flowed down the stairs.

She had seen so many deaths on the winding miles of hospital train, cradling the heads of dying men, the brave and the terrified, feeling their shell-shock going through her bones. Despite the hundreds of bodies she had helped to hand down to the side of the track in the darkness she still found it hard to believe that Dochie had been killed, though her husband could give her no details. Sometimes she felt an urge to cross the channel to try to find his grave, but where would you begin looking in all that mud and wreckage? He had taken her life with him too, because everything seemed so futile, so ordinary now, after knowing such a being with his strength and aura of perpetual sunlight.

She was still sitting there when the fiery circle of the Brigadier's cigar wandered across the mirror. He stood with his hands on her shoulders, and she could smell the combinations of drink.

'The streets are packed with people. It took half an hour for the car to get home. They're even climbing in the fountain at Trafalgar Square.'

'They have something to celebrate,' she said. In the glass she saw a face that hadn't endured any shortages in wartime.

'They were all asking for you tonight, including Winston. You can't sit here brooding for the rest of your life. It was a terrible thing that happened, but—'

Alanna's smile made her features even more grotesque.

'I'm not brooding.' She could never share her memories with this worthy dull man who was twelve years her senior and had never stimulated her in any way. She could only have married him for his money.

'I was thinking of taking a holiday to Invernevis.'

'I'll come with you,' he said eagerly. 'We'll leave it till the spring run. Do you remember that time we fished together before the war and that big fellow who was killed with the 8th Argylls pulled you out of the river?'

'How can I forget it?' she said with a wistful smile. 'But I'd rather go alone, to come to terms with what happened to me.'

He made a clumsy move towards her, but she turned away. After Dochie she could never let anyone near her. As he picked up his cigar with its wet chewed end, the ash fell to the carpet.

Invernevis also had his cigar as he sat in his armchair in the library, the curtains closed. It was too early yet to count the cost of the war, but he knew that it had been immense. Thousands of pounds had been wiped off the value of his investments, and it was likely that part of the estate – probably the upper reaches of the river – would have to be sold. But there was an even bigger cost. At least eighteen men from the estate had been killed, and a dozen others seriously wounded. There would have to be some kind of financial assistance for these families, probably reduced rents, which would put more burden on the estate.

The door opened after the sharp rap.

'Will you be wanting anything else tonight?' the new housekeeper asked. She was thin, in her forties, with her black hair cut short like a man's.

'No, thank you, Miss Carruthers.'

Before she closed the door she picked up the empty whisky bottle.

Up in the village the crowd had left the embers of the bonfire to go down to the hall, where food and drink had been set out on trestle tables. The wounded veterans who hadn't been able to climb the hill to the fire were already there, with missing hands and crutches in their oxters. One man who had been the best clay pigeon shot in the district hadn't been able to get away from the yellow cloud that had come rolling along the trench at Ypres. He sat in darkness, his hand out for a glass of whisky.

One of the other veterans was talking.

'The Laird should have been up at the bonfire, to make a speech.'

'He's skulking down at the big house because he doesn't know what to say,' another veteran said. 'There's not much point in thanking the dead.'

'Speak in your native tongue,' an old man pleaded, uncomfortable with English.

'I've been four years in France and Belgium,' the veteran of twenty-five said. 'I had to take all my orders in English, and I saw things there were no Gaelic words for. I didn't realize what a big place the world was till I went across there. English is good enough for me. Your health,' he said, holding up the glass of whisky.

In the spring of 1919 the river was running in spate. *Peigi bheag na biorraide* could hear it from her chair where she sat opposite the old man. He carried her up and down the stairs, but still put on her boots, though she was housebound now. He had fed her and had put the plate through in the scullery where he heard the sound of an engine outside. A motor car was shuddering in the rain, the driver in his grey uniform holding up an umbrella for the lady who was emerging from the back, her strapped shoe in the mud.

Alanna Richardson was wearing a veil in case her disfigurement frightened the old lady. She had to stoop as she entered the small house.

'I knew Dochie,' she explained after the old man had given her his seat.

'She has no English,' the old man advised the visitor with the sweet smell.

Peigi was studying the strange lady in the fine clothes whose veil made her even more mysterious. She stared at the rings on the fingers, as if she could see something in the sparkle of the stones. Then she began to laugh, rocking from side to side, raising her boots from the stone floor. Her husband leaned over her, speaking tenderly in Gaelic, reminding her that they had a visitor.

Alanna had been unsure about coming, and now realized that she had made a terrible mistake. The old woman's mind must have gone, and she didn't know that her grandson was dead.

'I'm so sorry,' she said to the old man as she rose. She went across and put a hand on her shoulder.

Peigi said something in Gaelic.

'She's asking if you want to see him,' the old man said.

Alanna was heartbroken for these two old people. She had no right to intrude on their illusion that the grandson they adored had come home from a French grave. There were tears in her eyes as she went to the door.

The old woman spoke in Gaelic again.

'You've to stand behind her,' the old man said.

Peigi was rising from her chair, steadying herself with a hand against the mantelpiece as if she was unused to her legs.

'*Dùin an uinneag air eagal 's gun tig an Sluagh a-steach,*' ('Shut the window in case the *Sluagh* comes into the house,') she ordered the old man.

He pushed up the window to the west.

Alanna could smell the rankness of the old woman as she stood behind her. She wanted to take the handkerchief out of her cuff, to hold it to her mouth but didn't want to offend her. She would go through with the charade, and then go out to the car.

The old woman spoke again in Gaelic as she put her left boot to the side.

'You've to put your foot on hers,' the old man said.

Alanna placed her elegant strapped shoe on the man's boot the old woman was wearing on a bare foot.

'Now look over her shoulder,' he instructed the visitor.

Beyond the pointed hat she saw Dochie sitting at the table, in a honey-coloured light, the light and warmth of high summer with its swirling motes. He was stripped to the waist, and the hair on his chest seemed to be on fire. There was a spoon in his fist, a blue plate of curds and whey in front of him on the oilcloth. He was laughing, but there was no sound coming from his mouth.

As Alanna fainted the old man shouted to the chauffeur to come in and help. They carried her up the narrow staircase to MacDougall's bed and she lay there for half an hour, under the grey slab of the skylight.

When she came down *Peigi* was back in her chair, and the old man was holding the saucer she was noisily drinking her tea from.

'She says you've to come back any time if you want to see him,' the old man told the visitor.

Alanna hugged the old woman.

'I'll be back very soon,' she told her, and straightened the pointed hat on her head before kissing her.

The car rocked up the rutted avenue to the big house, and as it braked on the gravel at the front she lifted back her veil because there was nothing to hide now.

Invernevis wanted to turn his face away when she was shown into the drawing-room, but she offered a cheek to be kissed.

'You've had a bad time,' he said.

'I'm lucky to be alive. Most of the men on the hospital train were killed. But how are things with you?'

'We lost a lot of men from the Invernevis company.'

'Including the big man who was my ghillie when I came to fish before the war.'

'Ah, yes. MacDougall was the last man one would have expected to be killed, but at least he didn't have any children. It's going to be very difficult for some of the families, with the breadwinners gone.'

They went into lunch.

'I'm thinking of moving out of London,' she told him. 'I'd like a place in the country.'

'Where were you thinking of?' he asked, surprised.

'Here.'

He was flattered, thinking that she wanted to be near him. He had always felt that there was a mutual attraction, though her looks had gone now.

'I think it would be too quiet for you,' he said as he helped her to more wine.

'That's what I want, peace. Do you know if there are any properties for sale?'

'Not at the minute. No, wait: there is a place, but it probably wouldn't be suitable. My brother built a house down by the river, and his widow moved away. The house has lain empty for years, and it must be damp. But I'm sure she would be interested in selling.'

'I'd love to live beside the river. When could I view this house?'

'They keep the keys up at the Home Farm,' Invernevis informed her. 'Do you think your husband will like living here?'

'He would stay on in London, because he's got his club and his

War Office friends.' She saw his look and added: 'Don't worry. It's not a separation. He'll come up when he feels like a break.'

They went through to the drawing-room for coffee and sat at the window overlooking the river.

'You seem depressed yourself,' she said.

'It hasn't been easy. I lost Maggie, my housekeeper.'

Alanna had noticed the difference in the quality of the welcome and the food.

'What happened?'

'She had a child and went away. I didn't want her to go.'

Alanna listened and didn't ask about the identity of the father. This was another casualty of the war, she suspected.

'Where is Maggie now?' she asked.

'In London. She saw the position in the *Times* and I had to supply references.'

'Who's she working for?'

'A family called Dugdale in Cadogan Square.'

'I know them,' Alanna said. 'He's a coalmine owner, very rich. I think I may call at the Home Farm to get the key for your brother's house, to look over it.'

She saw the house that afternoon. She stood for a long time in the principal bedroom, listening to the river, a soothing sound as it began to curve round to flow down in front of the big house. Upstream was the pool where Dochie had freed her from her dull life, removing the hook that day. She knew that she would be happy in that house and she was already arranging the furniture, putting the dressing table where the mirror would catch the light. She would have tell Freddie to get his lawyer to buy it as soon as she got back to London. But first she would have to get the village store to send down a box of food to the old man and woman.

Maggie didn't enjoy her work as much as at Invernevis. They were a different class of people, entertaining a lot, and the sons, who were both at Cambridge, were forward. Some nights she didn't get to bed until the small hours, after one of their parties, and then the baby kept her awake. At least Hector wrote, which was more than he'd done during the war.

'The boss is a different person since you left. He's drinking too much again, and he hardly goes out. I don't like the new housekeeper. She's a bitch, and grudges every potato in the servants' hall. Once I've saved up some money I'll come down to see you. I've gone off the pipes, after the war, but likely I'll take them up again some time.'

There was still no word of Sam. One morning the two Dugdale boys rang for coffee for their hangovers. She took it through herself to the morning-room. They were talking about the deserters at Etaples.

'They'll let them go now the war's over,' one of the brothers said.

'Will they hell. They'll round them up and shoot them. Why should they get away with it when others had to give their lives?'

Maggie spilled the tray as she was setting it down.

She was in her bedroom one afternoon, feeding the baby when one of the maids came up to tell her that there was someone to see her. She thought it was news in connection with Sam and hurried down the back stairs. There was a lady standing in the hall. When she turned round Maggie recognized Mrs Richardson. What in God's name had happened to her face? She wanted to go back up the stairs.

'How are you, Maggie?' she asked, extending a hand. 'I've been up at Invernevis and I thought I would give you the news when I'm visiting Mrs Dugdale. She says we can use the small sitting-room.'

Maggie sat opposite her. She knew Mrs Richardson had been a nurse in the war, and had heard Mrs Dugdale say how brave she had been. 'An angel of mercy.'

'Major Macdonald is missing you,' Alanna began.

Maggie didn't say anything.

'I know you have a child to look after, and it's none of my business who the father is. Major Macdonald wants you to go home. He says there won't be any problem with the baby. If you need help to look after it, he'll arrange it.'

'It's very good of you, ma'am, but I'm better here,' Maggie told her.

'You can't possibly be better off, bringing up a baby in London. I've got something to tell you. I'm going to live at Invernevis. I've bought Major Macdonald's brother's house by the river.'

Maggie wondered why a woman who moved in high society would want to go and live in such a remote place.

'I'll be able to spend a lot of time at the big house, to keep the Major company. It would be nice if you were there too.'

'I don't know, ma'am . . .'

But Alanna saw her faltering. She opened her bag and put five pounds on the table:

'That will take you home.'

'I can't take it, ma'am,' Maggie said.

Alanna had risen and was standing looking out of the window. The war had changed so much for her. She had heard the confessions of dying men, about deepest love. There was going to have to be honesty and openness from now on.

'Your brother was the best friend of Dochie MacDougall, wasn't he?'

'He was, ma'am,' Maggie said, surprised at the mention of the big fellow's name. 'I never thought that he would go.'

Alanna smiled as she turned from the window.

A month later her chauffeur drove Maggie and the baby to the station for the train north. They had a sleeping berth, and as she rocked across the border with her daughter in her arms she was thinking of Sam.

Maybe he would get home soon.

Hector was waiting at the station for her on the gig in the early morning.

'The housekeeper went on the early train,' he told his sister. 'Good riddance. So this is my niece? She's very like you.'

One of the women waiting on the platform to see who was coming off the late train, to give her something to talk about, managed to get a look at the baby's face before it was lifted up on to the gig. She leaned over the fence to tell the postmistress, who was shovelling manure on to her vegetables:

'It's got the laird's nose.'
The postmistress's spectacles glittered in the last of the light: 'That Maggie Macdonald always was a cute one.'

End of this Chronicle